DON/ COA

ABERDEEN
CITY LIBRARIES
www.aberdeencity.gov.uk/libraries

THE RECKONING

THE RECKONING

Patricia Tyrrell

Weidenfeld & Nicolson
LONDON

First published in Great Britain in 2002
by SixForty Press as *The Bones in the Womb*

© Patricia Tyrrell 2002

This edition published in Great Britain in 2004
by Weidenfeld & Nicolson

A CIP catalogue record for this book
is available from the British Library

ISBN 0 297 84891 7

Typeset at The Spartan Press Ltd,
Lymington, Hants
Printed in Great Britain by
Clays Ltd, St Ives plc

Weidenfeld & Nicolson
An imprint of the Orion Publishing Group
Orion House, 5 Upper St Martin's Lane,
London WC2H 9EA

I

Les called my mother that time from the only public telephone of a one-horse New Mexico township; I stuck my elbow in his ribs and told him he was acting damn stupid – what'd he do if somebody else showed up and wanted to use the phone, started pacing and overheard him? But Les snapped, 'Shut up, Cate,' and he dialled. The booth stood between an adobe post office and the highway; I squashed next to him so I'd hear her replies, because this call was more important than any of the previous ones. 'You don't need to listen,' he told me as usual, and scowled. 'Not trusting me, huh?' When I was little he'd lock me into the truck while he called, and anyway I'd no notion what the calls meant, but when I reached my teens he couldn't do that.

The phone rang her end, a mangy palm tree outside our booth rattled and a truck zoomed by. The hot air sat around us and I said, 'She's not home.' (With a wide grin to mean I didn't care.) I pictured her like in a movie, watching the phone ring and not answering it; that'd be much worse. But after four and a half rings the ringing stopped; I pressed close and imagined I could hear her breathing.

Les said what he always says, in one form of words or another. 'I got your kid here with me, you know. She truly is alive.' He took a moment to glance past me, making sure we weren't overheard, then he told her in that soft voice like he's pleading, 'Ma'am, I wouldn't lie to you.'

I hate when he uses that soft greasy tone; every time

after, I say to him, 'Just talk ordinary with her, whyn't you?' And he frowns, says, 'But I was.' Never has realised he's begging her – begging for what? For her to believe something that's the God's-truth, is all. But I pressed close past the grey desert dust and Les's sweat and the roar of another truck, and heard her say (as she most often does), 'Insane. Inhuman.' Her voice not interested, not a bit caring. Which has always hurt me, though Les tried to say there was part reason. Reason, the hell. She sounded like a robot voice, ready to switch off. And the next thing she said, in her bitty accent which Les claims is British, was, 'I'm hanging up now.' Click, the buzz of the empty line.

Les cussed but he'd already stacked the coins for his next try; was less than half a minute before her phone rang again, and this time she picked it up at once. Les said, 'You can't put me off that way.' Hoarse; he smokes too damn much. And breathless because he'd gotten jittery; after twelve years with him I can read his moods like my own. (Easier than mine, most often.) He said, 'This here's no nuisance call, ma'am.' A car on the highway slowed, saw the booth was occupied, speeded up. 'All these years,' said Les, 'I kept you informed, right, ma'am? Faithful I have.' No sound from her; he must have wondered if he'd dialled wrong, for he said, 'Hi there? This *is* Miz Janice I'm speaking with? Miz Janice Wingford that the daughter of got—'

Then she did answer, like talking from a clenched jaw, 'Say "murdered", why don't you? Might as well be honest.'

No matter how often Les has told her the truth, she's never believed him. He chuckled, but I couldn't view her as comic any more. Sick-minded or thick-brained or both, that's how she sounded to me. Les changed hands on the phone, wiped his sweaty palm on his jeans and said cosy to her, 'Thought I'd gotten the wrong number there for a second.' A pickup truck pulled in near us and the guy went into the post office. Not highway patrol or sheriff, but Les got nervouser and said fast, 'Ma'am, are you still there?' She grunted and he got to the meat of his call. 'Truth is, ma'am – and I do wish you'd quit fussing about a murder. They never found a body, right? Nor could they, seeing as she wasn't killed. But the truth is, ma'am, I need your help.'

He held his breath and I did too. If she hung up again, refused to talk this over, we could drive east and find her address and just arrive – but she might act furious disbelieving and call the cops at once. Which both Les and I had our reasons for not wanting to chance; we needed her co-operation. So it was a relief when she spoke again. 'You've a shitting nerve,' she said, 'my God, have you ever! You abduct my three-year-old daughter and do away with her, you spend the next twelve years tormenting me and then ask for my help? When the police catch you – and they will, I don't doubt they're much nearer now than you suppose—'

She paused for breath and I took a quick look from the booth in case she knew something we didn't, but the dusty surrounds and highway were clear. Then I thought, *This* is my mother? Her that's ranting on and not giving Les a hearing to put his side? So, I'm not saying him taking me away from that campsite was right, only – from what he's indicated since – he was lonely and unhappy at the time and seemed to him there was reason for what he did.

My mother went on, 'When the police take you in, I'll give my evidence with pleasure and try to make sure you never kill anyone else's child.'

I made a face at Les to mean, Same old stuff, and he nodded; he's closer to me than I can imagine any dad ever being. He keeps on telling me I'll for sure love my mother when I meet her, but I don't know how to go about loving anyone except Les. Especially this woman I can't even remember.

She said, 'A death sentence on you—' as if she could hardly wait – 'will mean full death.'

The man from the pickup truck came out of the post office with a bundle of magazines under his arm; he drove off without looking at us but I could tell Les was getting right jittery. Also I had a thought and wrote it, 'Traced?' in the dust on the window, poked Les's arm so he'd notice. And it did make him talk fast. 'Ma'am,' he said, 'hear me out, will you? The truth is, I want to hand the girl back to you.'

Every time he talked that way it didn't seem real; how could he hand me over to someone I'd no memory of, had scarcely really known? But there it was; he figured he'd got reason enough. I kept telling him no one'd found out what happened to Jeff and if by mischance anyone did discover – why, Les and I were living isolated in the desert anyway; we'd just shift on and no one was familiar with our habits or indeed us, no one'd be any the wiser. But I'd never realised how scared Les is of any sort of violence; when I told him what happened to Jeff, all of a sudden it wasn't any longer Les staring back at me but an old grey-faced open-mouthed stranger. Though seems to me there was reason for what happened, and no one could mostly call me violent. But there you are.

Anyway, when Les said that to the woman there was two thousand miles of silence for at least a minute and I thought, she doesn't want me, how could you not want your own daughter? Then she said in her stiff voice, 'This is a cruel scam.' I knew by divination when she said this that she'd noted down our number and was getting ready to put the cops on us; I joggled Les and pointed to the dusty word on the glass and he nodded. She said, 'You dare to inflict this on us after what you've already made us suffer.' She took a two-thousand-mile deep breath. 'What the hell piece of dishonesty has your crooked mind schemed up now?'

4

Les isn't in the habit of being spoken to so abusively; when we drive into town to pick up welfare money and food stamps the clerks mostly act polite even if they basically hate the guts of all us wanderers. And fast food outlets or gas station attendants mostly speak friendly enough; one bunch of dollars is as good as another. He's a sensitive guy too, although she mightn't think so. His cheeks coloured up and I wrote 'Trace us' on the back of his hand with dust; he scowled but there was no point in the two of us spending so long on the phone, trying to make arrangements, that we'd give the cops our end plenty of chance to catch up with us. No one'd found out about Jeff yet, as far as I knew – but how would I know? Les really did have a strong point about us needing to get out of that whole area, at least temporarily.

'Ma'am,' Les said, 'I got to stop talking now. You notified the cops to chase us, right? And I durstn't stay around in case someone shows. But I'd like—'

She interrupted; you wouldn't expect a woman that stiff-voiced to have so much energy in her. 'You, you,' she mocked. 'And please explain to whatever trashy girl you've persuaded—'

Then everything came clear to me; she didn't believe I was her daughter Cate, didn't *want* to believe. Wanted no part of any deal with Les or me, wanted us to get off the phone and leave her be so she'd never hear from us more. I nudged Les and pointed to the scar on my arm, and he nodded hard. Another car slowed on the highway; he turned to watch it pull in, then he said into the phone loud and clear, 'Ain't no point in you denying, ma'am. Because I can prove she's yours.' He hung up and we jumped into our pickup, got the hell out of there.

He drove fast, like I love to when he lets me, and after five minutes or hot whooshing air and red desert blur he said, 'Anyone following us?'

'You got paranoia. Nope, the road's empty. What'd you expect – sheriff and a posse of deputies?'

'You sure can joke,' he said past his teeth. 'Just a barrel of laughs, ain't you? Except when there's a knife in the room.'

'How often do I need tell you it was nearly accidental?'

He screwed his eyes half-shut against the glare and me; his voice went almost as clenched as hers. 'A man got killed, didn't he? And you right there with no clothes on. Went to him willing, didn't you? Snuck out, knew I'd forbid you.'

If I'd wanted to hurt Les I'd have said, Hell of a lot of difference your forbidding'd make. But he's always been like a true father to me and I'm really squishy fond of him, wouldn't hurt him just for the pleasure of giving pain. So I said nothing and we both stared at the road.

Trouble with desert is, there's no scenery. A fifty-mile drive in belting sun, amid grey sagebrush and rock, from that one-phone-booth town to the next buildings – a huddle of four shacks at a railroad crossing where the freight trains roar by and nothing but dust and scorpions hangs around for long. One of the shacks sells fast food and cold drinks and there's an ice machine on the front porch; I said, 'Won't we stop off here for a minute? I'm thirsty,' but Les shook his head and gunned the engine. Paranoid, like I said.

Another sixty miles of rock hills, and only a tattered few sagebrush, from the railroad crossing to the disused ranch we were hanging out on. A dirt track, a few shrivelled cactuses, three wooden buildings. We weren't messy squatters, we acted responsible; Les tidied up outdoors and I kept the inside as clean as possible. It was sort of a home and no one ever showed up to bother us, which was the important thing. We'd been there a good many months and I knew Les had gotten fond of the place, didn't want to leave; I felt bad that something I'd done was pushing him out. Lots of other empty places in those hills we could have shifted to; I lay awake that night, like I had lain quite some nights already, feeling extra sorry for both Les and me because I'd forced – without intending to – our moving clear away from that area we both felt comfortable in.

When we got home from the phone call that day I hugged him and said, 'Whatever happens, promise me that when we reach her you'll hang around there with me. Don't just hand me to her and walk out, right?'

He said, 'She for sure won't want me around,' but I made him promise.

2

I lay awake that night too thinking about Jeff. I don't dwell on the fact of what happened any more often than I must, but sometimes it rises up and swats at you. If anyone'd find out about him dying and they'd ask me how it felt to kill someone, I'd need to say, Astonishing, that's how. The total surprise of it, and yet at that moment I wanted him dead. But then you stare at the bloodied slit and he's not breathing and you think, Holy cow, where's the real alive Jeff gone? Did I without honestly meaning to send him away? And no hauling him back either.

Of course I had to drive away from Jeff's apartment in his car, drive up to the hills and wake Les, get him to follow me back down in the truck so he could help me clean up and between us we could get rid of the – what was left of Jeff. On that frantic drive toward Les I cooked up a whole different identity for Jeff, gave him another nationality and mindset so I could cry rape and hope Les'd more than half-way believe me. He did believe too, for quite a while, him being in the habit of always believing me and me not being much into the habit of lying to him – until this past year anyway. When I got to be fourteen I developed an itch to live like any other teenager. Boyfriends, discos, dances maybe? The works. Not school; Jeff and his friends were welcome to their college classes. But a bit of personal freedom and joshing around; Les is a reliable guy but he's never exactly been full of mirth. I owe him everything, okay, but doesn't he owe me some happy freedom once in a while too?

So, Jeff happened. And for a while afterwards Les would speak of him as, 'That no-good bum, that wetback from some muck-heap shanty-town – you said he was in this country illegal?' I say, 'Yeah,' but after a while I could notice – and dread – how Les's mind was starting to figure. Slow but determined when he gets into a project, that's Les. So, 'Along which stretch of highway'd he grab you? What were you doing in those parts anyhow and how'd you get there? You didn't have the truck.' Then – chewing his lip, flushing – 'Your clothes and . . . and you. No visible ripping or scratching of them, was there?' And the clincher, the question I'd hoped he'd never get to, 'What in all hell were you running around the countryside for, in the middle of the night and without telling me first?' There was no believable answer to that. So he got totally suspicious and, the more I lied and tried to cover up, the more he disbelieved.

The arguments rebounding from which, plus the fact of what happened to Jeff, were enough to keep anyone wakeful, but halfway through any sleepless night I'll shove Jeff firmly out of my mind; I'd never sleep at all if I dwelt on him. When Les used to say, 'A no-good bum,' I'd reply quietly, 'Sure was.' Telling lies about the dead doesn't hurt them, right?

So I switched my mind from Jeff to wonder about this woman my mother and how soon'd we set off to go meet her. I agreed with Les that it was a fine-tuned operation; he was scared and so was I that when we arrived at her place she might set the cops on us, but there's only so much persuading you can do over the phone. I needed to leave the timing to him though, he was the expert. He took me from her and he'd figure out how to safely return me. Sounds sadly like a package, doesn't it? But it couldn't – mustn't be allowed to – turn out that way.

At breakfast the next morning I said, 'Be a long drive when we do go, won't it?' And me never further east than the Arizona/New Mexico border – except for those first three years which I don't remember.

Les hunched over his coffee and cold sausages and grunted. He'd buy those cooked sausages at the super-market delicatessen and eat them with hot dog rolls for breakfast, never got tired of them. The same as he'd never laugh or want to go anywhere different or watch a tele-vision or buy a newspaper. Once in a while we'd catch part of a drive-in movie, but except for that we'd only the truck radio which mostly jammed itself up with mountain static and let wisps of music or news through like copperminers' ghosts wailing, and we'd the desert air and sun. And the welfare money when Les drove to pick it up. And we'd each other's conversation. Les let his grunt sit on the air a good five minutes, then he said, 'What're you staring at me for?'

'Wasn't. Only – when we go see her, it'll be all different than this, right? Different scenery, different sort of land.' I didn't say, 'Motels and all,' because I knew we'd sleep in the truck along the way; no money for motels, and I'm not sure Les would have slept in one even if somebody'd paid him to.

'Yeah,' he said past his sausages, 'different. Lots of trees. Hills like here, but so forested you can't see past the next corner.'

I'd more sense than to ask if he'd ever been east before; Les'd never talk about his previous life. 'What if she doesn't like me?' I said.

He took his nose out of his coffee mug and scowled. 'Didn't I tell you I got evidence for her? Not only the scar but . . . other things.'

Odd, to think there's a whole first life you recall nothing of. Those three years; Les says, 'How could you remember? Tiny kids don't,' but seems to me everything in a person's life should mark you with some memory, some feel. Noth-ing. 'I'm not talking about if she doesn't believe you,' I said, 'but if she doesn't *like* me. What if she agrees I'm hers but she doesn't care for the look of me?'

'She'll be crazy about you, soon's she sees you. Mother's instinct, ain't it?' He buried his nose in the mug again.

I sat there in the cold mountain dawn and forgot my own coffee and doughnut, imagining how the meeting might go. How she mightn't want to be bothered with me for whatever reason; twelve years gone is a long time. She might be busy with all sorts of other things now, other people. 'Suppose she's got a bunch more kids?' I said.

He set down his mug and said, 'You don't give me credit for much sense, do you? All those calls I made through the years, and never a kid crying or talking at her end, only her speaking or listening and a hollow silence behind her.'

'There's him – the man.' I didn't say 'My dad'; how could I, after being reared all those years by Les? The man'd get annoyed with me maybe, but that was the way it'd have to be.

'Yeah, well.' Les shoved his mug and plate across the packing-case we use for a table; always I got to wash the dishes. If you could call it 'wash' in an outside trough with no running water. I loved the days when we went to the laundromat and I cleaned myself up, washed my hair, in their restroom. Les wiped a hand across his mouth and said, 'I'd be ready to bet that your dad's not still living with her. For the last couple of years not, I'd guess.'

'No voice in the background?'

Les never has liked me teasing him; under the tan his colour rose. 'Laugh if you must, but I can prove he was there those first years. She'd tell him what I said, or he'd say something to her. Telling her to hang up on me, most like, but *something*. Nowadays there's no one. Just her.'

'Why would they split though? You'd think after they didn't have a child any more they'd hang closer together.'

'Unhappiness takes people various ways.' He chopped

the words off sharp, then he got up and hitched his pants, pulled his heavy jacket on, went outdoors.

That afternoon he stayed indoors, he spread out our tattered Rand McNally atlas and a bunch of maps he'd gotten from gas stations and he began studying them, so I asked if I could take the truck riding into the hills. He gave me that shaky doubtful look he'd never used before the Jeff trouble; it made me sad because it meant he didn't wholly trust me. I put my arms round his neck and said, 'Only into the hills. I promise,' and because I gave my solemn promise he finally decided to believe me. He threw the keys to me but I wonder if people ever start trusting again once they've stopped? Because I'd be bitterly unhappy if Les didn't trust me for evermore. After all, if the Jeff affair taught Les things about me, it taught me plenty too; you can't kill someone and not ask yourself questions afterward. During those hours when we cleaned up and buried Jeff, I surely grew up fast.

So in the blaze of afternoon I took our truck and drove up the potholed track. I parked on the crest of the hill, between two rock piles, and from the shade of a thorn bush I looked down from this grey dirt and scrub to the zillion miles of the red desert floor; it opened out in front of me like a great ripened fruit, stuffed full of all the savours and tastings a person could ever want. I stared down at it and planned how we'd stay a few months at most with my mother and then Les'd agree that him and me could safely head back out West. I guess when I said Les was all I loved, I was wrong. There's two things I love – Les and the desert – and I can't see how I'd endure getting torn away from either one of them.

After a while I picked my mind off the pain of that and tried to cast my thoughts eastward to where my mother lived. What she'd be doing at that exact moment; with the different time-zones it'd be near evening in Virginia where she lived. I'd asked Les once if she worked, but he didn't know about any of that. All he knew was that she and the man hadn't woken when Les, stepping softly past their tent, saw me awake near the mosquito-mesh and scooped me up. 'How old'd my mother be?' But he shrugged. Twenties then, late thirties now, at a guess. And the man – my dad – around the same. *Why* didn't they wake? I'm positive if anyone grabbed a child of mine I'd wake, no matter what. But Les shrugged wider and said the whole campsite was sleeping hard, that people sleep soundest those early-morning hours before dawn. He gave me his sickly apologising smile and said, 'I made no noise.' He can walk like a bird flying, that's true. Noiseless and quick like some bird going a long journey.

Anyway, no use; with all the guessing in the world I'd no notion what my mother could be doing at this exact moment. So I shifted my brain to make pictures of things which for sure must have happened recently around her. Like, after Les's last call my mother would get in touch with the man to tell him. He works only thirty miles from where she lives, her in the woods and him a teacher at the city university. Les checked that out from some education reference book in a Tucson library or on their computer; anyway he came out of the building muttering the job title and when I asked he said, 'Old foreign languages, that's what the man teaches.' Les looked at me sideways and said, 'Didn't suppose I could understand that much, did you? Thought I wouldn't know what his job title meant?' I felt cheap then because it's true I think of Les as being not any more educated than me – which is pretty damn little; I wonder how my mother'll feel about that. Gulches and rockslides ahead (as Les'd say), because she's most likely got a university degree herself.

So after she hung up from talking with Les, what'd she do? Call the man pretty fast, I guess; they'd still be on speaking terms. If you've loved someone and had a child with them, you don't stop speaking even if you move out, do you? So she'd call him up and he might go out to her place in the woods to talk about us; I can picture that. Or – and if he's moved out he might prefer for her to go visit him – she might drive to the city where he's living in a . . . what? Apartment, I guess. Here's where my picture gets blurred because I can't imagine how folks like him and her would move or speak; would he take her out to some swish restaurant for a meal or just offer her a drink? A drink maybe, since the two of them are split up. And she'd tell him what Les said. The man'd frown, listening hard, then he might ask her if she believes this is genuine, what's behind it and why in hell Les'd want to return me after so many years.

He's got a valid point there. Hope he doesn't start poking around and get in touch with the cops himself. If Les hadn't gotten cold feet I'm sure the two of us could stay on here and be fine and safe. Not that Les necessarily expects me to throw another dead body at him, but the limits he was positive I'd never go beyond – those aren't around any more. I can make all the promises I want, and act as gentle and biddable as I really do long to be, but I can't put trust in me back into Les's head.

My mother'd tell the man and maybe he wouldn't believe her at first; she'd need to say, 'His call was different this time.' Then the man'd believe and most likely he'd take her in his arms and kiss her – but I needn't think about that. He'd be glad for her sake; after this long time I don't guess he'd care about me. He'd kiss her and then he might say into her hair, not really interested, 'How did he sound this time?' And she'd say, 'Like a parent does, talking about a child that's tough to handle. That's how.' Because Les did sound that way, stressed but basically ordinary. Although fifteen isn't being a child any more and there needn't be handling problems, but he made me sound like a baulky head of cattle.

Then she and the man would have another drink or whatever, to celebrate them being happy with each other again, and when she's leaving his apartment he might say casual, 'So what's the next move?' She'll say she's waiting on another call and . . . yeah, I do believe Les ought to make that next call pretty damn soon: And the man'll put his arms around her, wish her good luck and hope to see her again soon; I guess some people do get pleasure out of mauling each other's body around like that. Jeff and I, if you ask me, went at it the wrong way from the start.

Then she'll drive back into those woods of hers and she and the man'll both be guessing what kind of proof Les might have that I truly am their daughter. More kinds than he's told me, for sure; the scar's not the only thing. Maybe it's not the really important one even. And Les went to some other library one day, read up on all the new stuff about blood tests, so he says we can prove it that way if they fuss about the other proofs. Yeah, I guess he did get educated somewhere; he seems to understand all this stuff I wouldn't have a clue about.

I sat up there on the ridge and thought about all this till the sun went down and the frost snuck back in, then I drove down the track and heated cans of beans and stew and we ate. Afterwards I said, 'How soon d'you plan we'll be on our way?' and he said, 'Depends.' I saw by his quick glance that he wanted to park me on her as soon as might be and yet he was unhappy about letting me go to her; his quick shy unhappiness made me sadder than ever too.

Les waited ten days before calling her again; seemed like an awful long time to me but he said, 'You got to trust me in this.' Give her time, he said, let her get impatient wanting her daughter back and needing to find out the truth of it all, don't stampede her or she might rush to the cops without giving herself a chance to believe us. 'All these years,' he said, 'I kept in touch with her, didn't I? Because I felt it was the right thing to do. Told her you were alive and well looked after; I couldn't force myself to return you then but seemed to me she shouldn't worry too much, after the first shock, if she knew you were okay.' And the pain of that first shock of loss, he said, the morning in camp when she and the man found I was missing – that pain must have been strong, there was nothing he could do to wipe out her memory of it. Only he tried to compensate by those phone calls he made through the years. And, he said, his approach had worked, hadn't it? She could trace his number but there'd never yet been cops or sheriff catch up to us. You had to get nervous, and he supposed he always would, but he'd jockeyed her along and kept her as near sweet as you could expect anyone to feel in the circumstances. Listening and talking with him private, that was as good as you could hope for.

So I said, 'Okay, circus man, I trust you,' (he likes me to call him circus man although God alone knows if he's ever worked in one) and I settled to sit on my impatience and wait. Then, ten days after that hot afternoon, he did call her again.

This time we drove for an hour through the desert to a dump consisting of two beat-up frame houses, one chicken-shit roadside diner and a gas station with phone booth outside. One solid hour of red-orange desert, then this hole with no sign of life except the gas station man sleeping in his shack and, far off amid red rock and scattered mesquite bushes and cactus, a silvery railroad train heading fast west. I said, 'You sure do pick the friendliest places for our chats,' and Les coloured up, he said, 'Think yourself lucky.' He said, 'You plan on listening in again?' and I said, 'Sure. Whose life are we talking about anyway?' I jumped down from the truck and followed him.

That tight voice she answers him with every time, it makes me wonder what in hell she's thinking and if she pictures me as an alive person at all. He started off – hoarse, poor man, with his cigarettes and nerves – 'You been thinking over what I said, ma'am?'

She cleared her throat; I'd imagine she might have a pleasant voice if she ever let it go. 'You mean about—'

'The girl, yeah.' He drew a long breath and my fingers tightened on his shoulder because I knew how hard this stuff was for him to say. And how neither him nor myself wanted to hear what he'd say next. 'I got the best of reasons, ma'am,' he said, 'for asking you to take her back.' His fingers reached up to where mine clung at his shoulder; his fingertips ran warm over mine, then he hauled them away. 'I done the best I could for her all these years,' he said, sulky like I imagine a schoolkid might be with a bad essay grade, 'but the truth is—' He stopped, took another long breath, went on, 'This is hard to say on the phone.'

She said in that way she talks past her teeth, 'Let me make clear that you're not going to get within sight or sound of me, not you nor whatever cheap bitch is trying to work this racket with you.' Meaning me; there's no one else. The words look tough, and even in her clipped British accent they sounded so, but something flickered in her tone then . . . as if a crack showed somewhere. A wondering, or at least the possible chance of a wondering. Les raised an eyebrow at me; he'd heard that change in her voice too.

'What'm I meant to do, then?' he said, and although I was standing right beside him he did sound a bit desperate. Like I say, you can do incredible hurt to someone like him without realising, before you've taken time to think what hands or knives are up to. He went on, 'Can't tell the cops on her, can I?' And his fingers climbed back to squeeze mine, saying, *That* at least I'll guarantee never to do. Whether this woman's helpful or not, I won't turn you over to the law.

'The cops?' she said. Blankly, thrown; this you could tell she'd not expected.

'Why yes,' he said, 'you must realise I can't go to the cops, ma'am. On account of what I did myself, all them years ago.' His fingers clutched mine and he said, 'Anyway I wouldn't. I've always treated her like she's my own child.' I whispered to him to hurry and wrap this up, that all this talk about the past was only wasting time. She made a sort of startled noise and he said, 'Yes, she's right here alongside of me, ma'am, she's been listening.' His hand clung at me like he was the one threatened and in trouble. 'Maybe she didn't ought to hear us talk about her like this,' he said, 'but I can't stop her. I've no one to leave her with.' I laughed out loud at that, because when has there ever been? 'Anyway,' he said while his fingers clung at mine like appealing, 'she's a grown woman, pretty near.'

I guess fifteen years old is, at that. Plenty old enough to have a baby if you're lonely or self-willed enough or stupid. Old enough to kill . . . well, there. A seven-year-old can hoist a rifle and do damage with it – but that's no excuse, Cate; I can argue to myself that I did have justification but I can't claim outright innocence. Guess that's what hurts Les most of all, that he realises I was, as you might say, willing. For all the lies I've told him, he's seen through them that far.

No sound from her end of the phone; there's never any background noises like traffic. Les says she lives on some rural route deep in the forests; he did pick up a newspaper once in a while, those first months after he took me, and he read the reports and interviews. Forests; neighbours, I guess, but not nearby. A dirt road like the ones in these hills. Not as lonely as here, Les says, but you wouldn't see anything for all those trees. I don't much like the notion of that.

After a long wait she said, 'How old is your child?' '*Your*' child, and she spoke dreamy as if she wasn't discussing anyone she'd ever met or wanted to. More as if she was being polite to some stranger she felt mildly sorry for.

'Why,' Les said with his hand clinging at mine, 'she's

fifteen, of course. I got her birth date from the newspapers, naturally, ma'am. Near enough, anyway.'

She went on in that dreamy not-interested voice, 'And what's she done that you think you ought to tell the police?' If she never talks to me except in this not-caring tone, I won't feel like she's my mother at all. I got angry because she damn well *ought* to care; I said so to Les, and between me talking at him and him trying not to tell her much all at once, maybe he spoke cagier than he need have.

He said, 'The reason I want to hand her back shouldn't be important to you, ma'am. Your daughter – you must want her.'

She laughed short and angry, not a good laugh to hear. 'Cate was a good child,' she said, 'and if she'd had a chance to grow up she would have grown up good and law-abiding. I'm certain of that. All this talk of police – what young criminal are you trying to palm off on me?' She gathered her breath and when she spoke again it sounded like spitting. 'Monster,' she said, 'monster.'

I shifted my hand to grasp his shoulder tight and show I cared about him, because whatever Les may have done there's not an ounce of truth in calling him a monster. His mouth and eyes twitched when she called him that; I held out my wristwatch to him and he said, 'Ma'am, I got to go now. We been chatting long enough that I don't doubt you got the cops out chasing me. But didn't I tell you I can prove she's yours?'

While she said, 'There's no proving,' I ran Les's fingers down the scar on my arm. But yes, he can surprise me and he sure did then; he shook his head at me as if, That's not important, and he drew out of his pocket a tiny yellow bracelet. Gold, I guess. He waved it at me, then curled it back into the palm of his hand, his pocket. Tiny links, and a heart or such dangling on it.

I say I've no memory of that first three years, and seems to me this is the truth, but once in a while – when we'd see something in a store window or Les'd make some casual remark – then something'd break up to the surface in my mind like a live thing breaking upward through the ice of a pond. And I'd say to Les, 'Wasn't there – didn't we once—' Then Les'd look at me odd, he'd say, 'Not since you been with me,' then he'd question me about it but the ice'd have formed again, there'd be no memory at all. I look back as hard as I can but it's blank, a plain whiteness where I might have been anyplace, living with Les or her or someone else and I know and can prove damn-all about it. So now he told me about this bracelet, how I was wearing it when he took me, how he'd taken it off my wrist and kept it safe all these years, and in my head there was maybe the very faintest of echoes, stirred up by seeing the bracelet and hearing what he said. The faintest possible echo – and I'm not even sure of that.

Les stopped talking and the silence at the other end of the phone went thick and crowded; I got a real odd feeling in my stomach then. Knowing that she was faced with me and she'd have to realise it truly was me at last. After a while she said in a thin slow voice. 'The bracelet was mentioned in the newspaper accounts. It must have been.'

But not like she truly believed so. Les said, 'No, ma'am, I read those reports after I took her and wasn't no mention of it then. The clothes she wore, but no bracelet.' He smiled his loose knowing smile into the phone and said, 'I guess they wanted to keep it secret so if anyone called them and mentioned it, that'd be definite proof.'

She raked together enough energy to say, 'Not so. You could have found it somewhere—' Her voice stumbled over this so I almost felt sorry for her. 'Isn't that what happened? And you're trying to use it as blackmail currency.'

I held up my watch again and Les said to her, 'I'm hanging up now, ma'am. You just think over what I've said, and the proof I've given you. You can check out the interview reports but you won't find the bracelet mentioned.' He promised to call her again, said we'd soon be travelling closer to her.

I said, 'If we ever get started,' and he said, 'We'll be doing that very soon.' Then he did hang up.

3

But for once Les had made up his mind and we started out a couple of days later. When we crossed into Texas I expected the sky would fall or something, all the country from then on being new to me. But nothing happened, only sagebrush and grumbling mountains like back home. I said to Les while we ate cold pizza in a layby one day, 'Are you *sure* we've travelled that many miles?' but yes, no doubt of it. And the sunsets, the nighttime noises of rustle and scurry and hiss, were the same in that northwest part of Texas as back home, with the smell of dust and sage and dry cottongrass in the air.

As I'd expected, we didn't use motels; where would Les find money enough? We'd pull off the road next to a clump of cottonwoods or a creek, and make ourselves as comfortable in the truck as we could — him sprawled out in the back and me stretched along the front seat. Not the first time by a long way that we'd slept so, and I figured it might not be the last time either. All depending on what the woman'd say when we'd arrive.

Texas gone, Oklahoma with its squared-off roads and cornstalks waving everywhere. Dry cornstalks rattling in the wind; the crop had been harvested and I realised this was early fall. There'd be cold weather coming in a month or so, and snow maybe as deep as up in our mountains. I said to Les, 'What'll we do if, wherever we are, the weather turns nasty?' and he took a drag of his cigarette, said, 'Happened before, hasn't it?' (but speaking quick, as if he was trying not to think about any of that). He spread out his maps and frowned. I said, 'Whereabouts're we heading? How much longer'll it take?' and he drew his finger across the map to show our route. But it was only his stubby finger moving on paper, and I did get tired staring at the dusty actual road while he drove; Oklahoma to Arkansas and Arkansas to Tennessee but I didn't care. Except for the hiccup of seeing the Mississippi. Les woke me from a doze on a morning sheeting with rain and said, 'I don't care how bored you've gotten with scenery, this at least you better notice,' and there it was, a big brown river. Wide, yeah – wide to end all rivers – but especially it was brown like all the floodwaters of the world.

Tennessee – mountains. Not like our bare rocks back home; these grew thick with trees like I'd not much relished the notion of, trees so thick crowded you couldn't see beyond corners or across to the next hill. We stopped to eat and stretch our legs one time in some cloudy gulch under a grey sky; I tipped my head to stare at the trees and I said, 'What's that steam rising off them?'

'Smokies,' Les said, 'that's what they're called. The Great Smoky Mountains.' He tried to cheer me up by telling me not to leave the roadside or I'd get eaten by a bear, but he knew he couldn't truly scare me because I'd grown up out West with all the tricky wildlife roaming around that you could ever expect. Anyway I was brooding on something else; as soon as he got through teasing I said, 'D'you plan on calling her again or will we just show up there?' I'd spent some of the time since his last call imagining how the woman'd run to that man her husband and tell him about Les's proofs, how the man'd maybe kiss her and say, 'That certainly does make it definite that she's ours, aren't we like to die of happiness?' I doubted that he'd truly feel that way, he'd just be saying it because he knew she did feel so, and I didn't want anyone that happy – or anywhere near it – on my account. I for sure wouldn't be the format they were expecting.

Les said, 'You never quit pressuring me, do you?' but he did call her next day, when we were heading up the damn mountains. Not the Smokies still; we'd driven out of that soft rotting stink and dankness as quick as could be. But more ordinary mountains, with bare patches and a falling-down cabin here and there, and in the background rows of hills, each one bluer with haze and leafage than the row before.

It rained and rained, a soaking mist; awful disagreeable weather if you've been in the habit of dryness and sun. In a hollow between two humps of soaking wet hills there was a roadside shack selling apples and a phone booth nearby. 'Last call,' he said as he slid from the truck, but of course I followed him as always. This was my life we were handling, so I'd an urgent need to know what was going on.

A brief call that time. 'We aim to reach your place in a few days, ma'am.' He didn't touch me, instead he'd a cigarette in his hand and he drew toughly on it between talking to her. 'I guess,' he said, 'you're not dumb enough to have the cops waiting for us. No point if you did – we'll look around cagey before you ever catch sight of us – but you'll be too smart to call them in.' He drew hard on the cigarette and turned his back to me. 'After all, you do want this child of yours back, don't you?'

A package, a package labelled and now pretty near being handed over to her. He said something to her about a mother's instinct and grinned down at his cigarette after he'd said it; I guess it was sort of a cutting remark, but I wanted so badly to stay on his side always (not hers) that I gave a sniggery laugh like I totally agreed with him. Anyhow I couldn't truly imagine how much pain she might be feeling – or not – at the other end of the phone, but Les's pain stood right close in front of me; I could see how much of an effort, under his hurtful joshing and grins, all this was costing him. So I sniggered good and loud, and it wasn't till afterwards that I thought, She's my mother, how'd she feel to hear me laughing at her like Les is laughing?

She said nothing, there was that deep silence again like she was shocked wordless, and Les said sharp, 'You listening to me, ma'am? Because I got no time to spare. A few days and we'll be with you, right?'

She started to speak then but he hung up; no point in listening to her dither. We walked back to the truck in those nasty drips of rain and I said, 'She'll know how close we're calling from, right? For sure she knows where, every time.'

He said, 'So what?' but while we climbed into the truck and drove off I imagined her saying to herself, They're much nearer, only one state away. She'd tremble a bit, I guess, happy at the thought. And she'd call the man, tell him, They've reached Tennessee, they'll be here soon. The man'd say – what?

Past the rain and the truck engine and the hiss of tyres, Les said sudden, 'She won't call the cops now. Handling her's like playing a fish, you got one on the hook and if you act cautious you land it easy.' He lurched the truck round another corner on the mountain road. 'She'll wait'll we arrive and she takes a good look at us. Can't hold herself back from longing to see you now, whether or not she fully believes you're hers.'

This brought me up with a jolt. I said, 'Why wouldn't she believe? You gave her those proofs, didn't you?' and he said, 'You don't understand too well how the mind of a woman like that'd work. Yes, she's got the proofs and she *ought* to believe, but an educated stiff-minded woman like that – she'll need run around inside her head searching for some other explanation, before she'll give in and believe.'

I said, 'You mean she mightn't want me after all? She might say no to me from our first sighting?' but he didn't answer, he was busy steering the truck.

I did think to say to him, an hour or so later, 'Maybe those aren't such complete proofs – couldn't she have told some interviewer about the bracelet and such?' But my heart wasn't in this because I recalled the shocked silence she'd gone into as soon as Les mentioned that; there was no mistaking. So I wasn't surprised when Les said no, he'd picked up the local papers after he took me and made a point of reading the interviews she and the man gave, the information released, and there was no mention of any such ornament. Les said the cops always tell folks to hold back some bit of information when a thing like that happens, so the person who did it can prove he's truly genuine.

I agreed when Les told me this; I stopped asking questions and let myself get a bit excited.

My excitement needed to hold itself in for a few more days though; up in those wet mountains the truck engine started creaking and turned out the problem was something Les couldn't fix, something needing a spare part that had got to be ordered from a town away off in the valley. So the truck was laid up but we slept in it anyway; what else could we do?

Les counted his dollars and frowned; he'd not bargained on this extra expense. But we just about had enough cash; I said, 'That must be meant,' and he said, 'Meant, the hell.' He dickered the repair shop man down on the labour charge and by the time we left there everyone, including us, was in a pretty foul mood. But the engine ran okay, we drove out of one lot of hills into another, and the sun came out.

That night we pulled off the road and slept in a falling-apart barn for a change; the nights here were cool but not frosty like out West. Next morning was a sky bluer than the world, and a hot sun which turned the forest all the colours in creation.

Les said, 'We'll get there sometime today,' and I said, 'What time exactly?' But Les went sullen again; those last few days he was taking a different mood every couple of minutes. 'No knowing,' he said, and pinched his lips in; when we left the barn to drive away, he kicked the truck tyres as if they'd betrayed him by bringing him someplace he didn't intend.

Anyway we drove down out of those mountains to lower ones, more like wooded hills. The woods were kind of pretty with the sunlight and the different leaf colours; I could see how you might enjoy living in them if you didn't mind never having a long view. He kept stopping to look at his map; we drove down the eastern slope of the hills and there across in front of us ran a highway. Les was a good navigator, we crossed the highway and left it behind us, then we took one little road after another, each one narrower and bumpier than the one before. First of all blacktop, then rocky dirt. Not many houses, only once in a while a beat-up empty old cabin or – a couple of times only in the whole miles-long stretch – a new brick house.

The road wound and dipped across little sheltered valleys and rock outcrops, but you couldn't see a damn thing distant for those trees. Then at a blind corner we turned off to the bumpiest and threadiest track yet. Les drove real slow now and after a couple of miles he said, 'We ought to be pretty much there.' He'd no sooner said this than we rounded a corner and there was her surname – which I guess is my name too – on a roadside mailbox.

Somehow I'd expected her to be waiting at the door to greet us. Stupid of me because, even if she felt like greeting, how'd she know which day (or week) we might arrive? But Les turned the truck up her winding driveway (you couldn't see the house from the road) and he'd gotten himself into a fouler temper than ever, he cussed something remarkable. His grumpiness made me nervous because of what-all he might be thinking behind it, so I said sharp, 'You've not forgotten what you promised me before we set out?' He stuck his mouth together mulish and squinched his eyes and I said, 'I'm not staying around the woman if you don't stay too. I mean it. If you try to dump me and drive out of here, I'll jump in the truck quick and ride right out with you. No way you're leaving me with this woman I never met before.'

He said, 'Course you've met her before. She's your mother,' and he squinched narrower.

I said, 'You know damn well what I mean,' and the two of us sulked while the truck rounded the last bend of the driveway and pulled up in front of the cabin. That's all it was, a big long cabin. Fancy and modern all right, but with low eaves and a pile of cordwood stacked nearby like the woman was playing pioneer. Les braked the truck in the turnaround and I said, 'You promise me now. I'm not getting out of this truck till you promise you'll stay around for always.'

He said, 'Oh Christ okay I promise, will that do?' Then he jumped down from the truck and slammed the door. He hadn't sounded believable but he did say the words of the promise and I'd never known him to lie, just as I'd not lied when I was a kid. He'd be mortal insulted now if I acted like I didn't trust him. So I got down out of the truck too, but slower.

He went up to the front door, which was all glass, and knocked on it; you could see the room beyond was empty and I said, 'There's no one home.' Not her, not the man. I don't know why I was so sure of that – she could have been in the kitchen or a bedroom, peeking out to take a slow look before she'd let us in – but the place, the whole clearing the cabin was built in, felt hollow, emptied of people. And so it proved. Les banged again at that door, then he went around the house looking in windows and banged again at the back. I stood away from the cabin, I leaned against the truck so it wouldn't get free of me, and when he showed up from around the other end of the cabin I said, 'There's no one home, right?'

He chewed his lip. 'Nope.' He moved his mouth around some more, thinking, then he came back to the truck, sat down in its open doorway and said, 'We'll wait. Nothing else we can do.' He fixed a cigarette and chucked the match away like he always does; I had a thought and went, found the match, stamped its heat out good and buried it in the dirt. I said, 'You better dispose of those careful, this place is a tinderbox ready to pop,' and when he looked blank at me I showed him how all the dirt was a network of tree roots and fallen leaves and pine needles and such. Which is another reason I'd never choose to live in a wood. However. And the smell of the place was quite different than out West; that's dry but this was damp and full of a million thick scents instead of just the desert sagebrush and coarse grass. Full of insect hum too – we kept brushing them off us and we tried everything to get comfortable while we waited for her. Sitting in the truck with the windows shut, but that got entirely too warm. Out in the clearing with the insects rushing happily from one to the other of us.

The sun began to slide downwards after a long time and the insects lessened; I said, 'Maybe she's not coming back today, whyn't we get out of here and try again another day?' I would have been pretty damn happy to do just that. But Les said no, a car was parked out back so it must be hers, she'd be out walking or such and we better wait. I said, 'Oh hell hell hell,' and I slid out of the truck again and propped myself against the side of it. Les got out too and slapped his hand where a small black something was biting him; he cussed and I laughed, but not by any means happy. We stood there grouching and sweating – and Les heard her first, he said under his breath, 'Footsteps.' Said it so quiet that she couldn't have heard.

She stopped dead when she rounded the corner, stopped and stared like she wished we'd just burn up and away out of her sight.

4

Les gave her the hungry-to-please grin he uses when he's scared, but it didn't do a bit of good. She said, 'You're trespassing. And hunting season hasn't begun yet.' The devil of it was, I could tell from the quick gritty way her eyes ran all over the two of us that she knew damn well we weren't hunters, knew at once who we were — or rather who we claimed to be — but she'd try if a fast brush-off would get rid of us anyway. Can you credit that — from my own mother? But that's exactly what she said and how she looked.

I yanked up my jeans and pulled my top straight so I'd feel halfway presentable. Neither Les nor I was in the most shining-clean shape, but on account of the sort of journey we'd made that hadn't been possible, and if she'd any sense she would realise so. Seemed like she hadn't; her eyes ran like small animals all over us and got colder all the time.

Les widened his friendly smirk — which I could have told him was a mistake, but there you are. He said, 'Your driveway, ain't it, ma'am? Your name's on the mailbox.'

I don't understand what makes her sort of woman tick, never have figured them out. Women who're scented like a city shopping mall and dressed smooth as butter, even way out there in the countryside, women who talk like you're a bit of dirt dropped under their nose. And you can tell by the sound of them that they've got all the words in the world stashed inside their heads, but they're picking the most ordinary and cheapest for you because that's all you'll be likely to understand. And they stare at you cautious and hating, as if you're a rabid fox. Women with faces as smooth as their clothes, and all their thoughts most likely smooth and hard as their faces.

She had on a pale tan shirt and long pants (not jeans) and slung round her shoulders a dark brown suede jacket with fringes like she was playing cowgirl. But you couldn't imagine her sort doing any hard work ever. Dark brown boots, and her face made up smooth and pale as ice; you'd wonder if she'd any real blood in her. Blonde hair pulled back smooth and her mouth a pressed-tight line, her eyes two alight spots of anger while she watched us. I'd seen women like that out West when we'd be driving along the edge of some tourist trap. I'd say to Les, 'Love to chuck her in a thornbush and wipe that sour smoothness off her face'; I'd laugh and he'd grunt agreement, then we'd drive on away from there to our own kind who might be sweaty and cussing or fighting but at least they'd be real; you could talk and argue with them and ask questions.

I watched her now in quick glances as tough and cagey as she was watching us, and I thought we might as well pack up right then and drive out of there, because we weren't going to make any sort of a dent on her. Also she looked very like the sort who might pull the cops on us, she'd that hard slick air. She said loud and brutal back to Les, 'I didn't invite you.' She took a breath which was as controlled as the rest of her, and she said, 'You'd better both get moving fast. We're expert at dealing with un-wanted visitors around here.' Meaning trespassers, of course. Meaning us.

Les's silly grin came and went like he hadn't fastened it tight enough and wasn't sure how to. I got disgusted with the pair of them – her because I couldn't imagine how she'd ever be or could have been my mother, and Les because after those phone calls of his he'd kept telling me how she was all sewn up, he could tell she accepted what he'd said, so we'd arrive and everything'd be just fine. He was adult and ought to know more than me, so I mostly had trusted him on this, but now it felt like I'd been wrong to trust, ought to have held to my own judgement and refused to trust either one of them.

I said to him from the side of my mouth, without bothering to look at him, 'You surely did explain to her so she'd agree, didn't you?' I turned away and sighed deep, kicked the dirt. 'Christ,' I said, 'what shitheads I do get mixed up with.' I kicked the bare red dirt again and thought how this red clay was wrong too, it didn't look or smell or fall apart like any dirt I'd known out West. I went on kicking it, didn't look at Les because I knew he'd have his hurt-dog face like he always does when I pick holes in something he's proposed. And I certainly didn't look at the woman – my supposed mother – because why would I?

'Yeah,' Les said in a niggly defensive voice, 'I did so too explain to her.' He swung around to me, and the woman made a small squashed movement as if she thought he might hit me but she'd decided not to interfere. I could have told her different, Les being so scared of any violence. He'll sometimes yell and cuss plenty, but he acts like he doesn't know what his arms and legs are for. I can give as good as I get in a fight, and better; I'm a hell of a lot more use at defending myself than he'd ever be. So when he swung around I got ready to yell back; we'd had a long wearing ride and none too comfortable, and you could say I was in the mood for a flaring argument. He sent his trembly gaze to one side of me and the other – didn't even have guts enough to stare me in the face – and he said, 'You heard me each time on the fucking phone, didn't you? Right there you was beside me at them last calls, nudging and telling me what to say as if you'd got any Christly right to order me around.' He gave a baffled glare at the woman's shiny cabin and I could see his anger was failing; he can't ever boost it to last. 'Where would you be,' he said feeble to me, like an appeal, 'if I'd not done everything for you, all them years?'

I got real angry then because no one had asked him to take me away from my rightful mother, he'd done it on impulse because he wanted to, and anything that happened afterward . . . just happened. 'Hell,' I said, 'you've no right anyway, no duty and no right. I never *asked* you to drag me up in one hovel or another all over the desert, did I?'

The woman made a sort of sound and we both turned to stare at her. A short sound, not noisy, as if she started to speak or cry out but then choked it back. She'd squinched her eyes shut like she was staring at private pictures, had forgotten us. When she opened her eyes again her gaze on me stayed hard and cold as stone, but that small private sound of hers had somehow made me realise all over again that she was my mother. I couldn't recall a look or a sound of her from the past, but if I could so easy grasp that she must be my mother, why couldn't she as easy accept me? We needed to clinch it by giving her proof, those damn proofs we'd carried halfway across the country.

So I said to Les from my mouth corner, 'Wake yourself up, can't you? And remind her we got proof.' He reached into his jeans pocket, dug out the little bracelet and held it dangling on his fingers to her.

She stared at it and took a step back. Forwards you'd expect, but she took a long stumbling backwards step like the bracelet was an insect and she guessed it might sting her. Kept her eyes on it though, and the hard glare had gone, she was wide and wondering almost like a child herself. 'No,' she said after that long backwards step, 'no.'

Les jiggled it in his fingers that are always brown with tobacco, he took a couple of strides towards her and dangled it in front of her face. 'Go on,' he said, firm-voiced and confident now, 'take a good look at it.' She shook her head and he said, 'You've not forgot it, surely? Anyway it's got her name on.'

She shut her eyes but her hand opened out of itself and he laid the little bracelet across her palm. A short length of gold-coloured chain it was, obviously a child's, and along with the links the letters C-A-T-E strung. She opened her eyes and looked down at it; the A hung a bit crooked from the others and she nudged that with the forefinger of her other hand as if its hanging astray meant something. 'And,' she said low to herself while her finger slid further along the chain, 'the link I mended.' All at once the bracelet was wound tight around her fingers and she jumped forward, she clutched at Les's throat. 'Where's Cate?' she yelled. 'What did you do to her?' She said, 'The blood on those clothes of hers,' and she shook him. 'Where did you bury her? I've got to know.'

You could tell she wasn't a woman that was in the habit of great physical effort, not a tough-muscled female like some of the types we'd known, and I figured she couldn't do a vast amount of harm no matter how hard she clutched his throat. But his neck is pretty skinny and, with him hating violence so, I guess he got scared. Anyway he croaked at me sideways, 'You gonna let her kill me? Whyn't you make her see sense, so she'll turn me loose?'

If she wouldn't listen to Les she pretty damn sure wouldn't listen to me, but his face went red and then dusky, so I opened my mouth to try. I shut it again because she yelled at him, 'No, *you* tell.' She'd gotten a solid grip on him by this time, she shook him fiercer and I did get kind of worried then because on that thin neck of his the head started wobbling. 'The blood on those clothes of hers,' the woman said, 'Cate's blood, and her night-dress stuffed under a rock in that godforsaken desert gully—' She wasn't noticing me or Les or what she was doing to him, she was off someplace by herself.

My heart started thumping like it had when I'd gotten angry at Jeff, only this time the anger was on account of what she was doing to Les, not for any threat to me. So I took three steps and stood beside her, I measured her height and muscle against mine and there shouldn't be any problem; if she wouldn't leave him alone voluntarily I could easy fight and overcome her. I said, 'You better hadn't quite kill him, had you?' I sounded so drawly and laidback, I couldn't hardly credit that this was me. I said, 'An awkward thing to hide, is a death,' and because I was trying so strenuous not to let any tremor of what we'd done with Jeff get into my voice, it came out sounding flatter and more uninterested than ever.

Anyway it stopped her, she took her hands off him and swung around, went over to a big tree trunk and laid her face against the bark. After a while she said, 'Oh dear God.' Les had gone back to the truck and was sitting in its doorway catching his breath; she walked across to him and said, 'Why are you tormenting me like this? Cate was my daughter and I've more right than anyone in the world to be told what happened to her.' During all this she didn't even glance at me, she acted like I didn't exist. Her colour rose up and she clenched her hands on each other. She said in the roughest voice imaginable, 'I'd gladly kill you if I felt I could get away with it, because you've shown me proof that you were involved in Cate's death.' The little bracelet was still wound among her fingers, and when she said this she tightened her hurting grip on it.

Les's face was normal colour again but her clutch hadn't done his voice any good. 'All these years,' he said to her hoarsely, 'and now I wish I'd never shown up here, ma'am. That's the truth. Maybe never kept in touch with you either. But what in hell am I to do with the girl?'

Both of them talking like I wasn't standing there next to them, or like I was a stupid animal that couldn't understand a word they'd say. I'd expected some sort of a welcome from her after these many years and miles, and beyond this it hurt me like crazy to hear Les – who I'd always felt warm and happy toward and welcomed by –

talk like I was an unfeeling piece of wood. A baulky piece of wood that wouldn't act right when you tried to handle it, and that he longed to get rid of.

So I flung around at him – truly I believe I'd not been so angry since what happened with Jeff – and I yelled, 'Where's all your fancy promises now?' Him and her both stared at me, but I was steamed up and I kept on yelling. 'You did too promise. Said you knew from the way she answered you on the phone. Said she was still raw hurting for me and she'd gotten disposed to trust your word. Said you could guarantee she'd be damn glad to get me back.'

When I got through shouting there wasn't any sound except the buzz of those damn insects and the rustle of leaves; the air sat on us hot and damp and I felt all over again that this woman couldn't possibly be my mother, because if she was she'd have to realise it by now, looking at me and hearing me; she wouldn't be able to go on denying. But she stood there slickly dressed and hard-faced, and her eyes on me had no more expression than water. Water not moving under the sun or wind, water not interested.

After a while Les said to me, quiet like he'd lost hope, 'Show her your scar anyway. If that don't persuade her, nothing will.' He leaned his head against the truck and sighed. 'Then we'll need to go away from here and—'

I said quickly, 'We can't go back where we've come from, haven't you kept on telling me how that'd be too dangerous?' The woman's eyes came alive then, they jumped from one to the other of us. Les didn't notice though, and I didn't care.

'I know that, dumbhead,' he said. 'Ain't that what this journey's been about?' He shifted his rear on the step, like the thought of where we'd need to travel next hurt him. 'Show her your scar anyway,' he said, and I could tell he was tired out. He's not young any more; our journey and this damp heat were getting to the pair of us.

So I turned around to the woman and pulled up the short sleeve of my top to show the scar that runs from under my left arm nearly down to the elbow. Ragged, an ugly scar, but that isn't exactly Les's fault.

The woman glanced at it, then she said to him, 'Is this supposed to mean anything?' Cool, like I say; not really interested. She said, 'Cate had no scar when I last saw her.' Like, End of discussion, now will you please both go away.

Les stared into space unsurprised, didn't move. I knew the facts of this because Les had explained them to me; how the gash my arm got, right after he took me from the campsite, accounted for all that blood being on the little clothes. I said to her, 'He—' I felt awkward trying to explain anything when she was so set on not believing us, but Les stared ahead of him and didn't speak, so I went on. 'As I had the story from him, my arm got tore accidental, right after he snatched and ran with – and that's why the blood was on the little clothes.' I fingered the scar; yes, it must have bled plenty. 'Bled like stink,' I told her, 'he said. Being deep and all.'

Les said dreamy, like he'd given up, 'I ought to have taken her to hospital and gotten it stitched, maybe plastic surgery or such, then the scar would've been tidier.' He fixed his eyes on the woman, with the clear pure gaze he wears when he's talking about those early days. 'But I couldn't take her anywhere official, could I?' Insects sang around us, the sun dripped and he said, 'You'll be welcome to get all the tests you want run on her, ma'am. Laboratory work, blood tests and such.' He shifted his head to stare at the treetops so there'd be no chance of him meeting my gaze with what he'd say next. 'I just want to get her off my hands. Too much of a live wire for me, she is.'

This was what we'd agreed he'd say, a safe easy form of words to hide everything about Jeff and not scare the woman, but hearing him really say it hurt me more than somewhat. I squinched my teeth into my lip and said, 'Oh hell, oh goddam hell.' I couldn't believe that now the moment had come Les would truly shove to hand me over to this woman I didn't remember and who didn't want me. But he was trying for just that, trying hard and desperate.

The woman stared from one to the other of us; at his mention of blood tests something shifted around in her face so she didn't look cool and unconcerned any more, and when she answered him her voice was troubled with little tremors and unevennesses. But not a welcoming or believing voice, never any note of that. I supposed that the reason his mention of blood tests had shook her was only, she'd not expected a ragged-looking man like him to know about such things – let alone use them to bargain with. Like, his lies were getting deep and she needed to figure out the best way to throw them away.

This wish of hers to get rid of us as soon as might be really got to me; in all the circumstances, how wouldn't it? So I said to her loud and clear, 'Les and me'll just go and not bother you again. It was all a mistake us showing up here, Les should've had better sense. Too many years, and neither you nor me rightly remembering the other. Never was likely to work, was it?' Beside me Les got to his feet like a stumbling old workhorse; he was suddenly too tired to fight her any more.

Her minchy little voice went on, saying she didn't believe a word we'd spoken to her, and I cut across it by walking back to the truck. I climbed in and Les started to haul himself up the other side; suddenly she was at the truck door and her hand feeling across the metal of it like you'd handle a stubborn animal. 'Wait a minute,' she said, 'you can't throw this – this threat of blood tests at me and then just walk out. You seem to be more skilful than most of the other tricksters who've contacted me, but that doesn't mean—' I ought to have realised there'd be other people claiming – there's plenty of dishonest folk around – but this did make me feel odd for a moment.

Les gazed down at her and said solemn, 'Did any of them suggest blood tests, ma'am?'

'One or two,' she said short, 'but when the arrangements had been made, somehow they never showed up to take the tests.'

Les said, 'We'll guarantee not to budge till you get the results, ma'am.' I guess he was realising, as I surely was, that we were damn nearly cleaned out of cash; the truck repairs and the last of the travel had taken pretty much all of what we'd had.

She went on fingering the metal of the truck and staring at him; there was a short tight silence, then she said, 'I don't believe a word you've told me – but this is what we'll do.'

5

I wouldn't know how to begin describing the inside of a house like that. Not a bit like an ordinary cabin inside, more like some fancy city house; bits of coloured glass ornaments and furry rugs and acres of shiny woodblock floor. With overhead a couple of huge imitation wagon-wheel lamps, playing at being rustic but, you could tell, real expensive. The living room ran right across the front of the cabin and its ceiling went clear up to the peaked roof; I realised the place hadn't half as many rooms as it looked from outside. Which might create a problem, but we'd face that when we got to it. The important thing was whether she'd offer to let us stay at all.

When we were all inside she shut the sliding glass door and Les shoved out his hand to her, he said, 'Lester Davidson, ma'am. Glad to meet you.' She looked at his hand like it was some stinky animal, and just then the phone rang. Les got his eager-to-please grin and he said, 'For sure it ain't me calling you this time.' She glared like he was more animal than ever, then she went across to the table under a side window and picked up the phone.

Sure I listened hard, why wouldn't I? Les and me had only our wits to help us, so we might as well use them as busy as we could. She said, 'Oh hi, Elly,' and this other woman's voice started yakking on. Smooth and glitzy and very sure of itself, pretty much like hers. City women for sure, the pair of them.

The other woman clacked on and on; I picked out stray words and it seemed the two of them had been out walking the woods that afternoon, then when this other woman got home there was a letter waiting about alimony or such. Marriage troubles, divorce. She chattered on like she was talking to the second half of herself, and the woman our end made sort of comforting noises but you could tell her heart wasn't in it, she was too damn occupied with keeping an eye on us. So, after what seemed like half an hour but was most likely about five minutes, the other woman must have realised she wasn't getting the response she'd expected; she said something and the woman our end said, 'Yes, I'll be free for another hike tomorrow. You can tell me the details of what he's asking then.' The other woman said something and this one interrupted, 'Elly, I'm not sure about an all-day hike.' With her eyes on us like we might be planning to run off with some of her fancy possessions as soon as her back was turned. 'No, not here,' she said fast, then she caught herself up. 'I'll meet you by your mailbox at ten tomorrow morning if that suits you. I'll know by then whether I'll be free for the day.'

It struck me that she'd her own life ongoing, a busy pleasant life we'd no notion of and that we were messily interrupting. I couldn't see how I'd ever fit into this life of hers, even if she changed her mind and decided to let me. Meanwhile the other woman's voice coaxed, questioned. Like, you sound strained, honey, are you sure you're not talking under duress? The woman our end – I guess I ought to call her 'my mother' but namings don't come that easy – gave a forced little silly laugh and said, 'Oh, Elly darling! You sound like a policewoman.' She said goodbye, she hung up and came slowly – like she hated the pair of us – back toward us across that shining floor.

'Blood tests,' she said, 'it'll take a little while to arrange those and wait for the results.' She sat down, folded her hands tight between her knees and said, 'Meanwhile I repeat that I accept none of what you've said. The bracelet—' one hand made a small brisk movement but she frowned at it and tucked it away again – 'there could be many ways you got hold of that. Most of them dishonest. Anything else—' her voice went whimpery till she picked it up again – 'I must have mentioned in an interview somewhere, sometime.' Les started to interrupt but she talked on and his voice faded. 'I'm calling your bluff,' she said hard and tough like hammering a nail into ironwood. Then she smiled, but a sneery grin, not pleasant. 'And,' she said, 'sooner or later, before the tests results come through, the pair of you will run away, because laboratory results don't lie. You'll run like rats, just as those other claimants did.' Her voice caught in the middle of this but she grabbed it. She got up and began to pace from us to the side window, to the glass front of the room, to us again. 'I told the police both times,' she said, 'as soon as the pretenders made an approach to me, and I kept the police closely in touch. Because I was determined to help them track down those vultures.' She halted in front of us and said sharp, 'You understand what I'm saying?'

Les didn't speak, he just hung in his chair limp and waiting, so I said, 'You mean you plan to inform the cops on us pretty soon?'

She and I stared deep at each other. Mother and daughter is an odd feeling, especially when the woman refuses to accept that she's your mother. 'I could phone them now, this minute,' she said, 'I ought to. Why shouldn't I?' But this was getting too odd for me, because she didn't say definitely if she would or wouldn't. So I shrugged, I grinned and tried to make my grin as unpleasant as hers, and I watched her. She didn't bear that too well, she started pacing again and giving us little quick glances. Especially me. 'You mustn't think I'm allowing you the benefit of the doubt,' she said. 'In my mind there's no doubt at all. If I treat you differently from the other imposters it's only because of a quirk I've taken, a whim.' She paced away and spoke back to us over her shoulder. To me, that time, more than to Les. 'It's been so long,' she said, 'this man has kept up his devilment for so many years that I can't help wondering what his motive is and what sort of girl—' she stood by the far window looking out and her voice only took the tiniest catch – 'would associate with him. So—' she turned and walked back to us and she'd toughened herself up – 'tomorrow I'll make enquiries about getting the tests done. Meanwhile—' she glanced toward the back rooms and I could see her figuring, calculating – 'don't expect to be given the free run of this place. I've more sense than that. The two of you can—' She stopped; her plans for trying to corral us were noticeably giving her trouble.

Les sat like he'd melted into the chair and was just waiting for her to throw us out; then he'd curve through the air and fall, would never move again. An old man he looked to be, what with fatigue and discouragement, although according to him his true age is his late fifties. With us having no money, we'd need to scruff around in these woods someplace till she made up her mind. I didn't understand too well about the lab tests, but when the results did come through she'd obviously deny, if she got half a chance, whatever they were supposed to prove, and she'd chuck us anyway.

I said, 'We'll go find a motel,' though we for sure wouldn't. We could sleep in the truck again but how we'd buy food I couldn't at all figure. We'd need to steal it; no other way.

She opened her mouth, shut it again, said, 'Wait a minute.' Didn't say any more.

I said, 'Ain't no great size, this cabin. How many bedrooms you got?' Didn't imagine there could be more than two; she agreed to that. Two. Seemed like she couldn't bring herself to lose sight of us for the night, yet her mind acted stiff about letting us stay. So I decided to shift her into making up her mind, I said, 'Then either Les or me'll need to—'

Les woke himself up at that and cut in with, 'I can easy go find some other place, angel.' His eyes on me were brown, huge; I couldn't read them.

'No,' I said quick; I couldn't free myself of the notion that once he got out of my sight he might just decide to keep on travelling because that would be simplest for him. Without me he could head back West and he'd be in no danger, he'd be free of me that had killed Jeff and caused all the complications. I got up and went over to him, grabbed his shoulders. 'You promised,' I said, 'damn you. I'd never have agreed to us meeting up with her except you did promise me you'd always stick around.' I sounded like a little kid, tearful and angry. But I didn't cry, I was shook up but mostly damn furious. 'All these years?' I said. Back over my shoulder to her I said, 'Tell him he can stay here. I'll sleep on the floor, or he will. Somehow we'll work things out.'

She said in that cool voice with tiny quivers running underneath it, 'Whichever of you has the spare bedroom will get locked in, and I'm certainly not trusting the other one an inch. But if he goes away for the night—' She gave me that sneery grin again and she said, 'You're not sure of him, are you? Neither am I. It would be so easy for him to dump you and run.' Then her face brightened, she'd figured out how to make life really difficult for him. 'Yes,' she said, 'the truck stays here. His truck and his luggage, and I'll keep the truck keys.'

Les ought to have flinched at this, for his truck was precious like an arm or a lung to him, but seemed like he'd shifted his mind so far into the future that he barely noticed. He said to her, 'How long did I ought to stick around overall, ma'am?' As if, for all her denials, he knew and she knew something that I didn't begin to know. 'Till the tests is done and you've the results,' he said, 'right? For sure you won't need me beyond then.'

So there it was, he'd never from the time we set out

intended to stay with me for always. Dump me and head away, that sounded to be his motto. After those twelve goddam years we'd lived together and no one else. Nearly my whole life.

So I shook him by his thin shoulders and I said, 'You *can't* run out. You *promised*.' That didn't have much effect, so I got cunning. 'If you go off and don't show up again, I won't stay with her either, why should I? She's no one I exactly know. I'll—' inventing, but I could have done those things too – 'I'll steal a car, her car maybe, and head out after you. Back exactly to where we—'

'Hush,' he said, 'you hush now.' His finger stood warm and fiercely warning on my lips and I needed it, I was nearly mad enough to have told her everything. 'Toughen yourself up, will you?' he said. 'God knows you got enough toughness inside you when you want.' He was angry too and maybe he said more than he should have. 'We both know how tough you can get, don't we?' he said. Soft, but she'd hear. The room went very quiet.

After a while she said, 'Oh yes. There was some mention of your not wanting to hand her over to the police, wasn't there? Not because of the fact that you'd kidnapped her when she was an infant, but because of—' she turned her hard smooth glare on me – 'something she's done recently.' She said, 'Before either of you spends a night here I'm going to find out what that something was.' She waited, swinging her hands loose at her sides like the two of us were just a nuisance interruption to her.

I was still steamed up but started to realise that I ought to act a bit cagier. I said to Les, 'You going to tell her?' I clutched his arm tight and said, 'You promised not, didn't you?' Because if she found out about something the size of murder, she'd go running to the cops right away; you could tell in a moment she was that sort of woman. Even if I'd already been proved her daughter, mightn't she go running? Les had told me that if the woman pressed us we'd cook up some minor thing and pretend it was that. So I let go his arm, I turned around to the woman and I said, 'Your daughter, right?' Her face took a sort of twitch but she stopped it. Tough luck on her though; we were there to prove that I was really hers. I said, 'What'd you guess your daughter might ever do wrong to get in trouble with the cops?' Les started to speak but I put my whole hand across his mouth and said, 'At worst, I mean.'

Like she was playing a game with us, that's how her face relaxed. When I puzzled over that afterwards, I decided that she was damn sure her perfect daughter Cate could never have done anything to land herself in cop trouble, so in guessing she really was playing a game with this brash uncomforting kid who was trying to jump into her dead daughter's place. 'Oh,' she said, 'let's see.' Of course she picked the most likely first. 'You could have been into drugs.' Nope, that didn't faze me; Les and I lived alone to ourselves, away from the streets and schools and dealers and such, and anyhow Les was never inclined that way. She said, 'Or a minor robbery. Or underage driving. A traffic violation?' I near laughed out loud because although Les complains I'm the fastest thing on two wheels, rounding corners, I never had an accident yet. Even Les admits I'm a damn good driver when I want to be.

It was pathetic, these things she'd dreamed up that she supposed were cop material. So different they were than the one big thing I'd truly done. But I got a hold of myself and said loud to Les, like triumphant, 'Didn't I tell you she'd not be fazed by a bit of cop trouble?'

Les cleared his throat and said to her, 'I really better be moving off now, ma'am.' I clung to him again and yelled but he said to me, 'Only for tonight. I promise to be back again in the morning,' and I made him give me his solemn promise. When Les promises a thing – which is rarely – it's set like in concrete and you know he won't break his word.

So I did finally let go of him and he stood up, he gave her the truck keys.

He looked skinnier and tireder than ever, so I said to him, 'Where'll you eat?' Hinting fiercely; she mightn't have enough rooms for sleeping, but there must be enough food around to feed the three of us. After all, we'd travelled a long way and she'd surely be glad past all the world when the test results were in and she realised I truly was her daughter. So I hung onto Les and kept hinting at her loud and clear.

And she did take the hint; first she gave us stuff like Cokes and corn chips, cheese flings, then after she'd watched us wolf those down she said, 'I might as well fix a meal.' And it was a good one – spaghetti, different flavours of icecream with chocolate sauce and little cookies.

When we finished, the sun was going down behind the trees and I knew Les'd be in a hurry to go find himself an empty cabin or such before dark. He wiped his mouth off, pulled his jacket tight around him, said, 'I thank you, ma'am,' and started toward the door. I went after him and said, 'You give me your solemn promise again so I'll be sure of it,' and he did. I hated to see him go but wasn't my house.

The woman said, 'There's some small motels out on the highway which wouldn't charge much.' He thanked her politely as if how much they charged was of any interest to him, then he went out, slouched off down the driveway and was gone. I was alone with the woman my supposed mother.

6

I'd kept telling myself that her caginess and obstinacy might somehow be on account of Les hanging around, that when he'd gone she would break out of her tough shell and . . . take me in her arms, I guess. Acknowledge me, whatever mothers do after so long of a time apart. But her face didn't change or flicker, only after a long silence she said, 'You're so young – how did you get involved with a man like him?' I opened my mouth to burst out at her, but for sure that wouldn't have done any good and I didn't get a chance anyway. She interrupted my first words by saying in a tone like all the rivers freezing up, 'No, don't bother telling me your history. I'm not interested.' I guess I was tired like Les, and her disbelief crushed me past arguing with. I didn't cry but I sagged into the chair Les had used and I stared at nothing. The woman carried out the china we'd used into the kitchen, then she plonked herself in front of me and said like an ultimatum, 'You want to help me do the dishes?'

'Oh,' I said, 'yeah.' Daughterly response, I guess. Her kitchen was glitzy as you'd expect, all bright shiny colours and imitation marble tops. She shoved a drying cloth into my hand and I said, 'We never bothered with much in the way of dishes or housekeeping.' Fast food and junk food do save an awful lot of work.

'I can believe you didn't,' she said real catty. She rinsed suds off a plate and shoved it at me. 'I'll start making arrangements for the tests tomorrow,' she said. In so damn rude a voice that I couldn't let it pass.

'You don't *have* to want me,' I said, 'there's always choices.' There was too; rather than have her so damn fussy about what sort of a daughter she'd accept, I'd go travelling again, I'd force Les to take me. Where to I hadn't figured, nor how we'd live; on welfare handouts most likely, same as always. I put the plate down and faced her. 'If you're so all-fired reluctant about being my mother,' I said, 'what in the hell makes you suppose I'd want to be proven your daughter anyway? I'd rather opt out of the whole relationship, wouldn't I?'

'There's no point,' she said, 'in discussing what – in assuming—' Her mouth took a long tremor but she got it under control fast; she was one stiff-boned lady. She said, 'We'd better leave any detailed discussion till after the results of the tests, don't you think?' But not as if she was asking me. She kept rinsing dishes and shoving them at me and she said fast, 'You do understand about these lab tests and how much they're supposed to prove?'

Basically not; I left all that stuff to Les. He got excited about them, said she'd be forced to accept their results, but seemed to me this woman would accept damn-all she didn't want to. So I shrugged and said, 'Not my department.' The kitchen was brightly lit but the night outside pressed at the windows. And all those damn tree branches reaching . . . I said, 'You could go on acting suspicious for ever though, couldn't you?' I buffed another of her damn plates dry and laid it down careful; there'd be hell to pay if I broke one. She might even try to get the money from me for a replacement, but she'd be on a losing pitch there. The tree branches reaching, tapping, got to me thoroughly and I said, 'You got a careful little place here but there's a hell of a lot of trees, isn't there? Are they all yours? Don't you ever feel smothered in among that lot?'

But clearly she accepted her trees as natural and unthinking as I'd hoped she would accept me her child; she looked startled and then annoyed like I was just chatting to avoid something. She said loud and distinct like I was acting slow-witted, 'The laboratory tests will prove whether – whether it's possible you could be mine.'

They'd prove much more definite than that, according to what Les had yakked on about. A billions-to-one chance beyond the ghost of any reasonable doubt; I did recall he'd said so. But there was another important factor which she'd not yet mentioned, so I said it. 'How about him then – the man? Where's he fit into all this?'

She clattered a cup in the sink and said, not looking at me, 'You mean the man who brought you here?' Damn well she knew I didn't mean Les.

'Nuh-uh,' I said angry. 'No, *him*.' I laid down the drying cloth; it was more important that we get this parentage sorted than that her blasted dishes get dried smear-free. 'The man who,' I said, 'I'd need to call him my father?'

Her hands went motionless. 'You mean Brad?'

And she wouldn't face me, didn't have the guts to meet my eyes while we talked. 'If that's his name,' I said, 'yeah. How about him, what's he say about all this?'

After a long pause she said, 'I haven't told him.'

'Why the hell not? Or isn't he around any more?' I recalled those airy calculations Les had done, based on nothing really, after each phone call; how for years, according to him, the man her husband had been definitely there and then all of a sudden not. There's death, of course, but she seemed too uptight about the mention of him for that. I said, 'Nothing happened to him, did it?'

'No,' she said, 'he – we—' She emptied the sink and started scouring it out real hard. 'Not that it's any of your business,' she said, 'but he and I began to rub each other up the wrong way and it seemed best for him to set up house on his own for a while. We're still very good friends, of course.' She added hasty, as if she wanted Les and me to know she'd got backup, 'He lives in the city, only half an hour from here.'

'And you'd told him previous that Les kept on calling?'

She said, 'Yes.' I got the strangest feeling then, that I was in charge and she was the kid unsure of itself. 'Of course he knew that,' she said, 'from the years he lived here with me after . . . and I . . . yes, I've kept him informed.'

'And you told him we planned on showing up here?' Like I'd pinned her against the countertop and she was trying to dodge me, but no place she could run to. 'About the lab tests and the other proofs we got, you told him any of that?'

'No,' she said, 'no. Only the call when your – when Lester said he wanted to hand you over, I told my husband about that and he said—' She stopped and wetted her lips.

'Said he didn't believe a word, huh? Yeah, I can just imagine.'

'How could you?' she said. 'You don't know Brad.'

'Not in detail recently,' I said, 'but, blood on blood, I ought to, didn't I?' And she scowled at me something fierce.

'For God's sake,' she said, 'stop shoving your claim down my throat. You're here, Lester's said his piece, and under protest I'll arrange to have the tests done. But I can't – I won't—'

'Till you're forced, you won't go beyond that?' Which riled me, how could it not? So I said, 'Whyn't I pick up this phone right now and call him, tell him I'm here and who I am? What'd he say to me if I did that? Would he be glad or would he tell me to get lost?'

'Of course he'd want his rightful daughter back,' she said stiff.

'Then whyn't I just call him?' I was bluffing to make her furious, I'd no notion of his number and although she'd not called the cops on us he well might. I made a quick move toward the phone extension which sat at the far end of the countertop and I said, 'Watch me call him and genuinely blow his mind.'

She gripped hold of me, she got in my way and the world was full of her perfume, her warm scented flesh on mine. I realised what had never really hit me before, that I'd once been a tiny baby and this body of hers was the body I'd truly been inside. The notion made me dizzy and I stopped moving, we stayed so with her arm on mine. I don't know what she was thinking but I felt like bursting into tears, not gladness but an enormous wave of disappointment and wanting. Wanting her to hold me in her arms like you'd hold a real daughter that had never gone away from you, that's how. Then she let go of me, she stepped back, stared at me and said, 'What's the matter?' I shook my head and she got tough again. 'No,' she said, 'I won't let you call him. He's had a very difficult time these past years and I refuse to trouble him with an episode which – there's no proof at all.'

'So we're back to those damn lab tests?'

She said, 'Exactly. What else could there be?' She went back to the sink and finished cleaning it out, hung up the dishmop and cloths; she sure was a very tidy-minded lady. God alone knows what she'd have said to some of the places Les and me'd lived in, nor the way we'd lived in them. You can't be extra fussy when you've the sort of non-money and surroundings we'd had.

I went into the living room, had seen enough of her damn fancy kitchen and her tidy ways to last me one long lifetime. It was full dark outdoors and all those damn tree branches stretching toward us like they grudged the lights we'd got inside the house. Like they grudged us breathing space too. I went to the glass front door and stared out and it struck me, with a hollow feeling as big as the world, that for the first time in memory I'd no notion where Les was nor how he'd spend all those hours of the night. There's a soft core to Les that'd rather lie than tough things out and say openly, Yes I plan to, or No I don't intend doing that. I've always prided myself he can never deceive me on this, though he'd deceived other people, because I recognise the squelchy look his face gets before he firms it extra hard for the lie. But this time, with our whole future at stake and although he'd promised me solemn, I couldn't be sure, would he show up next morning? Did he fear cops and the woman, and want out of the whole situation so bad, that he might just abandon me and run? I sat down in the chair he'd sat in and I bit my fingernails; Les'd surely yell if he saw me chewing away. But if he was never going to show up again, if he'd ratted out on me . . . oh hell. I chewed them but I didn't cry, that'd make me seem weak.

She switched off the kitchen light and came into the living room, she glared at me like I was a package which could explode at any moment. She sat down opposite, on the edge of a chair and glancing nervous. I tried to figure out how difficult it'd be for me to find Les if he truly was hanging around. He'd allowed her to suppose he would hitch a ride to the highway and some motel, but I knew he wouldn't make the full distance, he'd leave this road at the first old lumber track or disused driveway. Shouldn't be too hard then, and if I called his name he'd surely hear.

So I got up and said, 'What say I go find where Les is spending the night?' To sound convincing I invented, 'A motel, they'll most likely have room for me too.' I felt better moving around; her house was too damn tidy and prissy. Out on the road I'd feel purely like myself again, and that'd be good. The dark was a friend to me anyway; even with all those damn trees it'd never spook me.

It struck me afterwards that she most likely wanted to keep me there overnight as a sort of hostage, to sort Les and me from those others who'd made claim but hadn't hung around for the tests. But when she said, 'He'll show up again in the morning. Don't be afraid,' something new and other than that walked around in her voice. Like, although she didn't accept me as her daughter, yet she did realise I was a person in my own right and might have attachments and worries. She said, 'It wouldn't be safe for you to hike on these roads in the dark.'

No, her and me were coming from two different areas – and I don't only mean geographical. I said, 'Christ, if darkness and trees was all the problems I'd got!' Then I told her – brief because it was none of her business – how Les and me had lived, plenty times, with no city nearer than a hundred-fifty miles. Scorpions and snakes and biting ants and poison spiders, you learn to cope when you've no choice. I said, 'I've had problems much bigger than wondering if the moon and stars'd show up on time.'

Jeff's body, the look and strange feel of it, came into my mind; yes, if anyone found him, there'd be problem indeed. No ID tying me to him, but I pictured how, if the rocks didn't do a good job of weighing him down, he'd rise up and cry out my name, would come running, try to get his hands on me.

I shivered and she said, 'Are you tired?'

Tired and fretting over Jeff and imagining how, if I went hunting for Les along these different roads, I might easy miss him in the dark. So I gave up on that notion and said, 'Yes ma'am'; at least that way I'd get to be in a room by myself for most of these waiting hours. She got up as if she'd be glad not to look at my face any longer too; she explained how she always had the downstairs bedroom so I'd be up above. At least like that I'd be above some of those damn tree branches.

She suggested I take a shower before bed and that was okay, plenty of hot water and jars full of all different scented lotions and such. Then she took me upstairs and into the bedroom, high-ceilinged, set in the roof peak. I dumped my rucksack and looked around; she stood in the doorway and said short and tough, 'Goodnight to you.' She didn't leave then, just stood there twisting the doorknob; I remember the waily little grind of it. It got to me so that I said as short and cold as herself, 'Was there anything else you wanted to mention?' And she twisted the knob, twisted it, stared down at it while she said, 'You're observant and there's no reason why I shouldn't be honest with you. I was thinking that if my daughter – the real Cate – ever did arrive here and I behaved towards her as I have to you, I could never forgive myself. That's all.' Then she turned and went out of the room; the key grated around in the lock.

7

Next morning at breakfast Les hadn't shown up, so I was in a foul mood, and she kept niggling at me about how him and me'd lived before. 'Drugs?' she said, 'I suppose.' No, she for sure didn't care how much she insulted us. So I told her, long and furious, why not drugs, how we were short of money and lived outside the urban scene and how Les'd be too scared anyway. She said, 'He wasn't too scared to steal – either my child, or her bracelet from whoever else took her – so I don't see why a bit of drug-dealing would bother him.'

Her face was hard; we ate on the outside deck at the back of the cabin because the morning was so mild, and a bird sang fit to bust itself from a tree near us but she never glanced at it. Nothing entered her scheme of things except the girl who couldn't possibly be me, and I didn't see how I'd ever be able to break through that. She glared at me real tough, like I was a delinquent she was sentencing, and she said, 'Did you ever go to school out there?'

I said, 'You don't one bit understand. Les and me, we were never – we didn't—'

'You weren't part of the system?'

'Too damn right we weren't.' I stirred the syrupy remains of a hotcake around on my plate. 'We picked up food stamps and other benefits and such, but if anyone started asking questions we lit out.' She scowled and I said, 'There's plenty of folks live the way we did. Just because you never met one before, you needn't suppose I'm lying.'

'I'd have thought,' she said low like talking to herself,

'that the last thing a man such as him would want would be to take on the burden of a child.'

I jumped up and yelled, 'He never thought of me as a burden, Les'd never see that in me.' I backed against the deck railing, furious so I kept on yelling. 'Maybe you did though, or why'd the notion just now pop into your head?' She stared at me like I was a wild animal, she didn't speak and I got a hold of myself, I said, 'Whyn't we call this damn reunion off right now? Seems to me you and me'll never get along.'

I took a deep breath and the rail was firm at my back, the whole damn world waiting for me beyond it. Les and me could go, keep on travelling, we'd make out somehow. I didn't need stay and maybe spend years facing her nasty grudges. 'Been too long, I guess,' I said quieter, 'and both you and me switched our minds away from fretting about the past. Us showing up here has done damn-all but remind you – and not in any happy way either. So whyn't him and me just take off soon's he shows up this morning? Then you won't ever need see us again. Wouldn't you rather that? Won't it be simplest?'

'You forget,' she said, 'he brought my child's bracelet.' *My child* that was thieved away in the past. 'I'll shake the truth out of him,' she said, and I went down into total despair.

'Oh Christ,' I said, 'oh bloody hell.' I gripped the railing and the ground was only three feet underneath; it'd be easy to jump the railing and go. For please-God sure I'd meet Les somewhere along this side road; if he hadn't nerve enough to steal a pickup truck somewhere I would, then the two of us'd be together again, and she could go sink.

Those cool eyes of hers raked me and her voice was calm and tough like a cop's again when she said, 'You've admitted that the police want you. For something you yourself have done, not him.' She tried to soften her voice to wheedling, but because she disliked me so she didn't make a good job of it. 'You can tell me now,' she said, 'he's not around. I promise not to pass it on if you'd rather not. What have you done, that the police need to get hold of you?'

I did jump the rail then, I ran down the driveway and the pine needles hissed under my sneaker soles like they were saying Go, Cate, go quick away from here. I reached the dirt road and turned toward where Les should be, somewhere in the miles between her mailbox and the highway, and I'd a damn good feeling all of a sudden. Clean and honest, nearly as if I'd never killed anyone. Away from that false wheedling voice of hers that'd grab the truth and run to the cops with it if she found out.

I was my own person again, the person I'd grown up to be. Not Cate her daughter, real or pretend; Cate was dead in me now although, blood and bones, I was still here. But the false fake Cate that would have worn expensive clothes and been cleaner and gone — been accepted — into those rich-smelling arms of the woman's without any hesitation, that Cate was dead; I guess she died at the moment Les grabbed me out of their damn tent. Why didn't they take better care so he couldn't have grabbed me, if they were so damn fond of me? That's what I've often wondered. Seems to me if you'd a child you would watch it day and night, seems to me you'd hardly sleep for fear something untoward might happen. But they slept sound inside the tent — and me near the flap of it (that damn flap was open too, Les swears), me awake, peeking out and grinning when Les came by.

I've asked Les why, basically, he took me, why he was wandering that campsite in the before-dawn hours, but all he'll answer me is that he was looking for guidance. He's not the least bit religious but that one word is the only explanation he'll give me. Guidance. So I can't truly fault him — most likely he'd a muddle of problems in his head and seemed to him that there was weighty reason enough for what he did — but I can surely fault my parents. All the ways there are.

So I ran and ran along the dirt road, but when I heard boots trudging along toward me I knew whose they were; there wasn't going to be an easy out for any of us. Les swung around the corner and his wide-apart arms stopped me from getting past him. He said, 'What the hell're you up to?' He turned me around by the shoulders and his arm forced me to walk in step with him, back along the way I'd run from. 'Going wild,' he said, 'were you? How about if I'd not come along, huh?'

I said, 'I'm not Cate her daughter, I don't want to be. Whatever proof you've got and whatever those damn lab tests show, I refuse. Me and her'd never get along together.' I took myself out of the circle of his arm because the damn woman'd be capable of thinking him and me were smooching as we walked along.

'Been acting harsh to you, has she?' he said softer-voiced, and he was Les my father and mother and friend; I didn't want any other.

'Acting hateful.' We turned into her driveway and I started picking bits of grass and twigs and such off his clothes; no need to ask what sort of place he'd spent the night. 'Far from here?' I said, and the shorthand him and me talked was cosy for both of us, we understood each other right away.

'About a mile,' he said. 'Old half-wrecked cabin with a couple of fruit trees and a well.' Busted windows too; in this mild air his hands were still cold.

'The sort of place we might find further on, if we decide to shack up for a while in these parts?'

He halted then, at that last bend of the driveway before her cabin, and he turned to me. 'Look,' he said, 'I didn't drive two thousand miles here for fun or to see if you'd enjoy the area. She's your family, you're hers, she's got a right to you and I never should have took you. That's all.'

'Oh no,' I said, remembering Jeff, 'that's not even a tiny

part of it.' I hid my face against his shoulder because for what I was going to say next I needed to speak into an emptiness. 'I wish I hadn't done it. Him and – what I did.'

'We sorted it though, didn't we?' said Les angry, 'Between the two of us we tidied your mess up. So I don't see why you need keep dragging it in.'

'But I never told you exactly the true reason and you guessed I hadn't, way back there. The reason I gave you at first—'

'I don't intend to keep discussing that happening,' he said and walked on. The woman stood outside the cabin watching us and Les said to me from his mouth corner, 'Will you please get that through your head. You can stop cooking up stories, because I just plain don't intend to hear them.' We arrived in front of the woman and Les said to her with the loose easy smile she stiffened at every time. 'Goodday, ma'am.'

So that was it for Les and me and truthfulness. I could see his point; he hated what I'd done and it terrified him, he didn't want to think about it more than he must. There wasn't any point in me trying to get honest with him about it so's to clear my own mind.

The woman looked Les over pretty close and I guess she'd sense enough to realise he'd not spent the night in any motel. Anyhow she said, 'Come indoors, the pair of you,' and when we were inside she asked if he'd eaten that morning. Les is the world's worst liar and he didn't even try then, he said, 'No, ma'am.' So the three of us trucked into the kitchen and she fixed him a fry-up; she was a pretty damn good cook toward a hungry man when she chose to be. While he ate she told him (with little jerky glances at me, like she'd expected me to run for ever and not show up again and she wasn't too sure if she'd have been for or against that) how she'd spent some of the night reading up on those lab tests. The three of us sat at her big kitchen table and she leaned her chin in her hands while she talked; that way she looked a hell of a lot younger than I felt. A kid she looked, with her elbows stuck on the table and her trying to recall her lesson right.

She said the way we'd do it was, she and me'd get tested first, then depending on the results of that we'd bring the man her husband into it. My father, yeah, if I must think of him that way. I felt like he was an enemy, because of Les, and she felt to me more than half enemy too, so I tried riling her. I said, 'You won't tell him till the last minute because you're scared of him,' and Les told me to shut my face.

'No,' she said, her voice holding itself tight in so she wouldn't get real mad at me, 'there's a scientific reason for my being tested first.' She explained how some sorts of this damn DNA stuff get passed on from the mother, not the father, so we might as well get her part of it over with before we disturbed the peace of her chicken-livered husband. Not her words, of course, but the general drift came across pretty plain.

Les said damn-all; he was eating kind of noisy because he was hungry, and I could see this wasn't sitting too well with her, so to cover his noise I said, 'The whole testing bit sounds like a bunch of hogwash to me.' Which basically it did, though I accepted Les's assurance that it truly wasn't.

He swallowed his mouthful and said to me, 'Remember what I told you back in Arizona about the tests? How else'd you expect to prove to her who you are?'

There was one short and truthful answer to that: I'd expected her to take one glance at me and know for sure. More fool me, yeah. I looked at her and away, but not fast enough; our eyes hit and the colour came up in her face, kept coming. For once she knew damn well what I was thinking.

Soon's Les got through eating she cleared the table and piled the dishes, then she said, slow like she was reading this text off a wall or noticeboard and needed to be sure she'd gotten it right, 'When the – when those other claimants contacted me, I made arrangements at a lab down in our city. But this time—' She picked up a pencil, chewed the end of it and I was glad of this one little tiny thing her and me had in common, that we'd both reach for something to chew on when we got uptight. She said slow, 'Of course those tests had to be cancelled both times, which was embarrassing . . . so this time I'd rather not . . . But I've a scientist friend in a government laboratory in Washington who might—' The stuff on her mental notice-board was finished and she turned away from us to her desk, then to the phone; she dialled one number, then another, and both times she talked brief and official, with her British accent standing out more than usual. A whole world she'd got that Les and me knew nothing about; this made me feel sorry and lonely and wondering, and longing to explore her too.

She got through with her phone calls, told us the big boss, her contact, was tied up in a meeting and she'd left a message with his secretary; one or other would call her back and finalise the details. Les and me looked at each other when she said this, because him and me weren't the least bit into the sort of area where you've got high-up contacts in Washington. But she didn't notice, she was busy figuring her next problem. Namely, what in hell to do with us till the test arrangements were made and it came time to drive up to Washington.

I'd supposed she would want to keep tabs on us like the previous night, so we wouldn't disappear and make her look a fool like those others had. But she stared past us at the truck and said, 'I've no wish to keep you prisoners. If you walk out on me, that's a risk I'll have to take.' All day and every day she couldn't be bothered with the sight of us around, was what she meant. She pulled the truck keys out of her pocket and chucked them at Les like she hated the sight of them and us both. 'If you don't show up here before dark I'll assume you've gone and I'll cancel the test arrangements,' she said. 'Is that clear?'

At her question all the prickly anger in me dissolved away sudden and left me longing, bare and hurting, for this my mother, that someday she'd take me in her arms and hug me and we'd be good friends, we'd laugh together and she'd teach me stuff – and maybe I'd teach her too. But she kept acting so cold and unfriendly, which hurt me the more. And she'd this high-up friend she planned to lean on, to use his contacts or whatever; she'd at least partly the man her husband and she'd women friends too. Like, her life was plenty full before Les and me mixed ourselves into it.

I said to Les, 'She don't want us around for the day, whyn't we take a ride someplace?' At least the truck was familiar, was a sort of home, it smelled of the two of us and the way of life we were used to.

Les brightened up, then he gloomed again and said, 'What the hell d'you plan we use for money? We're damn near out of gas and those repairs took all the reserve cash I had.'

Our two pairs of eyes went around to stare at the woman – maybe this was impolite but who else around there had got cash? – and she coloured up fast, a real angry flare this time. She went back into her bedroom and came out with a couple of bills, she shoved them at Les like they were some of the dead armadillos we'd seen floating and rotting along our travels.

When him and me were in the truck bouncing out of there I said, 'How much'd she give you?'

'Thirty bucks.' While he drove he lit a cigarette, and I could tell from the fierce way he lit it what he thought of the woman and her money.

I said, 'What if these damn tests come out wrong?' and he turned to stare at me.

'What the hell d'you mean?' he said.

'You said they'll prove for sure whose kid I am, whose kid I couldn't possibly be. What if they prove I couldn't possibly be her daughter?'

'Holy God and fishes,' he said, 'but you are hers, whose else?' In between watching the road he kept staring at me. 'You disbelieve everything I've told you about what happened all those years ago, don't you?' He put his gaze solid on the road and said, 'I've a damn good mind to run the truck into one of these big roadside rocks and finish the pair of us. That'd solve every blasted problem.' He turned and stared at me again. 'You never have believed a word I've said, right?'

'I was just playing around in my head,' I said quick, 'no reason I shouldn't rearrange stories to see how they'd fit the other way, is there?'

'Look,' he said, 'there's no other way possible. You're her daughter, the child I took, and that's it.' He frowned and said slow, 'Sometimes, these past months, I just don't grasp what world you're living in.'

There was nothing useful I could say to that; the world had been a pretty mixed-up place for me since he'd said he planned on returning me. But I didn't aim to confuse him too, any more than I must, and the two of us had this day ahead clear. A sunny warm day too, and enough cash for gasoline and a bite to eat at midday. 'Where're we heading?' I said.

'How would I know? Taking this ride was your idea.'

Suddenly I got a truly brilliant notion. 'Hey,' I said, 'what say we go take a look at the man her husband?' Reconnoitre how things stood around him, like.

Les scowled deeper and said, 'That notion honestly stinks. You want to get us in bad with him before we get started?'

'Not tell him who we are, maybe just stalk him around and not let him know it's us. Like a crime series.'

'Oh God,' Les said, and his hands lay so loose on the wheel I grabbed it over them.

'Haven't I told you,' I said, 'I don't plan on killing anyone else? That Jeff was a one-off.' I pounded one of his hands where it lay on the wheel. 'I realise I did a wrong thing way back there, but can't you still trust me even a tiny bit?' Because surely that night about Jeff shouldn't have broken *all* of our major connections.

'Okay,' he said dull-voiced, driving and not looking at me, 'I believe you. So what d'you plan on us doing today?'

'We'll go look at her husband, like I said.' We reached the highway and I said, 'Turn left onto it, going down to the city.'

He did turn, but he said, 'Eighty thousand souls down there—' (and 'souls' isn't a word I'd ever heard him use before; don't ask me what was in his head) – 'how'll we locate where he's to?'

'You said he's a university lecturer, right?' I settled back and let the warm air, the sun, flow over me; that section of the scenery looked pretty good. Nothing but used-up cornfields stretching away to all the horizons, and after the closed-in-ness of her woods this felt great, it felt sensational. 'We'll find the university easy enough, there'll be signs directing.'

Les said, 'If you plan on walking into one of his classes you can count me out. And don't expect me to wait around for you either.'

'Not that at all. Just to see how – hell, his surroundings'll be a different sort of place.' But nothing I could say was right; it hung heavy in the air that Les, for all that he knew something about education, wasn't at ease in those highly educated places. And of course I'd gotten pretty much no education myself at all. Rightly or wrongly, we were both way out of that orbit. He got his scowl again and I said, 'Look, no sweat. The outside of a building, where's the harm in that? Then we'll find a phone booth and look his home address up in the book. He's sure to be listed.'

Les braked the truck to the road's shoulder. 'You intend

calling him up? Because if that's what you plan, we're not going anywhere near the city. Unless you walk from here to there on your own two feet, and you're too damn lazy for that.'

I didn't much want to arrive in the city without Les; cities are big places and, the kind of life we'd led, I wasn't that familiar with them. But I couldn't confess this, it'd sound cowardly, so I said, 'I'll hitch a ride.' I was rooting around in the glove compartment and found an old stick of gum, so I unwrapped it, popped it in my mouth and chewed. I watched him from the corner of my eye, blew the gum out and sucked it back in again.

'Oh Christ,' he said as if I might possibly mean it, as if everyone we'd ever met out West hadn't reared me on gruesome tales of what could happen to hitchers.

'Move over,' I said, 'and let me drive. You'd do better to let me handle this whole damn business, can't you see she's taken a major dislike to you?'

'Why would she do that?' he said, genuinely startled.

Poor innocent Les. Your smile at her, the fact that you sleep rough, also she doesn't approve your accent or clothes. And, surpassingly, you brought with you the little gold bracelet; that's enough, in her book, to make her hate you for always. 'Hey,' I said to cheer him, 'don't *believe* me, can't you recognise a joke when you hear one?' I grinned because what I was going to say next was the rock-bottom truth. 'She may not take to you, but she sure as hell hates the very pants off me. Now shift over, so we'll get some-place before today's gone.'

'You've got no driving licence,' he said.

'That's never bothered you any place else.'

'There's more people around these parts than back home, more cops to notice.' He gave me that weak wanna-be-friendly grin and I wondered, as I sometimes have before, what was in his past before he took me. 'She'd better not hate you,' he said, 'she'll need to learn adjusting.'

'Sure she'll adjust.' I'd have said anything then to make him happy. 'No, I don't plan on calling the man her husband up, I've got better sense than that. Only to look him up in the book, see where he lives, drive by there and park a minute, try to figure out what sort of a person he'd be to live in whatever sort of a house or apartment he does. That's all I've got in mind. Harmless, wouldn't it be?'

So with coaxing and promises I did get him to start driving again and we chugged along, finally got to the city.

That was a greenish goodish but puzzling day, all big stretches of close-mown grass and single trees huge as if they thought themselves mighty important. I'd better say right away that of course we never saw the man – not to know him, anyhow – only lots of college students strolling like there was no hard work to be done in the world, like having a pile of books under your arm could be more important than holding a regular job. And big pale stone buildings all curves and pillars; I said, 'Looks like a fine waste of time and money,' and Les said, 'Oh, you don't begin to understand.' Which riled me, because who snatched me away and made that understanding impossible for me?

I guess this visit to the university rubbed us the wrong way and made us both, for our various reasons, sore. After not many minutes of watching, I said, 'Let's get the hell out of here,' so we drove a couple of blocks and found a phone booth. The man's number was in the book, and his address; I tore the page out of the book because I'd no pen to write them down with, and we found a drugstore that sold a city map, then we went hunting.

But not far; where he lived was only three blocks from the university. Old houses, painted up pretty but to me they looked old enough to fall down. I said this and again Les said, 'You don't understand. They've got class.' At which I said if that was class, they could keep it. White frame houses and big, with porches and extensions poking out all over them. Tall, and windows everywhere; dormers shoving out of the roofs. We parked opposite the man's number; it was divided into apartments, with a row of names beside the front door, and Les figured from the apartment number that the man's must be on the top floor. Whether front or back, we'd no way of knowing.

So we sat there and I stared up at the top windows with their fancy scalloped blinds and I couldn't be sure if that was the man's windows or not. Which seemed typical of the whole mess; seemed like me being their daughter Cate wouldn't bring happiness or solidness to either one of them. So after not very long I said, 'Bloody hell, can't we go get something to eat?' and Les understood that it wasn't him I was mad at; he acted kind and gentle, saying what sort of place should we pick? We rode around and fixed on a drive-in hamburger joint; we felt like real fancy people, thinking we'd got choice, but the truth was that after we'd bought gas and the food there wasn't much cash left.

I said, 'What'll we do when we need more cash?' and he said, 'She'll give us some,' but not like he was sure of that. Him and me looked at each other and seemed to me I saw the same little thoughts moving around in his eyes as was squiggling around in my brain. I said, 'Would you take money out of her billfold if you'd got the chance and you was broke?' and he went a dark red colour, he said, 'I don't want to think about anything like that.' We kept on looking at each other and he said, 'Was you thinking you'd take some, if we really needed?' and I felt my own cheeks go a dirty red colour too. I said, 'Not necessarily in so many words,' and he agreed, he nodded his head and said, 'No, we wouldn't want to think of it that way.' Which mightn't mean anything to a stranger, but I was pretty damn sure him and me marched alike on this.

After we'd eaten we drove partway back out of the city and pulled into a layby where there was picnic tables and we sat in the truck and dozed a while, then we started back toward her woods. Just before we turned onto the dirt road I said, 'She'd never miss a few dollars once in a while, and we know which room she keeps her billfold in.' He said, 'I don't like to think of it that way,' and I said, 'Not unless we truly must.' The silence between him and me then felt warm and agreeing, it felt wholly comfortable.

When we pulled up in front of the cabin she was standing outside saying goodbye to another woman, dark-haired but slick and city-chic dressed − in all tans and browns − like herself. Elly, she called her, and I recalled how they'd arranged to meet for a hike that day. Les and me sat in the truck while they said their goodbyes; I reminded him and he grunted, wasn't much interested, but the woman Elly sure stared hard at us when she left. I said to Les, loud enough so she'd hear, 'She'll know us next time,' but when he got himself into a noticing mood, she'd gone.

We locked the truck and followed the woman my mother into the cabin, ready to find out when we'd go for those tests.

8

She'd finalised the arrangements; this high-up friend of hers in Washington DC had pulled strings and gotten the necessary appointments into place. Talking with this friend of hers had excited her; she coloured up when she told us and her eyes shone like she was a kid waiting for the Fourth of July. 'He's an old friend,' she said, and I realised she was basically a damn good-looking woman. So I thought, Not too old of a guy, likely, and maybe planning on being more than a friend. Anyway she and Les and me were to go up there in a couple of days' time; the tests would get done and then we'd go back to her woods to wait on the results. I said, 'How long'll that take?' and she said, 'Might be several weeks.' Us hanging around not wanted while she waited for the damn phone call? A real uncosy arrangement.

But meanwhile she was all happiness at the notion of meeting up with this guy again. Apparently he'd made a motel reservation up there for the three of us; we'd drive up in the afternoon and she'd leave Les and me in the motel watching television or whatever while she went out to dinner with her friend at some fancy restaurant. Next morning we'd go to a laboratory and get the tests done, then we'd drive back down to Virginia. I began to realise all sorts of things I'd not pictured closely before – like, Les and me wouldn't be going up there in his truck, the three of us would go in her damn car. She finished telling us the arrangements and stared at us like extra problems were hitting her too. 'The two of you will need to go shopping for clothes before then,' she said, 'you can't wear those things for a visit to Washington.'

At that I started to realise all sorts of other possibilities, like how she'd got so much money and – if I was proven her child and she accepted me – she'd give me money to buy clothes I didn't out-and-out need but wanted. Hungered after, like. Not just a pair of jeans because I was near splitting out of the pair I'd on, but extra jeans in other colours that I might take a fancy to. Shirts and other tops. Maybe I'd even take a fancy to a dress and she'd give me plenty of money to buy it? I couldn't exactly imagine me in a dress, but you never can be sure. So I shut my mouth and opened my eyes wide and listened to what she was saying.

But Les got purely insulted, his tone made that clear. 'We don't need get new clothes, ma'am,' he said, and his voice was whiny like when he's real desperate.

'But,' she said, 'you must, Lester. If you take a look at yourself you'll realise why.'

The wrong thing to say to him; didn't she realise he's got his pride too? He ran a finger around the neck of his grey T-shirt like he wanted to be sure she hadn't peeled it off him, then he remembered me and got cunning. 'How about *her* though, ma'am? Suppose someone in the store that knows you sees her alongside you, before she's been proven yours, and starts to think? Wouldn't be too tidy of a situation, would it?'

She brushed that fast aside. 'We'll go to a store where I'm not known. There's plenty of shopping malls down by the city.'

But how fancy'd the clothes be? I said, 'What sort of clothes?' and Les glared like I was a traitor. I fingered the jeans I'd got on, they'd faded uneven and the dirt was sort of grimed in. Les or no, I could see her point.

But Les refused to go with us, he stayed home – or rather he went off on foot to wander her woods for the day, since she didn't suggest giving him the run of the house. She drove me in her car to some mall on the bypass the other side of the city; her car smelled so different inside from our truck that it made me shy, which is a thing I practically never am. That smell of polish and leather and no dirt or oilstains anywhere made me realise the difference between her and us. She didn't speak all the way there; guess she figured she didn't need to make an effort to behave halfway decent to this kid that was going, pretty damn soon, to get shown up for an imposter. I only spoke once; when we'd pulled into the mall parking lot and she swung the car into a space (she was a pretty nifty driver, I will say that for her) I said, 'You don't *need* spend this money on me,' and she cut the engine, put the keys into her pocketbook and turned to me.

'I do what I want,' she said, 'it's my money.' I couldn't argue about that, and for some reason she suddenly started studying me like I might be partway human after all. 'Do you have any idea what kind of clothes you'd like to get?' she said, and rainbows burst inside my head at the notion of what might be inside that big grey hump of buildings. Clothes, and she'd the money to buy them with.

'I'll know when I see them,' I said, 'I'll soon pick out what's right for me.'

She smiled then, a real honest-to-God grin I'd never thought to see on her face, and she said, 'Kids!' Then she pulled herself together and got rid of the smile, but it had truly been there. She said, 'You do understand what sort of clothes you need to buy? Not those eternal jeans, something more upmarket but not noticeably fancy.' (Since then I've noticed that people wear jeans every which place and they're acceptable, but there you are, they weren't her style.) She smoothed her own clothes; she had on a tan skirt – some sort of fine wool and goat-hair, she said – and a brown wool jacket with a yellow and white scarf. She said, 'I'll be watching nearby to make sure that you don't—'

Make purchases she'd think silly, I guess; expense didn't

seem to be any problem. So she wouldn't be standing right next to me; she, in her own way, was jittery too. That made her seem a touch more human; I didn't dislike it. Anyway she gave me a whole wodge of cash – safer in our circumstances, she said, than a credit card – and the two of us marched inside.

Of course Les and me ordinarily got our clothes from thrift shops; we could never afford any other than fourth-hand. So it felt odd to be buying new, and with so much cash. A kid in a candy store? Yeah, but not wholly so; a sort of shock at the choice I had, and the prices they all were, held me back. Also this was her money and I felt account-able to her for how I spent it. I'd *seen* quality clothing before – I always kept my eyes wide open out West when Les and me were driving around places – but *buying* them, that was different.

On the way back, a couple of hours later, she kept looking at me. I still didn't feel exactly close to her because she acted so chilly, but those stares did amuse me. So I finally said, 'You've not expressed your opinion of what I bought.' I'd used the store's restroom to change into some of the clothes because once I'd gotten them on I damn well hated to take them off. I couldn't avoid giving her a quick grin to repay the one she'd given me, and I said, 'Surprised you, huh?'

Her own smile spread again; it looked sheepish and I could appreciate that. It damn well deserved to.

I said, 'You don't give me credit for a hell of a lot of sense, do you? Or for taste or anything else.' I fiddled with the long white scarf, slung it closer around my neck over the black straight pants and a black wool and goat-hair sweater like hers; the clothes had a good belonging feel and I enjoyed touching them.

She said, 'I'm sorry.' A pretty damn guarded apology; her tone made that clear. Apology for thinking me a thick-headed dumb-skull, and for nothing else. But there got to be a sort of warmth in the car, not exactly between us but not totally unattached either. Then she had to go spoil it all. She said, 'How will Lester like your new outfits?'

For those couple of hours I hadn't totally forgotten Les but he wasn't running around in my head shouting; I was listening a hell of a lot more to myself and all the sorts of person I might turn into than I was to him. What she said shoved me back into being the dumb young broad from the desert, that didn't keep herself clean unless she was told to, and wasn't likely to recognise good clothes from bad. So I mumbled, 'They'll demolish him totally, I guess,' and after that neither of us spoke again all the way home. Once again she'd marked off our difference from herself and I couldn't dispute it.

9

The drive up went okay; she had Les and me sit in the back of her car so she didn't need talk to either one of us. Good-looking countryside if you like that sort of thing – corn-fields drying up, and green meadows and woods. Then a wide busy highway she called the Beltway, then a lot of streets and this fancy motel we'd stay at, just into Maryland beyond the District line. But streets everywhere, going on for ever.

The motel was four floors like a hotel; it hadn't struck me till we walked inside that her and me would be sharing a room. (And Les of course next door.) She kind of hesitated like it hadn't struck her till then either. But the room was big, two kingsized beds and any gadget you'd want. The three of us went down to the restaurant; Les and me ate hearty but she nibbled, then when it got dark she said we'd all better go back upstairs because it was time for her to get ready. Her blasted dinner date with this influential guy, yeah.

In the elevator I said to Les, loud enough so she'd hear, 'She plan on locking us in while she's gone?' She glared at me but she didn't speak.

Les and me settled ourselves in front of the television in the big bedroom; she took her toilet stuff and new dress and such into the bathroom and fixed herself up there. She looked okay when she came out but not like the woman I'd been getting accustomed to, she looked slick and city-shiny. And I thought all over again, She can't be my mother, we've not a damn thing in common. She had on a dress that went different shades of blue-purple in the lights, it had a fitting top and a slinky skirt. And high heels; she wasn't any longer a person whose thoughts I could relate to at all.

She picked up a silvery purse and went out, and Les and me watched television. I'd *seen* television sets on before, of course, in windows of stores that sold them, only Les'd never let me stay to watch. And often enough, when him and me were driving along some street after dark, I'd notice the televisions all flickering at us from people's living rooms; it felt strange to be indoors now and watching just like anyone else. You get accustomed to the notion of them easy enough, but to sit and watch them – that's different.

I said to Les, 'See what good programmes we been missing all these years?' To tease him, not because I'd necessarily made up my mind to their being that good. But it was the wrong thing to say to him; he grunted and made a sour face. He watched the set though, just as close as me. After a while I got bored and devilish; I said, watching him, 'I've a mind to go chase after her, peek into that restaurant and see the two of them together.'

'The hell,' he said, 'you wouldn't know where to find it or them or anything.' Which was true enough, she'd not told us the restaurant name. I only said that to rile Les. Then he said, 'We're in strangers' territory now.'

This depressed me so much I can't explain how. As if him and me were exiled from where we truly belonged, as if we could never hope to find our way back there ever. I went over to where he sat on a long couch and I took his face between my hands, I turned it away from the television toward me. 'You can't truly mean that,' I said.

His eyes connected with me then and they gave a sort of twitch, but they stayed on me and honest. 'Ah,' he said like he'd used to when I was a little kid and bumped my knee or whatever, 'don't *worry* so.' He put his arms round me and rocked me; I shut my eyes and he was the Les he'd always been, while he stayed around I'd be safe. So he rocked me a while and then he said, 'You're a sight too old to need this treatment.'

He loosed me and sat back, watched television again, but he'd calmed me; I stayed beside him and although he smelled different than his usual – those damn new pants and the shirt she'd bought for him, and the fancy soap in his bathroom – yet he was Les and everything was basically okay. The television chattered on and I let my thoughts roam, imagining what her restaurant would be like inside and what this boyfriend of hers was like, what they'd talk about, if he'd lean across the table and kiss her. Whether she planned on getting a divorce from the man my father and, if so, whether she might marry this city guy. If so how soon, and what that'd likely do to my future with her – or lack of one.

She came back around eleven, still shiny-bright and happy; Les went off to his room, and her and me undressed and climbed into those huge separated beds. She switched off the lamp but there was traffic headlamps outside and various noises; I couldn't sleep worth a damn and her silence was wakeful too. So after an hour or so she said, 'You can't sleep?'

'No, ma'am.' That 'ma'am' slipped out, there was no reason for it and plenty against, I guess, if I was really who Les claimed me to be. Anyhow it riled her or got to her someway, because when she spoke next her tone was sharp.

'I'd rather you didn't call me that. It sounds wrong, whatever the circumstances.' After another pause she said gentler, 'How do you feel about tomorrow?'

Those damn tests, she must mean. 'Nothing special. Got to be done, haven't they?'

She said, picking her words, 'I wondered if you were nervous about having blood drawn. If you don't like needles. Or about the result of the tests.'

I got loyal then, I'd plenty of fierce reason. After all, Les was the only person I'd yet had cause to feel loyal to. 'No, I'm not worried. Les'd never lie to me.' That was all there was to it by my reckoning; it's only now I can realise that for her it was never so simple.

After I'd said that she didn't say any more, and the two of us eventually went to sleep.

The tests next morning. A white-tiled room in some tall glittery building, and a woman in a white cotton coat who stuck us both in the arm. I got stuck first, and before it my supposed mother said, 'Do you stand the sight of blood all right?'

I'd never had much occasion, that I could recall, except for what happened to Jeff, but on account of him I was plumb sure. So I said, 'No problem,' and her and me got stuck, we got it over with. She'd told me first thing that morning how she'd be taking all these tests alongside me; she'd gotten them done before, in Virginia, when the previous what she called claimants showed up, but she didn't want to trouble the lab there for the results. (She was embarrassed because those other claimants had gotten away with lying to her, yeah.)

And there were other tests besides the blood – hair and such, if you'd got it, they wanted a tiny bit of it. Afterwards we went back to the motel and she checked us all out of there, then she drove us around Washington some.

I said, 'We seen other cities too, various places,' because Les had done his best at rearing me and I didn't want his pride to get hurt again.

She tightened her lips on that but after a while she persuaded herself to unclamp them; I guess you could say she was making an effort to act civilised.

Driving back down into Virginia I said, 'How long before you get the tests results?' and she said it might be a couple of weeks. I can't truthfully say that reaching her house felt like arriving home, because there was never any of that to it; it was just a place she lived in and Les and me definitely didn't belong.

Those weeks of waiting we hung around; the truck was almost out of gas again and I said to Les, 'I'll lift some cash from her purse if you'd like,' but he kept saying, 'No, let's wait a while, we can maybe hold out till the results come.' She was feeding him as good as she did me, I made sure of that, and wherever he spent his nights they didn't cost him a cent. But the weather turned cold and I worried over him; he said I was as bad as a mother for fretting, but I kept right on doing it — because if I didn't fuss over him, who would?

She fixed a solid breakfast every morning for the three of us, and a hefty meal each evening when we got fed up with the cold outdoors; she acted like she was cooking for a pair of greedy lumberjacks and I guess to her it did seem that way. Les and me tried to mind our manners around her at mealtimes; I learned to eat slower but Les was so accustomed to shovelling the food in. No one said much at meals; what would the three of us talk about? Once in a while she'd say something about the woods, but Les and me were always looking at different things there from anything she'd notice. I mean, a ruined cabin could be dreams halfway come true to us, but to her it'd always be just a shack.

After the evening meal her and me would either do the dishes or shove them in the dishwasher, then Les'd take himself out of there before he could fall asleep in front of her. I'd pick up a newspaper and make it last till bedtime; anything rather than see the hurtful little glances she kept giving me. I don't mean I didn't enjoy the good meals and hot water and all, but there was no real peace or the sort of comfort that'd matter the most, because she mistrusted me and wouldn't believe who I truly was.

So Les and me spent our days roaming the neighbouring

countryside on foot; I'd supposed she spent all her time enjoying herself but turned out she did work, did jewellery designs and made the pieces up out of metals and various coloured stones. Not precious like diamonds, but ones you might think were pretty colours and markings. So she kept busy with that. After a couple of weeks we got back to the house one evening and she acted real snappy and short with us; I said about the tests and she said they'd told her there was going to be a delay, further tests had got to be run. I said, 'Does that mean they want more bits from me?' and she said, 'No, no.' Said it like I was totally stupid.

From then onward the three of us jumped every time the phone rang, but when the call did come it was a day that Les and me had gone exploring a couple of beaten-down old cabins back in the woods further along the road. I was poking around them and telling him how easy they could be fixed up if you didn't bother with stuff like electricity and running water, and he was calling me the optimist of all time; we were happy and laughing pretty good together. We walked back along the road and the sun was going down through the trees, with frost sneaking in on the air. I said, 'Wonder what she'll fix for supper tonight?' and Les sounded a bit sad when he answered me, 'You don't suppose you're getting a mite spoiled here?' I said, 'Nothing of that. Might as well freeload while we can, right? No more questions asked, no responsibilities, just easy living.'

We walked up her driveway and in past the glass door; she stood in the living room waiting for us and as soon as I saw her face I knew the freeloading was over with for always.

10

But I guessed wrong about the reason for her change, I only knew she stood there looking at me like she'd never seen me before. I stopped inside the door and stared back at her, and after a while she walked forward like someone dreaming. Walked slow like she wasn't inside herself. She put forward the fingers of one hand and touched my hair, cautious like I was an insect, then she sent the fingers travelling like an inspection down my arm – not the arm with the scar on, the other. She took her hand away from me and made a long step backwards, kept looking at me. 'Cate,' she said at last. 'Cate.' With no expression at all.

It hit me that those damn test results must have arrived – and *this* was how she felt about them? Thanks a whole lot, mother, for nothing. I said to Les, 'See? Didn't I tell you she might not believe anyway, or if she did she wouldn't want me back after so damn long? It's been a hell of a lot too long separate for her and me both, any fool could realise that.' I said, 'You and me better both get out of here, Les, and pretty damn quick too.' I was so hurting sore at her attitude, I only wanted to get as far away from her as could be, and as damn fast as possible. I started toward the door but Les grabbed me.

'Shut your fool mouth,' he said, 'and give her time.' I guess that's where being adult helped him; I'd no experience to judge by, but he could somewhat understand what might be trucking around in her head and give her a chance to bring it out. He held my shoulders tight so I couldn't move, and he waited.

'The odds,' she said, moving her mouth stiffly like it hurt, 'are astronomical, I couldn't dispute them however much I wanted to.' She talked like she was acting in a movie and couldn't without an effort recall the lines she ought to say. 'The DNA sequences—' And she went on dreamily about this technical stuff; I finally did with a sort of shock to myself unearth that she truly wanted to believe and accept that I was who Les said I was. Her daughter. I stood there under Les's hard clutch and told myself I'd a technical interest only in seeing how she faced the fact. Basically I knew there was a hell of a lot more than that to it for me, but I didn't know how to start finding the right emotions. And she'd held us off from her, she'd disliked us so. Wasn't she still holding us off? Maybe Les could understand this stiff quiet-voiced manner of hers, but I couldn't.

When she stopped talking about the blasted DNA and such, there was the sort of silence you need to fill with *something*. I said, 'Those damn test results came through, huh?' Of course they had, but I couldn't come up with any other remark.

'Yes,' she said, still in that distant dreamy voice, 'and I've just told you what they showed. Cate,' she said again; she walked forward and put her arms round my neck but I was tall as her and the way we stood felt to me like a pretty odd tangle, with my brown bare flesh against her slick clothes and that careful make-up she'd got on. Anyway she left her arms there, and they felt to me like two bits of wood lying on me. I guess I'd expected the feel of a warm close mother bending over a really young child. Which, as Les pointed out to me afterwards, didn't fit either her or me. She smelled good, I did have to admit that, but in the way that a woman with lots of money and fancy clothes can smell good, not especially like a mother.

She said past my ear so I couldn't see her expression, 'We'll have lots of work to do, getting to know each other.'

I didn't answer because I plumb didn't know what to say, I simply couldn't imagine this getting-to-know at all, and she dropped her hands to my shoulders, she held me at arm's length and looked at me. 'What's the matter?' she said. Real soft-voiced now, but I wasn't sure how much of her softness I could trust. And Les, standing there gawping and listening, was no damn help.

'Nothing,' I said. 'Nothing's wrong.'

'Didn't you expect,' she said, 'that I'd believe the results?' With that terrible new softness like treachery, it seemed to me. Like the flowers and bright green grasses of a swamp; like I say, I'd no standards to judge her by. 'Oh Cate,' she said, and gave my shoulders a tiny squeeze like a question. 'Cate Cate Cate.'

The touch of her hands on me confused me too; no one had ever touched my body except of course Les – and him ordinary reassuring, never the least bit sexual – and a few boyfriends, which they were totally different. This touch of my mother – I couldn't guess what she might want, in the way of my responding words and actions. No word or movement toward her came into my mind or body, but I was pretty damn sure she'd spot the difference between a real *felt* response and counterfeit. So the only thing I could do was stay honest with her, which meant no gush of words from me, no jiggling around of my hands to rush into hers. I couldn't imagine what me voluntarily touching her body might feel like; she was my mother, okay, but that body of hers didn't seem to be my territory at all. We're talking really wooden postures now; I stood under her hands like a stick of wood sap-frozen in a bitter frost.

She dropped her hands from my shoulders, she'd got that much sense. And Les said, 'You'll need give her some time, ma'am. I doubt that she truly imagined how all this'd turn out, for all that I kept on telling her.'

I said, 'Sure I believed. I've got enough sense for that.' But I couldn't force a hell of a lot of expression into my voice. She noticed, of course, and yeah, I guess it did hurt her; there was no way the two of us were going to avoid hurting each other right along the line. Maybe in that I was wiser than her, because I suspect she intended to clean up my accent and get me educated and the two of us'd adjust together easy, but I saw plain it was never going to be that simple. And something was still adrift in the whole situation, because when the phone rang then she jumped a mile and her face went tight. It was only that damn Elly, and my mother did say, 'Sorry I'm busy,' she did cut the woman off short. For that one time at least.

She hung up and her face softened again; I watched her and kept telling myself, This is truly my mother. Hauling herself around me had mussed her hair some and she looked warmer, vastly more human. It was going to hurt me like all hell if her and me got close and then she changed her mind about me being her Cate, so to get things clear between us I said, 'The man – my father – there'll be tests he'll need to take too, right? Just to make hundred per cent sure.'

She flushed all over her face then, and the stiffness and softness came and went while she gave us this complicated confused story; she wasn't lying but she sure didn't make things very simple. Anyway I gathered in the finish that she'd gotten the results from the Washington lab after only two weeks, as they'd promised; this further delay had been because she put some heavy pressure on her scientist boyfriend to send those results to the Virginia lab that still held not only her results from when the previous claimants had run, but held her husband's too. And she'd told this local lab – most likely she was on buddy terms with some white-coated type there too, I didn't ask her – asked in her name and her husband's for them to make the comparisons and let her have the results.

'So,' I said, 'they've told you? It's all checked out both ways?'

She nodded. Yes.

'And he doesn't know yet? You've got to tell him?' Like that'd be an ordeal, but she'd her hands pressed at her mouth like it would.

This time she shook her head. 'The lab — they thought they were helping. They left a message for him at the University telling him the results.'

'So he's contacted you, right? Or — no, he hasn't.' I felt sorry for her then, she was hurting so bad. 'Maybe,' I said to her, 'the message missed him.'

She took her hands away from her mouth and said like difficult, 'I checked with the desk there. At lunchtime he picked that and his other messages up.'

Lunchtime . . . and by now dark had fallen. There was no tactful way I could ask this. 'And he's not contacted you?'

She shook her head. No.

She fixed a meal and we ate hurried, none of us much appetite, and she kept giving little startled glances at me. Then she said, 'I can't stand waiting any longer.' She went to the phone; we'd eaten in the kitchen and Les and me still sat at the table, so she said to us, 'You might as well hear my part of this.' She dialled and when he answered she said, 'Brad, it's me.' She'd said no more than that when — click, the line went dead. She frowned and said, 'Must be a technical fault. He wouldn't—' She dialled again; this time his phone rang and rang, no answer. Then she put her phone down on its rest and she said to us bewildered, 'He's never hung up on me before.'

Les cleared his throat and I felt like crying; we were both so embarrassed for her. I can't say that being rejected by the guy her husband meant a hell of a lot to me, because somehow I'd not expected much of him anyway. I'd gotten the impression that she was the forceful one, who made the decisions. But I got so furious and upset for her that it quite surprised me. My mother, yeah, I guess there was something of that to it. Sort of: how dare he act so uncouth to this woman who's my mother and is basically doing her best for all of us in a damn tricky situation?

She bit her lips and fumbled her fingers a minute, then she said, 'I must drive into town and see him. Now, this moment. Waiting would only make it worse.' At which Les took his cue like a right little gentleman, he said goodnight like he always did and shuffled out into the cold, went off down the driveway with his dim old torch.

I said, 'It's getting too cold for him, we'll need come to some other arrangement,' but she looked at me like she wasn't even hearing. I guess you couldn't expect her to, right then; she was so set on what she'd say to this damn man her husband. It stuck out all over her that she still cared like crazy about him, troublesome and useless as he was.

So after Les had gone she hustled around getting her coat and car keys, then she said, 'You can stay here and amuse yourself till I get back. Cate – I must remember to call you Cate,' and she gave me a brilliant startled smile as if the fact of it kept hitting her afresh but hadn't yet gotten completely inside her. A smile that was like a foretaste of happinesses to come.

I didn't aim to spoil that, but I had to say, 'Nuh-uh to me staying here. I'm coming with you.' That stopped her in mid-rush.

'Oh no,' she said, but I didn't give her a chance for any more arguing.

'My dad,' I said, 'isn't he? I'm coming too.'

'For the ride, then,' she said. She was in such a hurry that she'd already opened the front door and gotten herself halfway outside. 'For the ride, if you want to, Cate. You can sit in the car while I – and I promise not to be with him very long. Is that it? You don't want to stay here at night by yourself?' Which was a pretty stupid question; no matter what I'd told her, she just couldn't grasp how Les's and my past life had been. But I didn't bother arguing, I just went outdoors with her, she locked the house up and we climbed into the car, took off. I'd imagined we might pass Les plodding somewhere along the road, but we didn't spot him; I suppose he must have turned off sooner. I'd a notion which old cabin he might be camping out at; it was back in the woods not far from her place. Nevertheless she'd need to find him a bed before the worst of the winter set in; I meant to make damn sure of that.

So we drove down to the city; when she turned off the bypass near his place she started to tell me whereabouts he lived and I said, 'I already know.' She gave me a really odd look then, like I was a package of explosive, but maybe you can't blame her.

'How so?' she said.

I told her how Les and me had driven down and poked around, that first morning while she was fixing up those lab tests. She breathed quick and her fingers tightened on the wheel.

She said, 'You didn't speak to him? I would hope to God not.'

'Hell,' I said, 'we didn't even *see* him. Not to know it was him, anyway. The idea was only to see what sort of a dump he lived in.' Guess I could have put that more tactful; anyway she flinched like she'd hit some small animal on the road.

'Yes,' she said, 'well—' We arrived then and she parked the car. 'I won't be long,' she said, 'I promise. He'll want privacy to—' But I was out of the car before she could say any more.

'All the way,' I said, 'I'm going up there with you. My dad, isn't he?' She faced me across the front of the car in the frosty night and I said, 'No point in you arguing. I've got a right. How long d'you think I've waited for this?'

Which wasn't exactly what I meant, only things don't

always sound as you intended. The truth was, she needed support from *someone*, and being her daughter it seemed like I was the person who ought. I felt she was one lonely lady starting out to fight a tough battle, and for once I was on her side. She said, 'Cate, don't you trust me?' and she sounded more like a confused little kid than ever. She said, 'Oh, if you must. I refuse to come to blows over it.' And she turned her back on me, walked off toward that big old frame house with her shoulders drooping.

The door was open and a guy in the hallway saying hello to a downstairs tenant; her and me went upstairs and she rang his bell. While we waited she said, 'I still think of Cate as a little girl. A child who loved me unquestioningly and would hold out her arms to me.' Her twisted small grin showed she was hurt somewhere by how I'd acted, but if she'd tried for a month she couldn't have said anything to hurt me deeper than this did. Maybe my face showed it, for she took my hand in her two cold ones and she said, 'I'm sorry, my dear.' And I was thinking, kind of frantic, It's been long enough since she pressed his bell – he ought to have opened up. He's not going to; we'll go away from here with nothing sorted. Then his lock clicked, the door opened and he inspected us.

A lined face and fair hair going grey, getting thin. Not a lively face like hers; he looked like he'd gotten tired in the year one and just stayed that way. He glanced at me – didn't look long – and the tired hardness of his face never changed, it was like I was some pebble he was getting ready to kick out of his path. Some pebble that had no business being where it was. He let my mother go into the little hall and I was all set to follow but his arm barred me. He didn't waste breath saying no; just that lean surprisingly strong arm barring me out of his life. He banged the door shut against me and the lock clicked again; he surely wasn't taking any chances.

So I stood waiting outside and told myself I was wrong to have insisted on showing up there, I should've listened to my mother and let her go talk with him alone. Insisting meant that I'd fouled things up all around and made this meeting vastly difficult for her.

I stood there and wondered what in hell the two of them were saying to each other; the door was solid and beyond it I couldn't hear but the barest murmur. But – I guess my senses were sharpened because Les and me had lived so long in the desert away from people – it came to me that there was a smell of perfume on that landing. Not my mother's, some other woman's. And not out of another apartment, because the man my father had this whole atticky top of the house. Anyway the smell had surely – hadn't it? – been stronger when his door was open.

Soon I forgot about the perfume because her voice sounded suddenly louder, fierce – and, right after, so did his. Then the murmurs again, but short. When I heard the click of the lock I walked away to the stairhead, so he wouldn't suppose I planned to rush him and force my daughterness down his throat.

The door started to open; beyond it she said, 'We'll talk about this again,' and he said, 'No.' Just like that, no expression in his voice at all. She came out and he held the door for her from inside, I didn't see him again.

Her and me went downstairs – he didn't offer to see us out – and I tried to figure why he disliked me so. True, I had on the old jeans I'd worn for walking in the woods, and my sneakers were battered and a bit grubby; we'd left her house in such a hurry I didn't think to change them. And my hair – she'd kept on at me about getting it cut, but I liked the long tangle of it and I hadn't brought myself to hand its styling over to her yet. She might come up with something altogether too fancy for my taste. Anyway, were clothes and a hairstyle that important?

We got into the car and she told me in a low mutter, like

she was ashamed, how he refused absolutely to believe. How he'd said he realised the odds were zillions to one but he insisted on riding on that *one* and nothing she said could shift him. How she'd begged him to talk the results over with the test lab but he refused. I said, 'Why, why? Is it that he can't stand the looks of me?' and she said, 'Oh no, my dear, he made up his mind as soon as he read the results.' (This was only the second time she'd called me 'my dear,' and the words warmed me clear through.)

She went on to explain how he'd told her so, hard and clear; she argued with him about the scientists' findings but he wouldn't shift. When all her explaining words to me died into the frosty night I said, 'Even if that one-in-zillions chance didn't exist he'd want no part of me. Prove it into hell, but he'll never believe.'

She said, 'He had a bad time after the kidnapping, he blamed himself as being the man of the family, who should have been able to prevent his daughter getting grabbed.' She started the car motor and said, 'I know you're attached to Lester but I'll never be able to forgive him. He wrecked Brad's life and mine throughout those years and he turned Brad into a neurotic untrusting—' We swung out of the parking place and she shook her head. 'Probably,' she said, 'Brad's scared of finding his new quiet life wrecked, poor man. The life he's so carefully constructed. But he'll come around to accepting you.' Yet I could tell she truly doubted that.

When we got on the highway and left the city behind I said – not meaning to be cruel, but I was trying to act open and straightforward with her and these words came out without me thinking – 'There'd been another woman there tonight.'

She said, 'I know.' I saw her face in the dashboard light and all of a sudden it was shining wet. 'I'm so naive,' she said, 'won't I ever learn? I'd expected there might be difficulty at first over you, but the other I never expected, not in a million years. I always felt he and I still belonged wholly to each other.'

Then she pulled the car onto the shoulder and cut the engine, because she was crying too hard to see where she was driving. She put her head down on the steering wheel and her hands each side in her hair.

I didn't know what in all hell a daughter ought to do, but finally I put one of my hands on her arm kind of gentle. She'd behaved pretty much okay to me since we heard the results, and I wanted to be a loving daughter to her. After a while she brought her hand up to cover mine, so I guess my doing that had been more or less the right thing. And neither of us spoke.

11

After that evening a sort of warmth sat between her and me; I can't describe it any more exact. A hint of loosening up; we knew we could reach out to each other in an emergency and find something there, because we'd already done it. One time, anyhow. And during those next quiet days at her house we got to know each other better than before. Especially after we got one big question cleared away: she hinted how she'd wondered if Les ever put his hands on me the wrong way. After I got through yelling at her that he wasn't that sort of man at all, she said sorry but it was natural for a mother to wonder and be afraid. We cleared up that wonder of hers pretty damn fast and got to talking about other things we felt easier with.

For instance, her jewellery business; she told me she must get back into working on that because she'd commissions to fill. She showed me her drawing-board and the raw stones and such, the wheel she used to polish them. Big fancy bits and pieces for women that wanted something sparkly and would pay well, and she sold them mostly to stores, which was less hassle. I thought running this business was pretty damn clever of her. I kind of admired the style of some of the smaller pieces; I said to Les one day that I was beginning to think of her as one gutsy lady, and smart in all sorts of ways. I instanced the jewellery, but Les said, 'Who the hell wants that sort of thing?'

He was way out of touch with her world and you'd never get him in touch, but seemed to me I was – sneakily and in a small way – starting to understand where she was at. I said that to Les also (which wasn't, I guess, the most tactful of me) and he didn't scowl, he just looked all of a sudden like he was far off. I said fierce, 'You recall you promised to hang around for always? Don't you dare try to rat out on that,' and he said, 'Who the hell said anything about ratting?' And so on. But the thought was in his head, I could see it walking around there. That because her and me weren't enemies any longer, I didn't need him.

I hugged him tight and said, 'I'd *die* if you left me. Kill myself, chop myself away, whatever.'

For a moment he looked scared, as if he might believe me, but then he sighed and got his weary-animal look. 'You'll get accustomed to her,' he said, 'and that's good, it's what I wanted.'

But I clutched his neck like she had when we first showed up and she'd gotten so mad at him; I clutched and made him promise all over again.

I also pointed out to him – and this was true – that, even if me and my mother were getting warmer together, we were still – most times – pretty damn timid around each other. Not so stiff any longer but quiet, exploring. Which, as far as I could figure, we certainly were. And I couldn't with all due respect take to any of the other people around her. Certainly not to this Brad her husband my rightful father; why should I? How could you take to anyone who'd acted in regard to you as he'd done to me? He was shook about the past, okay, but didn't I have a right to be ac- knowledged now I was here?

Moreover, when her and me went shopping in the city – a happening I wasn't yet accustomed to, it felt strange to me every time – the salespeople acted courteous to her – something in her manner seemed to prevent them from acting any other way – but they either ignored me or, if I was feeling awkward and wearing some of my older clothes that day, they acted like I was a pile of shit in the roadway, that's how. As if they'd need to step around me prissy and flinching, and hurry on so they didn't need look at me more.

I said something to my mother one day about this and she said, 'People do judge by appearances, you know. People who do their kind of job.'

I said, 'Then they fucking oughtn't,' but that got her flinching too, because she wasn't in the habit of hearing that sort of language. I said, 'All they care about's who's going to spend how much money with them,' and she couldn't entirely deny that.

One evening, after Les had gone off to whatever old cabin he slept in, a thought hit me and I said, 'You must have pictures? I'd enjoy seeing them.'

She stared and said, 'You mean you want to watch television?' (which she did rarely, though she'd a set there) but I said, 'Nuh-uh, I mean pictures of you and my father and me when I was tiny. You must have those.' Because I'd often seen tourists out West taking pictures of each other; seemed like all families did that.

But nothing could ever be straightforward between her and me; she coloured up, shifted her feet and said, 'Unfortunately we – he – I'll show you what I have.' And when she got the albums out I understood; masses of pictures of adults in them, yeah, but then I saw that lots of the little transparent envelopes were empty, and towards the end of the second album all of them were. No pictures at all, as if my parents had stopped having a life when I disappeared.

I looked hard at my mother, I didn't want to ask but I ought to have been in there and she needed to tell me what'd happened. So she coloured up some more and she said how my father'd destroyed them all, a while after I disappeared, how he'd made up his mind I wasn't ever coming back and he said he couldn't stand to see the pictures when I'd gone and he should have prevented it. All of which seemed to me crazier than ever, but I managed to keep my mouth shut about that because my mother was already so upset. Instead I said, 'Okay, let me see the other pictures then.' Because they might be of people that, when I was tiny, I'd known.

It had never struck me that, besides my mother and father, I could have other family, but turned out this was so, although nobody that seemed to matter much. We flicked through the envelopes in the first album and one was of an aunt, another a bunch of cousins. All of them in England, my mother said, and their way of keeping in touch was a Christmas card once a year. My mother looked grieved and said the gap wasn't of her seeking but she said the truth was, people drift apart. Especially when they live a long way separate and their lives go different directions.

I said, 'So you and my father had parents too.' Which sounds really dumb but none of this had hit me before. She said yeah and she showed me their pictures, an old one of her own mother who'd died at thirty – when my mother was only six – and a not so old one of a guy in full diving gear, holding his diver's helmet in his hand and grinning on some jetty; he looked like a fun person and I felt I could relate pretty close to him. 'My mother's father,' she said, and he'd lived safe, took good care of my mother till she went to university, then he started doing all the things he'd enjoyed again, like diving onto wrecks, and one day he went on a diving expedition – and something went wrong, he came back up too late. After which my mother finished university in England and then came to Virginia on a postgraduate course. And that was how she met my father.

I said, 'So he wasn't British?' and she said good heavens no, he was Virginia-born and as proud of it as could be. Virginia the first permanent settlement, she said, the Old Dominion, all that stuff. She showed me pictures but they were mostly when he was young, college-age along with her, and he looked like any other skinny college student only more absent-minded, with his long arm around her and a sort of half-smirk on his face. As if he might not be too bright but he knew he'd found the best bargain of his life and he meant to hang onto it.

I said something of this to my mother and she said, 'Yes, until you came along.' She laughed and said, 'He went on loving me, of course, but he really doted on you.'

I wished I could recall something of him having played with me like she said he had, or when the two of them went hiking and he carried me in a backpack slung from his shoulders; I searched my memory but found nothing there. My mother's face glowed when she told me how much they loved hiking and camping, and how they always took me along even when I was tiny. Then her face got all closed up and hurt. She went on quickly to tell me about his parents, how his father had run off to Delaware with another woman and lost touch with them, how Brad's mother filed for divorce but never remarried, kept busy with real-estate selling and her friends until she died of intestinal cancer three years before Les brought me back. I looked at the pictures of her and said, 'I only just missed meeting her. I'll bet we'd have gotten along great together.' Because in the pictures she was always smiling. But her husband that ran off, he looked more like my father, skinny and not much life to him.

There were various other distant relatives scattered all over the country, who got in touch with each other if one of them died, but that was all. I said, 'Did you tell them about me being gone?' but she said no, she couldn't bear to write the words, and these weren't people that ever called her up. She said, 'I kept telling myself that if I ever met any of them I'd break the news then. But now I don't need to.' And she reached over, hugged me hard.

The days went by and Brad my father didn't call her. I could tell that this made her damn unhappy, she was still fond of the guy and she couldn't decide what to do to make him see sense. But she'd friends in various cities up and down the east coast that called her to chat once in a while or that she'd call up; she'd laugh and her face'd shine pink while she talked on the phone with them. She even had friends in England she kept in touch with by phone. But these Virginia woods were nearly empty of houses – whole inhabited ones, I mean – and as far as I could make out she'd only the one true friend living nearby. Which was Elly, the woman she'd been hiking with, chatting about Elly's marriage problems, the first day we arrived. And she'd been due to meet with Elly again the next morning; yeah, I recalled how when we'd arrived back that day she was saying goodbye to a woman all city clothes and clanking gold-coloured jewellery much fancier than any my mother designed.

So I said one evening, when I was helping her do the dishes, 'What happened about your Elly that morning? Did you and her take your hike in the woods?' Meaning, Did you tell her about Les and me?

But she took her hands out of the soapy water, she stared at me and then she laughed. 'You funny girl,' she said, 'whatever made you remember that, all these weeks later?'

I made my voice real quiet and smooth (like Les pointed out to me I do when I'm trying to lie my way out of something really noticeable) and I said, 'It came into my head, that's all.'

'You odd girl,' she said, and then she did a thing which shook me all over, she put her soapy hands around me and kissed me full on the face. 'Oh Cate,' she said, 'I'm so glad you're back with me. Thank God Les came to his senses after all these years and brought you back. You and I are going to have such a good life together, aren't we?'

Like I say, shook me rigid. I'd planned on being able to cope with getting accepted by her but the truth was, when any sign of the acceptance showed, it was almost as hard to handle as the opposite would have been. In some ways harder; I could imagine toughening myself against her rejections, but this reaching out of hers toward me made me feel unanchored altogether. Like I was drifting around in her orbit and not unhappy – indeed, pretty damn happy at times, I guess – but no firm harbourage in sight. Which, for a person brought up like I'd been, wasn't the easiest to handle. So when she said how good of a time we'd have, I finally answered into her soapy hands, 'I don't know what to say to that.'

She grinned and took her hands away, went back to doing the dishes and handing them to me to dry. 'We'll learn,' she said, 'you and I. We'll learn together, won't we?'

Then while she finished the dishes she told me about this Elly. How she'd been a damn good friend of my mother's through some rough spots, apparently the difficulties with my father which led to him moving out. But she'd not been around too many years and hadn't been told in detail about what happened to me. Only that they'd lost their child and Brad blamed himself, couldn't settle. If you ask me, the chats were much more about Elly's supposed problems than any of my mother's; she'd got this high-pitched yappy voice and she seemed to be a female who loved the sound of it, who rated her problems more important than anyone else's; she waved her hands around a lot and her jewellery clanked while she talked about her troubles. Also my mother was a damn good listener. Anyway, no, she'd not told Elly the whole story nor who I was, only that she'd got these two friends from elsewhere staying with her.

I said, 'Elly's one slick lady but I wouldn't trust her too damn far,' and my mother frowned, she handed me the last plate to dry and said, 'You mustn't be jealous of my friends, Cate.' Which wasn't at all the point. Then she said she couldn't imagine why I'd mistrust Elly. I said, 'Because of her stare.' Les and me had met her along the road a few times when we drove out in the truck, and she stared not just nosy but like she wanted to shove us out of her nice clean woods. I said this too and my mother said carefully,

'She's only here for three months each year and I think she feels rather—'

'Like the woods all belong to her?'

'One of these days,' she said smiling, 'I'll teach you some tact, won't I?' (To which I thought, Not necessarily.) 'Elly's very,' she said, 'I don't know how to put this, but – security-conscious.'

'You mean we look to her the sort that might be a risk around here?' Fire hazard, crime hazard maybe. My mother hadn't asked recently why the cops out West might want me; I hoped she'd forgotten it but I suspicioned she was maybe too damn smart to. She might be biding her time, waiting till I'd trust her enough to tell her the truth.

My mother screwed her mouth tight. At last she said, 'Elly checks up on the empty rundown cabins along the road, that sort of thing. Makes sure nobody's hiding out in them.'

'Oh, she does?' I'd need to warn Les. But my mother would need to do something permanent about him pretty soon, he couldn't be expected to go through snow and ice in some half-broken cabin without heat. 'She's a very smooth woman,' I said, 'but I don't like her.'

'She's a friend of mine, Cate.'

Then it burst out of me, the thought I'd not realised I was thinking. 'And you're too ashamed of me to tell all these friends of yours I exist?'

Then she left the sink and turned around to me, she took me in her damp soapy hands and rocked me like Les had the habit of. 'No,' she said, 'no no. Only trust me, will you?'

To which there was no truthful answer except, I'll try but it'll take time. I guessed she wouldn't want to hear that – it sounded too much like setting conditions – so I said nothing.

The weather stayed fine by day, so Les and me went out

and roamed the woods and the dirt road; seemed both of us felt more comfortable doing that than hanging around her fancy cabin. I felt like I was halfway into her life but still halfway outside it. The evenings after Les had gone off to his cabin, the nights and the early mornings when I'd wake early and listen to the outdoor sounds until I heard my mother get up – all those times, when there was only the two of us, seemed like we had a relationship. But I wanted to be with Les too, so he wouldn't decide I didn't need him any longer. Because I surely did need him, he was my basic security. And I told myself that anyway she needed time for her jewellery work.

A couple of days during that next two weeks it rained and we went back to the cabin early, before the school bus passed; when she heard its rattle and saw the yellow gleam of it through the trees she looked at me like weighing me up, but she didn't mention the subject. Had more sense than to, I guess; knew what my answer to *that* would be.

And one evening after Les had left, this guy from Washington – this scientist that had arranged the lab tests – called her up. Vince, his name was. She talked kind of shy and sweet to him at first, then he got pressing her and she let out at him, showed how tough she could be. I was proud of her for being my mother then, she sure could be one gutsy lady when she put her mind to it.

He asked the results of the tests apparently, for she said, 'Fine, fine. I'm very happy,' with that shy sweet glow and a sideways glance which included me. He must have asked how this Brad was adapting to the result, for she said, 'Not yet.' With some of the glow gone, but some of it still remaining. Then this Vince started pushing her – when she baulked I could hear his voice easy from where I sat at the other end of the kitchen table – about her going up to Washington again, not Les and me, of course, just her. It'd been so good, he said, to see her again, and he made clear how much more than just seeing her he'd like to do. 'After all,' he said, 'Brad's not really a significant person to you any longer, is he?' And he started chatting on about he was surprised she was still married; didn't she have it in her mind to get a divorce?

She said quiet, 'It's not as simple as that, Vince,' and her gaze came around warm on me, like I might be afraid this Vince'd be a threat to her and my future and she meant to tell me pretty damn honest there was no danger of that. Which I was glad to know, because he sure was a pushy one.

She thanked him a dozen times, if she did once, for arranging those damn tests, said how grateful she was and all that. Finally I said loud and clear, 'No sweat. If he hadn't done it for you, someone else could have, easy.' Meaning, Don't need feel obligated. She gave me a quick grin like the two of us were real good friends as well as mother and daughter; she was too polite to talk to him the way I'd said, but through her politeness it did come to the same thing in the end. Finally she scraped all her politeness together and said, 'Vince, I'm profoundly obliged to you, and next time I'm up there I'll be sure to contact you.' He got all enthused at that but she interrupted, telling him she'd no immediate plans for travel up. She got in a little dig too about the number of women he'd already got available; I was glad to see she'd that much spirit. (And he laughed, he didn't argue over it, so I guess she knew what she was talking about.) Then she said goodbye and hung up, she wiped her hand across her forehead and said, 'Whew!'

I said, 'He's too pushy a one.'

She said, 'He's been very helpful and I'm grateful but – yes. I ought to have expected that he'd claim there was a price of that sort to pay.'

'But you're not going to pay it?'

'No.' She sat down across the table from me and pushed her hair back from her face. 'No, Cate. I don't like black-mail. I'll feel bad with my conscience but—'

I said, 'A person can get accustomed to that, it's no major

deal.' My past rose up then and it was true – you could live accustomed just fine, but the process of getting that way was like thorns dug into you.

This was (I realised afterwards) a dangerous thing for me to say, because it might remind her what Les had let out about me and the cops. But fortunately she was busy with her own thoughts and not deep listening to me; she said dreamy, 'Yes, I suppose so.' Then she told me about Vince, how him and her had met at college and kept in touch ever since. (That was in England, he'd been there on some scholarship.)

I said, 'If he wanted you, there's been a hell of a lot of time,' and she said yes, she wasn't worried about that. Was certain sure he'd never wanted her much till she became unavailable – which was her way of saying she'd married and stayed faithful to this Brad my father.

Another evening late – after Les had left, again, and I was flicking through a magazine – the phone rang; I answered because she was taking a shower and asked me to. I guess she'd pretty much given up by then on her husband phoning. This wasn't any voice I recognised. A female, but not that Elly nor any of the friends who lived elsewhere and might call up. Must be one I'd not heard of before. So I asked the name and the woman said Louise. I called into the bathroom and my mother, all muffled in a big towel, said she didn't know any Louise; was I sure I'd gotten the name right? Which I was, but I had the woman repeat it. So my mother pulled a robe on – it was fluffy pink; she looked like a piece of candy wrapped in it, and her hair falling loose; she looked like a pretty damn good mother for a girl to have – and she came into the living room where I'd answered, she picked up the phone and said, 'I'm sorry, who is this?'

The woman said, 'Louise,' again plain and clear, then she said, 'You don't know me,' and I couldn't catch the rest of what she said.

Only my mother's face went white above the pretty pink robe; she let the robe's edges fall apart and she stood there shivering, listening. She said after a while, in a stiff dead voice, 'You've a key? Because I haven't.' Then she said, 'Tomorrow morning, very well. Ten o'clock. I'll meet you outside.' She hung up the phone, turned to me and said, 'It's about Brad. Your father. He's disappeared.'

12

Most likely my mother didn't sleep much at all that night, and to be honest I didn't either. Not that I'd any reason to warm toward this Brad my father, but him disappearing was a bit drastic. He'd known about me for several weeks, it wasn't as if the fact of me hit him and he disappeared next day. I was pretty damn sure his going and me were directly connected, and that kept me awake; it belts you one in your stomach to think that a person took off on account of they couldn't stand the notion of you. At least Les, who wasn't even my real father, had stayed around.

At breakfast next morning Les showed up as usual and she told him what had happened, how she must drive down to the city but him and me could stay around her place, have the run of her cabin for the day. It was a stinking wet morning, so I guess she figured she was acting kindly. But I was determined not to get left out of these happenings that involved me so close, and before Les could answer her I said to her, 'I'm going with you.' She opened her mouth but I said, 'Forget the arguments, my mind's made up.'

Les looked from one to the other of us and his eyes went sort of weary and accustomed. I dived into his brain as I sometimes had in the past, and I divined that the expressions on her face and mine were ones he was beginning to see there pretty regularly. Me, mulish as I'd been with him on occasion in the past, and her – that shine on her face which meant she was angry at having her wishes thwarted (I was learning that her will, in its way, had its moments as strong as mine). But she wasn't going to allow her anger free rein, oh no. Technically because I was her daughter returned from the supposedly dead and it wouldn't be happy-parent-like to argue, but also because I was *me*, damn it, that she was getting sort of fond of for my own sake. (From little things she'd say or ways she'd act at times, I'm pretty sure I'm right on that.) Les knew all about the formal technicalities of relationships but this warming between her and me somehow kept him outside and there seemed no way I could bring him into its comfort where, on account of my true affection for him, he did belong.

So this time she said nothing to me except a quiet 'All right.' Then she realised and glanced at Les and caught him looking at her; the two of them stiffened up. Enemies, like. Not fighting directly over me now, only she'd plainly realised that if I went down to the city with her, that would leave Les in her house alone – and even after these weeks she didn't trust him. That was the unfancy and un-pleasant truth.

He flushed a deep red like the wattle of some old turkey and he said, 'I planned on taking the truck out today any-way. Errands I need do, down along the highway.' Which was as unlikely a story as I ever heard, but my mother was upset over her damn husband and she quickly accepted Les's excuse, it'd solve a problem.

So after breakfast Les rattled off in our old truck – taking the long route which meant miles of winding dirt-and-rock road, not the direct-to-the-highway route her and me'd use. The two of us left soon after Les; she drove hard, frowning, toward this empty apartment of her husband's, and I didn't aim to bother her. Only, about halfway there, I said, 'Who's the woman that called you? This Louise?'

She said, 'How should I know?' In a tough voice but none too steady. Then she brisked herself up and said, 'Oh, Cate, you can guess who. She'd got a key to his apartment, she visits him after work. I guess,' she said, 'they sleep together when they're not too busy doing other things. And she checks on him in between, she's got – or she found – my phone number. She called me from his apartment to say she's in possession but there's a slight problem.'

'Hell,' I said, 'damn good thing she did call you, isn't it? Otherwise you'd not know he'd gone.'

'Yes, of course,' she said. 'Don't mind me, I'm feeling bitchy. That and a lot of other things.'

We drove some more and got to where the first shopping squares are, with a few old frame houses tucked into the trees next the new malls and looking silly, like the bulldozers should have swept them away too. Soon we'd turn onto the bypass heading toward the university and his nearby apartment.

I said, 'Why would he rat out *now*? He's known about me being his for a full three weeks.'

My mother frowned at the highway signs and said, 'Delayed shock, I suppose.'

I said, 'You mean the news has only just hit him?' and she nodded. Seems crazy to me; if you're told something, wouldn't you take it into your brain straight off instead of shoving it away from you for three weeks and then letting it swipe you so hard it knocks you over? But he was what she'd called an intellectual, and maybe folks like that are different. She says not, but the truth is I've no handle on how that man my father might possibly think. Or act or anything; thin hard faces like his was when he kept me out of his apartment that night – I don't understand those at all.

While my mother turned us from the bypass and we neared his apartment, I wanted to say to her, Hey, thanks and I really do mean it. Because she'd been so tough against me at first but after the test results came through she swung totally to believe and there'd be no shifting her. I'd never felt truly grateful before except to Les – there'd never been occasion, that I recall – but I surely was beginning to be so to her. Only I couldn't figure how to express it, and we were nearly at his apartment, so I kept my mouth shut.

This time the street door was locked but the woman Louise answered the voice-check from upstairs and the door unlocked. My mother and me went up those creaky old stairs on the new red carpet, and I thought how a carpet that colour wouldn't much show blood. I never used to think about stuff like that before Jeff. Sometimes when I got shy with my mother it wasn't because of me worrying how to express my gratitude or any other picky thing like that, it was because there was Jeff in my past and what had happened to him; I didn't want to think about how my mother'd feel toward me, how she'd act, if she found out about that. Not in the way of her calling the cops, I mean; I somehow couldn't picture her selling me out that way. She'd be more likely, I supposed, to tell Les and me to get the hell out of her sight and her house and never show up again, never try to get in touch with her. Then we'd drive off and she'd stay home by herself and – what? Hate me and love me and hurt inside, all the ways there were; I didn't want to hurt her over any little tiny thing, let alone that bad. Yet I hated to keep inside of me all that had happened, because if she didn't know about it she was learning to love a person that wasn't the full me; a big chunk of what made me up, she didn't know about. And I don't mean that I planned on making a habit of murder, far from it. Only that it's a pretty major event and, as I'd found myself sharing much less important things with her, so I wanted to share that. But I couldn't manage to figure out the for and against of that sharing, let alone the how and when of it.

The woman Louise opened the upstairs door of the apartment to us; she was a plump young woman with wispy fair hair. You couldn't call her beautiful but everything about her looked soft, she looked like she'd be damn good at cuddling.

She said to my mother in a wispy little voice, 'I'm sorry, but I did feel you ought to be told,' and my mother said, 'Yes, of course.' Formal, like she was signing a document.

We went into the little entrance hall and – I guess I was nervous about setting foot in his place even though he wasn't there, it seemed like more of an intrusion this time than if he'd stood in the doorway and I'd pushed my way past him. Anyway I was nervous, for whatever reason. So from the end of the little hall I saw this girl staring at us and I thought to myself, That is one quite slick-looking female. Then I realised it was a full-length mirror, I was looking at me.

I had on a black-and-white check jacket, white high-necked sweater and black pants, black loafers, heavy low-slung metal belt. (What I wore each day was according to my mood, and jeans were still a favourite, but this had seemed the sort of peculiar occasion you ought to dress up for.) My mother wore a deep yellow pantsuit, buttery colour, with thin gold jewellery; she was upset, I knew, and she wouldn't have thought about what'd be right to wear, it was only that she always had that neat quiet *together* look. And the woman – this Louise – she wore a crumpled white shirt and a full blue skirt that she'd too thick of a waist for. And the straggly hair; I couldn't see how any man'd prefer her to my mother. I said something of all this to my mother afterwards, when we were out of there, and she said, 'Oh dear God, have I turned you into a fullblown clothes snob, Cate? That wasn't my intention at all.' And I must admit that the Louise woman looked like she'd be soft and warm in bed and for living around, wouldn't fuss. Which sounds disloyal of me, like my mother would. I don't mean that, only that there was a difference. But adults surely are confusing.

The Louise woman said hi to me pleasant enough, but she looked surprised and started to say to my mother,

'Who—' but my mother walked right on past her without giving an answer. She clearly didn't know who I was – or maybe even that there was a Cate to know anything about. And that was okay, there were complications enough banging around already. We all went into the living room and my mother said to her brisk, like there might be a problem with the imaginary document she was signing but she intended to sort it through, 'When did you see him last?'

'Oh,' said Louise, 'Brad?' Soft and close, like she'd known him real well for a long time; I saw my mother flinch. But I doubt that Louise saw, she didn't seem the noticing kind. She went on, counting on her fingers like a tiny child. 'Yesterday . . . um, first thing.' She flushed then, a delicate colour if you admire that coy stuff, and she went on in her tiny little voice, 'I left for work about eight thirty and he – and I—' I understood what she meant, she'd spent the night there with him and most likely plenty of other nights too. Nothing to blush over in that, but my mother's steady gaze somehow wrongfooted her. As if my mother had an overriding claim which didn't depend on a marriage ceremony, and they both knew it.

'Did he seem all right then?' my mother said coolly.

'Yeah,' this little soft thing said, 'I guess so. He was always sort of silent but . . . yeah, he kissed me at the door, like always.' She watched my mother's face and hurried on, fussing over her words. 'I work at the university too, in the registrar's department. I didn't sleep here every night,' she said pleading.

'Dear God,' my mother said, 'as if that matters. The point is, where's he gone and why?'

'He didn't say anything to explain,' Louise said, 'if he had, I'd tell you. We just ate breakfast and I left.'

We were in the living room, with big bookcases and white armchairs all around; she sat down in one of those white armchairs and started picking at the fabric of its arm.

I thought how angry he'd be to come back and find she'd picked a hole in it, then it struck me that he mightn't come back ever again. At this I got a sick feeling in my stomach, as if he would be stretched out dead somewhere and there was a lot of blood. I sat down quick or I might have fallen; my mother looked at me fast and then she pulled a straightbacked chair up beside me, sat on it and put her arm round my shoulders, realised I was upset. But she didn't know the half of why.

'When was he missed?' my mother said, and began to tap her foot on the floor as if she was saying Speed's important, we've got to find him before anything happens to him. But I had a warning feeling even then, a guess that none of it was going to be that simple.

'The university – he was supposed to lecture at ten but he never showed up. He had a lunch appointment with another professor but he missed that too. Then meeting with a bunch of new students at two o'clock, and when he didn't show up there the dean called me in, asked if I knew where he was.' She got that deep flush again, like it might matter that the whole university knew she was sleeping with him. Seems to me, if you're going to do that, there's no point in getting coy over it.

'And you'd no idea where?' said my mother impatient.

'That's right. So I – so the dean asked me to come back here and find out what gave. I rushed over here but there was no sign of him.' She got a couple of shiny little tears in her eyes. 'So I phoned from here, told the dean and called the police like they told me to, waited here till they came. Then they went to the university but he hadn't shown up there.'

'They haven't called me,' said my mother. 'Dear God, I'm still his wife, aren't I? Did no one think to tell them I exist?'

The Louise person started to cry real hard then. 'I called you though,' she said, 'last night, didn't I?'

'But the police didn't,' said my mother. Then she said

like stiff, unhappy, 'Well, let that pass. The important thing is to find him.'

The Louise person stopped crying and said, 'But supposing we can't?' For a moment I felt sneery at her because she'd dried her tears up so fast, then I realised it was fear had dried them; she and my mother were only just then getting around to imagining what I'd jumped on right away. Previous experience, I guess; there must have been people missed Jeff and went hunting him. Because he was no wetback immigrant but a local boy, had family and such.

Anyway my mother went to the phone and called up the police; Louise and me couldn't avoid hearing her end of the talk and seemed the police weren't too interested. He was a grown man and he'd decided to take off for someplace, that was all. People did it all the time, men as much as women. And he'd only been gone a bit over twenty-four hours.

My mother hung up finally and said to this Louise, 'You haven't *any* idea where he might be?' And Louise said no she hadn't; she and my mother talked some more but didn't get anywhere. After a while this Louise said she'd make us coffee, she went in the kitchen to fix it and my mother riffled through the loose papers that were lying in the open bureau. Looking for a clue, she said. She put one of the papers into her purse but when I said, 'Did you find a clue?' she said, 'No.' It struck me that she was in an odd position; she was still his wife so she'd a right to do this sort of thing, but you could tell she felt uneasy doing it from the fact that she specifically did it while this Louise was out of the room.

When Louise brought in the coffee, the two of us were sitting quiet again like we were waiting for someone that we didn't expect would ever show up. We drank the coffee – which tasted as wispy and uncertain as that lady looked – and my mother thanked her politely, then we left.

Outside in the street I said, 'Is she going to carry on

living at his place?' and my mother said, 'I neither know nor care.' Which I could see her point.

But when we were sitting in the car again she didn't start the engine at once, she put her clenched fists on the steering wheel and stared at them. 'I behaved so horribly to her,' she said. 'I'm setting you such a bad example, aren't I? Cate, don't ever be as brusque and cynical to anyone as I was to her. It's been a long time since I was in the position of being an example to anyone, but that's no excuse.' Before I could answer, her thought swerved and carried her onward. 'Regardless of that,' she said, 'and for the woman's own sake . . .' She looked at me, past me. 'Louise caught me on the raw,' she said, 'because I can see how she's much more suitable for him than I ever was. She's a kindly person and I was never kind, I was in too much of a hurry. From the beginning – when he and I were young and happy and you were still around – he needed so much reassurance, the needing was part of his character. And what did I do? I tried to toughen him.'

She started the car and while we drove back to her cabin she told me little anecdotes about him from early times as well as more recent, told me about his work (I'd seen books in his apartment in foreign languages, which confirmed what Les had said) and more little jokey bits about him and her and the young me. Picnics and trips up into these mountains and such. After a long time she said, 'You're not saying much, Cate. What are you thinking?'

How I was flesh and bone of him as well as her, that's what. I'd written him off as a useless nothing but these tales of hers fleshed him out, made him a living person; it had been as much his doing as hers to be a parent to me. She was too late warning me not to get brusque and cynical, I'd already done more than my share of those. I burned now to think how he was my true father and seemingly him and me wouldn't ever get to know each other; it shamed me that I'd thought him a nothing until then.

I tried to get some of this across to her and she drove one-handed while she took a piece of paper from her purse and laid it on my lap. The paper she'd taken from his bureau. 'Your birth-right,' she said.

I read it and it was a paper with some tabulated results, drawn up by a local lab. At the bottom of it, a conclusion. That the odds in favour of my being his and hers were so many to one, you could dwell on the one if you wanted but, in scientific language, you'd do better not to waste your time.

'Keep it,' she said, 'it belongs to you.'

But it seemed to me a double-edged gift because of what it had just done. I said, 'He ran because I was proven to be his.'

'Oh Cate,' she said, putting her hand on mine in that warm way she had, 'please don't feel bad about it. Didn't I tell you he had a much harder time adjusting to your disappearance than I did? He felt so totally responsible.'

'So he's run because he refuses to believe it's me? I disarrange his life too much just by existing?'

'Don't let it hurt you, Cate,' she said, so gentle that I couldn't argue more. She added, 'I'm sure he'll change his mind and come back when he adjusts to the idea,' and I could tell she wanted to believe this, even if her common sense was telling her different. But it seemed to me like a pretty damn long shot, almost too long to be possible.

We got home and Les wasn't back; fair enough, it was still morning. I hung around all afternoon instead of going out to the woods, hoped he'd show up. He'd need to show before dark anyway, both of us always did. But dark came; no Les. I paced in and out of the rooms of her cabin and I said, 'Can't you do something to find him?'

'Like what, Cate?'

'Call the cops or whatever. You were quick to tell them your husband had gone missing, can't you see that Les is all of that important to me?'

She started to say something and then stopped; it must be in her mind that he could've gotten fed up with the setup, figured I'd no more need of him and just lit out.

I yelled at her, 'He promised me, damn you! He never in all hell would run away.' But the truth was, I couldn't be sure. I got frightened of my own temper then, hadn't felt so angry and scared since the trouble with Jeff. Was ready to take it out, if Les didn't show, on whoever got in my way; I sensed her doubts and they stirred up my anger. When it got near eleven o'clock I crouched myself into a chair and knotted my fists together, because I was afraid like hell of what I might do.

13

About one in the morning my mother said, 'We'd better go to bed, Cate.' She'd sense enough not to talk gentle and soft, which would've made me yell at her for pitying me; she spoke sort of stiff, and that was okay. I grunted 'No,' but after a while I hauled myself out of the chair I'd scrunched into and I went upstairs; she did have a point. I might as well forget about sleeping that night but I could undress and sit at the window. At least then I'd be on my own to watch and wait, not have to sit around her and feel her concern.

I put the bedroom light out and wrapped myself in a thick robe, sat staring out at the darkness of the woods night, and I pictured whereabouts Les would have gotten to by then. He'd head back out West; without me, there'd be no problem for him. He'd have reached southwest Virginia by that time, he'd be looping the curves of the mountain roads in our crazy old truck that was more held together with baling twine and shortage of cash than with any metal fasteners. I gnawed my nails and hoped to God he'd have sense enough to pull off the road and sleep some; I hated the whole notion of him because he'd ratted out on me, yet I'd this sort of wistful care that he shouldn't get injured or too much disappointed. I leaned my chin on my elbows and watched the dark, listened to the short howls of a bobcat in the deep woods down by the creek, and I thought about Les and me, about the desert. Finally, yeah, I thought about Jeff.

About, I mean, what sort of person he really was. Too

clean-living and honest and upright for me, that's for sure. A college kid caring about me? You can forget that. But a tangled side to him also; is there a tangled part to all males? I wouldn't know. Not half as tangled, though, as the wishes and wants that turned out to be roosting inside of me.

I recalled how I'd told Les Jeff was illegal, a wetback, how I'd joked about his supposed family back in Mexico. No one but Les would have believed me for a moment. Not that Jeff couldn't have been Mexican by his looks; it was his dark slicked hair and deep tan gave me the notion. And Les was in the habit, till then, of believing every word I said.

But that apartment of Jeff's, where I went that night and where we had to roll him up in the rug to carry him out of there because there was so much blood on everything – how could Les imagine a wetback'd have cash enough, or knowhow, to get and pay for that? Because Les had trusted me always to tell the truth, is how. At which I put my arms down on the windowsill and my head on them and started to cry, not noisy because there was no sense in making a fuss. No one except my mother around and I didn't want to bother her because she'd trouble enough of her own. So I cried without much noise, only I kept saying inside myself, Les, please come back and get me, take me along with you, I don't care what the risks are. I don't belong around these smooth places and never will. And, much as I like my mother, these slick-mannered people either. Les, don't run out on me; if I can't believe that promise you made me, who in the whole range of hell can I believe? Who'd I want to, that is? I'd believe my mother because she seemed like she wasn't expert at telling lies either, but that was different. Although she was my mother she was, to me, pretty much a recent discovery, but Les had washed and fed me and that, all the time I could recall when I was tiny, and he'd always been around since; I couldn't imagine living without him.

All of a sudden my tears dazzled me because a light

shone through them; I jumped up and stared out the window but the clearing in front of the house was empty except for my mother's parked car. The lights swung up the slope toward us, then partway along the drive they stopped. From the downstairs bedroom my mother called to me very low. 'Cate,' she said, 'are you awake?' and I knew she was terrified.

But, like I say, one gutsy lady; I was real proud of her then. I pulled my robe tight around me and ran downstairs to her. The two of us watched from her window which overlooked the curve of the driveway, and I said, 'Them's not Les's lights.'

She said, 'I know it,' and the two of us, side by side, felt our hearts beating fast together.

No one out there moved, no one spoke, only the slow snorting of the engine of whatever vehicle it was. I said, 'Did anything like this ever happen here before?' and the air moved beside me when she shook her head.

She said, 'If they don't go away I'll go out there. I've got a gun.'

I said, 'The hell you have,' and the two of us gave a little chuckle together; despite the fear, that was a damn good moment.

She said, 'You didn't expect that of me, did you?' and pointed to show that the pistol lived in the drawer of her bedside table. That was pretty damn good too, her trusting me by telling me that. But then nervousness wiped away my pleasure, because those lights swung up and headed on along the driveway toward us. She said, 'We won't just hang around and wait,' and she broke from my side, went and got out her little gun. She said, 'You stay here, Cate. I'm going out to meet whoever it is.'

But to the definite hell with that idea. I said, 'Only over my very dead corpse you are.'

I caught at her robe and we faced each other; we were pretty much of a height so we stared face to face in the shadowy starlight. She breathed quick and excited and her perfume from the daytime lingered about her; it smelled pretty damn good. I thought again, I grew inside her body, I was a little baby growing in there and she's truly my mother, and I was just overwhelmed with a sweet flood of . . . I don't know. Something that makes pretty damn near all the happiness in the world, is how.

I said to her – the two of us breathing face to face in that quiet dark room – 'Don't you ever run out on me. I'd be totally demolished,' and she said in that warm low voice she sometimes took, 'I promise you, Cate.' Then she took a firmer hold on her gun and she said, 'What a time to realise how much we love each other!' But I still intended firmly that for her own safety she shouldn't go outside; I was holding her back and she saying, 'Let me go, Cate. The gun's only to make people realise we're not defenceless. I'm certainly not going to use it. And whoever's out there wouldn't harm me, I'm sure. But I must find out who's there and what they're up to.' Suddenly the vehicle stopped, its door banged, we heard a voice.

If you'd asked me before then, I'd have said Sure I'll recognise Les's voice anywhere, any time. But this yell and laugh and the mashed-up words that followed – no, I didn't recognise who said them. Didn't want to recognise, maybe. For my mother put her arm around me and when I said, 'Who in the hell?' she said, 'It's Les come back, Cate. And by the sound of him he's roaring drunk.'

You'd say drinking too much is no big deal; everyone's seen drunks falling or careening around and most of the time they're pretty damn harmless. If by mischance they're not – well, it's mostly not your problem because you're not responsible for or closely attached to them. Right? Yeah, when it's somebody other than the man who reared me, did every damn thing for me, *loved* me; you must understand that in all those years I'd never seen Les lift his hand to any alcoholic drink. Hadn't seen him do that, was damn sure he never had. So this person he'd suddenly turned into didn't seem to be Les at all.

We got no sense out of him that night, not even about who'd brought him home and dropped him off along the driveway; his body had arrived but the rest of him sure hadn't. And his body was repulsive in a way it'd never been before; I tried to say something of this to my mother next day, to explain my shock, but even she who listened so careful didn't grasp my meaning. She said, 'But you must have seen drunks before, Cate,' and I said, 'Not *Les*.' She said, 'I'm sorry, my dear,' and put her arm around my shoulders, but for once that wasn't enough comfort.

The two of us got him into the house that night – he sort of staggered in between us – and we dropped him into a chair, then I said, 'What in hell will we do with him?' My mother shushed me but you could tell he was beyond hearing anything we'd say. The two of us stared at him but his eyelids had fallen and he started to snore.

'He'll have to sleep here overnight,' she said. 'There's no other option.'

I said, 'I'll stay up and keep an eye on him, make sure he doesn't burn the place down with his damn cigarettes when he comes to,' but she said no, that wouldn't be fair. A growing girl needs her rest – the traditional garbage. Instead she went through his pockets, she did a real neat job of that but it showed nothing except the little bit of money he'd had that morning was gone – and the truck keys too.

I bent over him and shook him and I yelled, 'Where the hell'd you leave the truck to?' but he never answered except to snore.

My mother said, 'Leave him alone for now. Anyway the truck's not important,' but to me this felt like I was deep involved in some furious religion and she'd denied my god existed.

I stared at her and said, 'But the truck's all we've got – I mean it's the only transportation we'd – if we ever wanted to—' then I saw what difficult waters this was getting me into; I shut my mouth before I'd betray myself further.

'Him, yes,' she said, 'I grant you that. I'd give him rail fare though, to anywhere he wanted to go. That'd be no problem. But you . . . Cate, would you really walk out on me? Am I still on a trial basis as far as you're concerned?'

So over his snores we argued; of course, I said, 'There's none of that, I'm here and why wouldn't I stay?' She couldn't pin me down any closer though; it stayed in my head that I'd got to keep some escape route open in case the worst happened. In case she found out everything and didn't want me, that was what, although I couldn't say so to her. True, I'd insisted that she promise never to rat out on me, but she could well argue that the promise wasn't binding because she'd not known all the facts.

After a while we were both too tired and fratchety to argue more; she shook his cigarettes and matches into her hand, then I went back upstairs and she went to her own room. How much sleeping either of us did is another matter.

Next morning after breakfast I hauled Les out into the woods and used the roughest part of my tongue on him. Damn nearly used my fists too, I was so angry. In the back of her woods was a little pond all overhung with bushes; one of them had late flowers and the bitter-honey scent of it stood beside us while I talked. 'You've got to promise me,' I said, 'that never in your whole life will you act that way again.'

I'd supposed that people got drunk and then they got sober, I'd not realised how some of the drink could hang around in them for hours or days and make them silly, not listening. So the lees of the drink was still in him, it made him outspoken in a brutal way which wasn't like the Les I knew. Not lying, but not minding how much I cared about him and how strong he was hurting me. He said, 'You, you. Doesn't occur to you I got a point of view also?'

'A drunkard's?' I said, and his eyes got fiery like he'd hit me.

'Christ,' he said, 'that damn mother of yours – what hogwash's she been filling you up with?' His eyes narrowed and his mouth prissed up, cunning. 'One little drink,' and something in the way he said this made me sure the earth had opened under me, that this happening wasn't just a little crevice splitting apart but a huge gap that could separate him and me for always. 'I give you my word,' he said with a sob in his voice so phoney that it insulted me, 'one little drink was all I took.'

Yet there was something moved in his voice which made me believe he wasn't wholly lying, that some sizeable part of the happening I didn't understand at all. I said uncertain, 'Then one little drink must affect you pretty damn much,' and he sat down on an old tree stump, to my horror he started to cry.

'Too damn right it does,' he said past his wet fingers, 'poor little Cate, I never told you how things had been before I met you. So you trusted me, didn't you?' With his mouth slack and those tears running down; my stomach curled itself and I longed to throw up and run away from him, but I couldn't. I'd got to stay and listen and try to sort some sense out of this whole mess. 'Poor little Cate,' he said, 'why do you suppose I stole you?'

I backed away from him and said, 'Not because you were drunk when you took me. No. No.' And the coarse rich smell of that damn bush all about me; I very nearly did throw up then. 'Taking me would mean moving quiet and careful,' I said, 'you couldn't have been drunk.' I wasn't in the least sure if this was true.

'Poor little girl,' he said with his wet slack mouth, and I yelled, 'Don't call me that!' Some bird nearby flew away with a squawk and Les said, 'Goddam, you even got the birds of heaven upset. You speak quiet to me now, or you'll never know the truth.' That was the drink talking in him, and pretty damn near heartbroken I was to hear it.

'Then tell me the truth,' I said quiet-voiced, 'but I'll know if you're lying.'

The drink got him again and he said, 'Too damn right you will. Too damn much of your blasted mother in you, ain't there, sweetheart? You suppose I've not been noticing that ever since we arrived these parts?'

Which made me understand that he'd been feeling himself neglected and mostly unwanted for quite some time, longer and harsher by far than I'd supposed. I felt truly sorry for him then, but he spoke and looked so unpleasant – the drink blurring his words, and the way his eyes glared once in a while when he took offence at something he'd imagined – that it was easy for me to rein my sorrow in and act every bit as cold as my mother would've. Cold but a bit kindlier than her because, after all, somewhere inside this unhappy and bruising mess was the real Les. So I let him talk and I prodded once in a while when he slowed; he seemed to feel it a relief to tell me all this stuff finally, and plainly he figured I was adult enough to accept it. Which I can't honestly say I was, the pain of it was too great. Anyway he told me.

Sure, he said, I was an alcoholic, why'd you find that hard to believe? Before you came along, I mean. Did you never wonder, Cate, what I did with myself all them years? You supposed I'd worked like an honest God-fearing sort maybe, and then just quit when I grabbed you. Or did you never bother to wonder, Cate; was I only important for what you could get out of me?

I interrupted to protest then (by that time I was crying too, furious at myself for doing it but I'd no choice and anyway he didn't seem to notice, so what the hell) but he held up a finger to stop me and his slow thick voice went on. The bird had come back, or another; there were various squawks and fidgetings and bits of birdsong in the undergrowth, and I recall thinking how I'd never want to spend any time in those damn woods again. But might be I'd need to; I was starting to realise that life mightn't be so simple.

Yeah, he said, an alcoholic from the year one. He'd parents he didn't like and he ran away from home, all that damn usual stuff. He'd work a bit to earn money for drink and then he'd drink, no other options interested him. Worked various jobs where you didn't need use your brain. Lumber and chopping folks' wood for them and such. He got iller and iller from the drink; finally he passed out in the street one night and woke up in hospital where they told him he'd be a dead man if he kept on . . . yeah, all that usual stuff too. From the hospital they sent him to a rehab unit and an alcoholics' programme; he finished that okay and they discharged him but he sorely longed to drink again, what else had he got to live for? 'I did mean what I said just now,' and he looked up at me with those red wet eyes, 'I only took one drink last night. You see—'

'One that you recall,' I said tough, but he shook his head and sobered up some more, he was so earnest about explaining.

'No, Cate. I recall fine what happened till I was in the truck driving here. Then that one drink I'd taken hit me all of a sudden like a heavyweight standing behind me and slugging me. When a man's been, like me, a near-dead alcoholic, one drink is all it takes.' He brought his shoulders up and down real slow like he was opting out of any responsibility for that one drink or anything else he'd done.

'So where's the damn truck now?' I said ferocious; anything to block out the fact that he'd stolen me for one reason – purely selfish and no other – to solve his wish-to-drink problem. If he'd the responsibility of a child . . . yeah, I could see this might work as enough inducement. And if it hadn't been, if he'd kept right on drinking . . . I shoved my face close to his and I yelled, 'I never knew such a rotten-selfish person in all my life. On top of which you've gone and lost the damn truck too.' And he couldn't deny this.

'Must be someplace between here and the city,' he said, holding his head like the one drink was batting around in there as an off-course missile, 'you could go look for it, Cate, if you're worried.' He frowned, like thinking was hard work to him. 'Yeah,' he said, 'you're right, I might need it again one of these days.' (Not 'we' but 'I'.) 'Little Cate,' he said with that loose weak grin, 'you'll set me right, won't you? Be a nice little stroll for you, out along the highroad. Then we'll have the truck again and everything'll be okay, won't it?'

I ran away from him then; it was in my mind to hit him as hard as I knew how, and I got all sorts of gory pictures in my head how he'd fall over backwards from the blow and split his skull open on one of those damn upsticking tree stumps. Then it'd be the Jeff business over again, and no Les to help me clear things up. Les'd be lying dead in the woods and I'd need find the truck quickly, get going. But it wasn't the thought of my mother or prison that stopped me hitting him, it was that his face and hands were alive now – not good-looking, in fact the opposite, and his voice saying things I didn't at all want to hear – but I couldn't forget the *otherness* of how Jeff had looked, dead. I couldn't guarantee never to cause that look again, but the notion of doing so was like staring down into a spiked pit full of animals; it made me shiver.

So I cut and run back through the trees to my mother's house and sobbing upstairs to my bedroom; I locked myself in and lay on the floor because that was the most un-comfortable, and I bawled like a kid. It was in my mind that Les had partly won because he'd demolished the solid base I'd supposed his life with me was built on, but I'd won a sort of battle too because I'd held myself back from hitting and maybe injuring him. So far I had, anyway.

14

After a while I pulled myself together, I went downstairs and told my mother I was heading out to go find the truck. I planned on walking to the highway and hitching a ride down toward the city; if the truck hadn't shown up by the time I got there, that'd be too damn bad, I'd know for sure I could never trust anything Les told me ever again. And I'd hitch a ride partway back easy enough; there was always plenty of traffic on the highway. Through traffic mostly, coming from up north and heading to the Deep South, or the other way around, but what the hell? Hitching's always a gamble, and it did seem to me at that moment that I'd not much to keep on living for. Except my mother, of course.

But she got that odd dissecting look she sometimes had when she was studying me, like she wondered how in the hell her cute biddable little daughter could have turned out to be this wild of a mess. 'Get into the car,' she said, 'I'm driving you.'

All the way out to the highroad I grumbled, 'I could've hitched a ride easy, there'd be no risk in that.' Too late I realised that me sounding like I was familiar with hitchhiking would put a real shade on how Les'd reared me. And if I told her it hadn't been so, she'd not believe me.

But I'd got to try, so I said, 'That honestly wasn't the way we lived out West. I didn't mean—' then she turned to me, driving at sixty miles an hour she turned and showed me her face of pure disbelief, of bone-deep disgust at any way I'd lived before I came back to her.

'Oh,' she said, 'shut up, Cate.' She turned back to watch

the road and she said, 'You're my daughter and you're under my control now. You and I are going to hammer out some sort of a tolerable relationship and I don't care how much the hammering hurts either of us. Do I make myself clear?'

I said, 'Damn right you do,' and she gave me a little sideways grin. I said, 'But you truly hate Les, don't you? Although there's no need. He did his best for me through the years and I honestly never saw him drunk till last night.'

'Yes, I hate him,' she said, 'why shouldn't I? He stole my daughter, he robbed her father and me of twelve years of her life, he brought us enormous grief and heartache and broke up our marriage; how could I not hate him? If he puts even one finger wrong while he's hanging around here, I'll call the police about him and be glad to.'

The car zoomed along between rustling dried cornfields and I said, 'I don't greatly care for people who dislike other people so much.'

She said, 'That's too bad. I'm heartbroken.' Dry and tough as the dried cornfields. She was starting to expound on how I'd pretty strong likes and dislikes myself, but for-tunately at that moment we saw the truck.

Pulled up on the far shoulder; she swung the car across the highway and pulled in behind the truck, then we both got out and checked it over. Inside it smelled of Les and chilly night air and urine – yeah, he'd made free with that, too. I walked around the truck and wafted the driver's door to and fro to get the worst of the stink out, and I said to her, 'Never in a million years would I have believed—'

'Drink does strange things to people,' she said gentle, like she knew I'd taken all the shocks I could for one morning. Then the two of us stood there on the hard shoulder with the big interstate trucks roaring past and busting up our new argument. Yeah, we argued again, seemed we couldn't manage not to. About how to get the truck back to her place, that's what.

The keys were in the ignition, so seemed to me that when the smell inside had cleared some I'd jump in and drive the damn vehicle back; I'd driven it plenty of times before and I told her so. She said I mustn't because I'd no licence. I said, 'The hell with that,' and I laughed for the first time that day; it felt good to have something to laugh at. Anyway we yelled at each other till finally I jumped in and roared the engine and just took off; she'd got to follow me then in her fancy car. I rattled along ahead of her to the turnoff and along it; one time on the highway she tried to pass me and cut in front to stop me, but that old truck, when it was desperate or perverse, owned more go than she'd supposed. Also it took up a fair bit of width on the highway and she couldn't try much in the way of tricky manoeuvres on account of there was quite a bit of other traffic.

So I got back to her cabin first; I jumped down from the truck and when she pulled up I said cheeky, 'Oh yeah? *Who* plans to tell me what to do?' Then I noticed there was another woman stood there watching us.

'Oh,' said my mother, 'hi, Elly.' My mother, what with being annoyed at me and finding the woman there watching, looked pretty damn good; a high colour in her cheeks and she breathed fast on account of she was excited. I got a sudden rush of love and warmth toward her, and seemed to me this other woman might as well be told so. I went to my mother and slipped my arm around her waist and squeezed her to me.

'Hell,' I said, 'nothing serious to that last argument of ours, was there?'

She sort of glowed at me; she was softening toward me every day, I'm positive of that. She said, 'What *am* I going to do with you?' but not like she was waiting for me to come up with an answer, cheeky or otherwise. She said, 'Elly, do come indoors,' then she put her arm round my shoulders and said to the hard-faced woman, 'This is my daughter Cate.'

Which gave me the feeling a bunch of fireworks went off

inside me, all colours and stars, soaring upward. When we got indoors she went into the kitchen and I followed her. I said, 'That's the first time you ever introduced me as that,' and she said, 'Yes, I'm sorry, Cate. It's more than time I started.'

We went back into the living room carrying drinks and cheese nibbles and corn twists, we sat down and this Elly person said to her, 'I'd no idea you have a daughter.' Flicking her cool eyes across me and away like I was dirt on the rug.

So my mother started an explanation, how we'd been separated for years (not mentioning the hows or whys; she made it sound like I'd been away at some pretty peculiar school) and I drank my root beer and watched this Elly. Maybe it seems like I keep banging on too much about her and she was harmless only I didn't think so, but the truth is, she was all the things that scared me – or just plain turned me off – about the way well-off educated people like my mother lived. So I wish I could say that because she was my mother's friend I took to her on sight, but I'd disliked her from the start and always would. Slick-dressed like my mother only fussier, in smooth fabrics and hanging bits of jewellery, with a lot more make-up and with bad-tempered lines trying to show through – a frown and harsh marks at her mouth. And every word she said was about herself or her possessions, how she was still trying to get more money from the man her husband. (Flashing the big diamonds on her hand and fingering her gold necklace while she spoke.) And what a damn nuisance the deer hunters were that year – their season had opened a couple of weeks previous – how she'd found a couple of them on her property and she'd called the game warden three times and meant to keep on plaguing him. How she was engaged in a boundary dispute with the folks the other side of her, how much she disliked that couple and how unreasonable they were. (I could read my mother's face pretty well by then and although she dutifully said yes and no to this part

I could tell her heart wasn't in it.) How badly the county had repaired the road last time, how she was still sending in complaints about potholes and rocks – but seems to me if you live on a dirt track you've got to expect some problems.

I opened my mouth at this and said, 'This here road looks to me a paradise compared to some we got out West,' but she gazed past me into the air and said very calm to my mother, 'What school did you say she'd been at?' so I had to watch my mother flinch.

I said to my mother, 'Oh hell, I'm sorry.' I slipped my hand into hers and she said, 'No apologies needed, Cate.' Which I thought was pretty damn good of her.

So this Elly says to my mother, 'I assume you haven't had much chance to work lately? You mustn't give up doing the jewellery designs, you've such a talent.' Her calm disliking eyes travelled on me and beyond again, like she felt I'd be getting in the way of anything my mother wanted to do. I longed to say Mind your own damn business, this here's strictly our affair; but I didn't because that'd make my mother flinch deeper.

Elly stayed quite a while yakking and drinking iced tea and gazing past me; when she finally left my mother said, as we watched her strike into the woods for a shortcut home, 'She's lonely.' But I said, 'I don't damn well wonder,' and that was the end of that subject.

Only my mother and me both did worry that Les might still be hanging around in the backwoods and Elly'd see him; there'd be more explanations needed then than any of us could handle. So, to comfort my mother, I ran along the road to the old cabin I'd guessed he was camping in, and sure enough there he was, sprawled on a pile of old rotting sacks and snoring his head off. I went back and told my mother he was safe out of the way; she didn't ask his exact whereabouts and that was okay, I guess she truly didn't want to know. One less responsibility for her, one I was happy to take on.

*

There's no point in dwelling on the next messy couple of weeks. Les was right when he said one drink was all it took with him; the two of us were out riding in the truck one day, and him cold sober, then he pulled into a layby, said, 'You'll hate me for this, child, but I got to do it,' and he whipped a beer can from under his seat, pulled the tab off and drank the beer. You could watch it travel through him like fire; five minutes later he was grinning-silly and a couple of minutes after that he started to get belligerent, angry, raring to have a go at someone, anyone. Him that had always, in my knowledge of him, acted scared of the least little bit of violence.

So I calmed him and I drove the truck back to that rundown cabin he was camping in; I helped him stagger indoors, laid him down and wrapped him in his old blanket and straightaway he was snoring. Then I drove back to my mother's cabin – she was good, she didn't ask any questions – but when I walked back along the road after dark to check on him the pile of sacks was bare and his blanket tossed aside; he'd gone. He never would tell us who'd brought him back from the city that first night of his drinking; me and my mother suspected he'd gotten in with a no-good crowd, and that made us both uneasy. But, like I say, my mother was damn good and more patient than you'd expect; sometimes she'd tighten her lips but she didn't say to Les like she could have, You damn well get out of here. Didn't say it on account of me, I guess. But, how he was acting lately, I felt guilty all ways around.

My mother had other stuff to worry her too – like the disappearance of this Brad my father. She and that Louise kept sort of in touch but there was never any news. Which didn't worry me overmuch because, from the looks of his apartment and Louise, he seemed the sort that would make even his disappearing arrangements comfortable.

Only, one afternoon when Les had gone off someplace

without telling me and I was feeling blue, I took a walk further along the dirt road, beyond my mother's cabin and beyond the creek, to a place where there was a swamp beside the road and you could stand on the grassy sidestrip and smell the evil rotting stink and watch the thick bubbles rising. While I stood there it all of a sudden got to me that I was being entirely too casual about the disappearance of this man my father. I recalled how my mother had told me, on our way back from his apartment, those little alive anecdotes which made him a real person and my father indeed. Instead of being holed up somewhere comfortable, with a tame shrink to consult and maybe a new woman in his bed, he might have decided to do himself in and have chucked himself into a stinking hole very like the one in front of me. And all – or mostly – on account of being confronted with me, his daughter.

When my figuring reached that point I turned tail and ran, hared back along the dirt road, pounded across the wooden creek bridge and up the hill to my mother's driveway and cabin. She was in the middle of doing a batch of jewellery designs and I felt bad because I was busting up that aspect of her life too, but I'd more important things than jewellery on my mind at that moment. I charged into the living room where she sat, and it was a toss-up whether I'd burst into tears or start telling her how I'd imagined her husband might be messily decaying in the nearby swamp. But I'd just about enough sense not to do either one, instead I said, 'I better get out of your life right this instant.'

'Why,' she said, 'Cate, what on earth's the matter?' She put her pen down; the jewellery design was all spiky and twisty like wires and, although I might know which designs I liked better than others, I'd sense enough to realise that I truly knew damn-all about this work she enjoyed so much.

'Before I do any more damage,' I said.

She came across to me and her arms were warm and all that, but I couldn't forget the rising bubbles in the swamp. The desert was dry and different, you could imagine how people would fall in pieces without any mess. But seemed like all I could think about by that time was bodies – and of course I couldn't tell her. Not only because of her husband, although I was pretty sure the chance that he'd done that sort of thing to himself was pretty damn small.

Anyway she held me and murmured and I guess she figured she'd soothed me. After a bit I mumbled an apology and went off to take a shower, and she got back to her work. That evening she said, 'Cate, I hate to keep fussing at you but we really are going to have to do something about enrolling you in school.'

I put my fork down with its handle in the spaghetti and I stared. 'You have absolutely got to be kidding,' I said.

'No, Cate, I mean it. You're bored and restless and I don't blame you for that—' I opened my mouth but she held up her fork to mean she'd not finished talking, and she went on. 'Apart from that, what we're doing isn't legal. You're supposed to be in school unless I've applied and been approved to educate you privately at home.'

'Just do that, then,' I said, 'because no way am I going to go.' Les had taught me to read; when I was little I started puzzling over the newspapers folk dumped in trashcans at roadside rest areas, so he said, 'I guess I better halfway educate you,' and he taught me, although he'd grunt scornful every time. I said to my mother, 'If you enrol me and shove me in the school's front door, I'll run right out the back.'

She said, 'I believe you would too.' She took another mouthful and chewed, finally swallowed it; she said, 'I don't always know how to handle your return. And it doesn't help that Brad—' then she took another forkful and chewed some more.

'Oh, the hell,' I said, 'that's what I meant. I've busted

your life up all the ways there are. The only useful thing now is for me to clear out and let you stay peaceful for all your future years.' At which she laid her fork down good and hard so I was scared she'd crack the plate.

'Peaceful be damned,' she said, 'I want my daughter with me. If she runs out, all the peace in the world won't give me happiness.'

'But will my staying?' I said.

'Oh yes,' she said and laughed. 'Don't mind my complaints, Cate. I've got what I wanted – my daughter home again – and if once in a while I give way to my motherly instincts and try moulding you into shape . . . well, we both know you're too tough to be moulded.' The two of us grinned at each other and it was a warm happy feeling. Then the damn phone rang.

'Elly,' I said, 'blast her.' But it wasn't Elly, it was some man's voice. My mother listened and said a quiet yes or no once in a while, then she hung up and all the life had gone out of her face, it was spiky and thin like one of her jewellery designs. I was terrified for her, fearing it might be bad news about this Brad her husband that she still cared for. But after she put the phone down she came back to the table and sat down and stared at me like she was seeing me for the first time.

'No,' she said, 'that wasn't Elly. It was a bondsman.'

'A what?'

'A man who arranges bail for people accused of crimes, if their guarantors are willing.' My head was still so full of this Brad, I didn't get the point, so she went on, 'It's about Lester, Cate. He's been arrested and he'll have to wait in jail until his trial unless I stand guarantor for him. Which I refuse to do. I'm sorry, Cate, but—'

'Trial for what,' I said, 'in God's name?'

She was still giving me that intent look and she said the next words like she hated having to shove them out at me. 'For,' she said, 'attempted murder.'

15

My mother stuck out that she wouldn't post bail for Les; I got furious and sick at heart about him being cooped up in the city jail, but I could see her point. What I found nearly impossible to get into my head was the notion of Les getting involved in any form of violence. Because, as I explained to my mother, that was the one thing he'd always shown a dread of.

She said sadly, 'But, Cate, he wasn't drinking in those days.' Which I had to agree. Then she said, 'Did you ever wonder *why* he disliked violence so much?' but I hadn't, I'd supposed it was because he was basically an all-round decent guy – even if he was a natural loser in the money-earning stakes.

I said, 'You mean there could have been reason before?' and she nodded. I'd no answer to that either.

We visited him in jail. A big solid building southwest of the city, with high walls and a spike-topped fence. When I first saw it I toughened up and said to myself, At least they don't have chaingangs in this area nowadays like they still do some other places; here there's only gangs to fill potholes along the dirt roads. I'd seen them once from my mother's house, a prison truck crawling ahead, then the double line of men in green tracksuits walking with guards each side of them, and another truck crawling behind with guards in it and their rifles trained. At least that work'd be open air, be better for Les than indoors all the time.

I thought I was real tough and accepting – until we got inside the jail and there were so many doors to be locked after us, it felt like walking into a trap. And Les sitting across the table from us in the interview room; he looked sort of shrunken, as if only a part of him was there. He didn't have much to say to us either, only thanks for coming and that he was still trying to sort out what had happened that night. It hurt me to see him sitting there hangdog like that, almost seem better if he rose up and shouted. But not better for him, I guess. After the first visit I said to my mother, 'Someone else did the hitting and, because Les was hanging around drunk with them and got hazy about the events, they've delegated him to take the blame.'

She was unlocking the car and her lips went tight in the way I was getting accustomed to. She said, 'Perhaps so, but he was there – he admits that – and he's stuck. Most likely no one will ever know the truth.'

For sure Les didn't; he was stone sober now he'd been in jail these weeks, and he acted mortal sheepish – but as if the drinking had been the worst part of it for him and he'd not a clue about what happened with the other. I said, 'Such a damn sordid little crime—' a warehouse break-in it was, banging the security man on the head a bit too hard – and my mother said what I'd expect of her, 'No violence is little, Cate. And if the security man should die—'

So we went through Thanksgiving with the security man still pretty sick; between the two of us we fixed turkey and all the trimmings, but I looked at it on my plate and said, 'I don't have no damn heart to eat this.'

Only us two in the cabin; that Elly had finished her long vacation and gone back to the Carolina coast for the winter, and my mother hadn't heard anything yet from Brad her husband. Once in a while that wispy Louise his girlfriend would call up and say, 'Heard nothing yet.' She called up the Thanksgiving evening too and I said, 'The hell she cares about him or you. She's only trying to remind you who had him last.'

My mother looked tired and strained; I guess she'd been remembering other Thanksgivings good or bad. She said, 'Cate, sometimes I wish you wouldn't say everything that comes into your head.' Then she said hasty, 'No, I didn't mean that. Say whatever you want to. You and I must stay close and open with each other, no matter what.'

When she said that, it hurt me all over again – hurt me deeper than ever, on this family feastday – that there were huge gaps in what she knew of me, and that I didn't dare say a word to make myself clear to her.

The weather got cold, frosty with biting little flurries of snow; Christmas came near and she said she always cut a tree, decorated the cabin. I said, 'No odds to me, I never had a Christmas tree so wouldn't matter if I never got started,' and she gave that weary little flinch like I'd hurt her and she was accustomed to me doing that. She said, 'Well, I have a tree every year, damn it, and I don't see why your being here should make me stop.' So we stomped out furious to her woods and by the time we'd chosen a tree and cut it down, hauled it back to the cabin, we were pretty good friends again; that was how it went between the two of us in those weeks.

I put the ornaments on the tree – delicate bits of thin all-colours glass – and she draped the little lights across; partway through she said, 'And you *have* had Christmas trees before, Cate. Even if you don't remember them.' She'd a right to say that, reminding me.

I said, 'Yeah, sure. Sorry.'

But she said short, 'For God's sake don't apologise. That's not at all what I meant.' Then she hugged me and we laughed together. We lived like we were knocking the rough sticking-out places off each other, a painful process for her and – as she plenty of times clearly realised – for me too.

And presents for Christmas; I never saw so many. Separate presents from her to me, I mean. Mostly clothes and a new purse and such. I'd not had a clue what to buy her, so finally I bought fancy soaps and such, figuring at least she could use them. But they looked little indeed beside her presents to me. She bought Les a present too, which I thought was kindly of her, considering how she felt about him. Nothing big, a little wallet and calendar, but when we both made our Christmas visit to him and she gave it, he coloured right up and couldn't hardly speak to thank her. For a moment there was a closeness between the two of them which didn't include me and, boy, was I jealous. A real hot flare of jealousy. I gave him a present too, a whole stack of those damn cigarettes he was so partial to, but he said the hours they'd let him smoke in jail were pretty restricted. Seemed like her present to him was every bit as useless as mine, but there you are. I was all of a sudden eaten up with jealousy and didn't go searching for the cause.

She and I spent our Christmas at the cabin and it was pretty good, all things considered; as good for me as it could be without Les there. And she got a piece of news the day before which cheered her up considerable – this Louise called her and said she'd heard from the Brad man at last, a Christmas card – big deal, yeah – and a short note in it telling her he was staying at some resort up in the mountains of southwest Virginia, that he was being treated by a shrink there and had sent a medical certificate to the university, straightened things out with them.

I was glad that at least I didn't need wonder about him being at the bottom of a swamp somewhere. My mother looked a bit shook – I guess she'd kept on hoping he'd come back pretty damn soon and we'd all be happy to-gether – and she gave a little sigh like she was grieved.

Then this damn Louise had to stick the knife in my mother by saying, 'You've not heard from him?' and my mother had to say no. But my mother told me, after she hung up, that she was glad just to know he was alive and sorting himself out, nowadays she didn't expect more of him than that. Which I took to mean, among other things, that he totally wiped out his responsibility as my dad, but that – although it made me feel kind of lonely for a moment – was basically okay by me; from what I'd heard of him that was just fine. I'd got my mother; she was enough. Whether I'd be enough for her, I wasn't yet sure of.

We got Christmas and the New Year over with, then Les's trial came due. The warehouse security man didn't die but he lost the use of an arm, wouldn't be able to work the same job again; at least though it wouldn't be a murder charge. No one was facing trial for hitting him except Les, because the cops couldn't find out who else might have been involved.

We visited Les the week before the trial and he was sure he'd be found guilty; he seemed less worried about that than you'd expect. I said so to my mother on the way home and she said, 'I think that in a way he's given up, Cate, and not being free comes as a relief to him. At least he won't need to feed or clothe or house himself for several years. Prison may not be perfect, but I'm sure he's lived in messier places. And maybe with the same sort of people.'

There wasn't anything I could say to that except Not while I knew him he didn't. And one other thing, which burst out before I could stop it.

'You mean he's given up on me too?' I said. 'He doesn't care about me any more?' Because it had always been in my mind, as a final reinforcement, that if my mother found out about Jeff and either tried to hand me in or totally chucked me, Les would still be around and him and me could work out our future.

'He knows I'll look after you,' said my mother, and that was unanswerable – except for the huge fact about me which could change her mind.

They found him guilty, of course; no choice. He got a lightish sentence because they knew there must have been other men involved – and of course, to be honest, because my mother kept her mouth shut about that long-ago kidnapping. Eight years he got, which is still quite a stretch. Eight years with time off for good behaviour, if nobody riled him in jail or got him into a fight or breakout try. I hoped he'd have sense enough to stay clear of all that stuff; next time we visited I'd need to tell him so. But at the least there'd be quite a number of years with no Les close by, drunk or sober, no Les to roam the woods with and tease and know he thought the same as me most always, about most everything. No Les to turn to for help and a way out if things should go wrong between me and my mother – and how could I be sure they wouldn't, when she still didn't know the one big thing about me that'd made him bring me back to her? Anyway, eight years or some-where near, and no arguing with it. They shifted him into the regular part of the jail and we went to see him the next week as usual.

But something different happened – he refused to see me that time. Only wanted my mother; I objected pretty forcible in front of her and the prison guard when the guard told me. But I wasn't a little kid that could fling itself to the ground and bang its fists and yell, so I went sulkily back to wait in the car and my mother went in alone. I sat in the car and gloomed, didn't speculate much about the reason for Les doing that to me, thought maybe he was just doing it to be awkward.

Only when my mother came out of there and walked across toward the car, she moved stiff and her face was white like the underwing of a bird. A dead underwing. She got in the car and sat stiff beside me and I said, 'Was it that bad?'

She didn't turn around to look at me, she just said in a stiff dead voice, 'No, he's settled in well. Only he told me about you and the young man out West. About the murder.'

16

All I remember of the drive back to her place is the snow, falling thin at first then fast and steadily, thickening till the windshield wipers could hardly push it away. And me saying – yelling before long – 'Why in God's name did Les tell you?' Over and over, but she didn't answer me. All the way back she never opened her mouth, didn't even say Oh shut up Cate, like she sometimes did when I rabbitted on and annoyed her.

On the dirt road the snow was already thick enough so the car slithered despite its snow tyres. She pulled the car to a stop in front of her cabin, she cut the engine and went indoors, didn't wait for me. Still didn't speak. I followed her in. She took off her coat, shook the snow from her boot soles into the sink and put them on a newspaper to dry, then she faced me.

'All right,' she said, 'I'll tell you why he spoke. Because he's scared, that's why. He's going to be shut up in prison for quite a while and he doesn't know what you might—' She didn't need to finish that phrase. 'You've insisted that I spell it out to you,' she said, 'there's no point in your trying to look so demolished.' But I wasn't trying any damn thing. I just *was*.

'Oh,' I said, 'sweet raging Jesus.' The snow was coming down thicker than ever, great fat flakes like they fed on the air and meant to swallow it and us up. I went over to the back porch, got my own boots and started wriggling into them again, hauled my coat off its hanger.

She waited till I'd gotten them all on, then she said very quiet, 'What are you doing?'

'Leaving here. Quitting. What other option did you have in mind? Won't want me around here any longer, will you?' Because if Les, that'd known me all those years, couldn't trust me, then I surely couldn't expect her to. Even though she was my mother, that much trusting was something you just couldn't ask for.

'Where do you plan to go?' she said quiet like she was a gravestone and might speak a carved word once in a while but no more.

Plans, how would I have any plans, how could I? 'Oh,' I said, 'I'll make out.' I couldn't say Don't worry, because obviously she must be worried now that I mightn't leave, that I might hang around and she'd need to wonder what violence I might get up to next. Kill her, maybe? Christ, that did hurt; nothing in my whole life hurt so much. Hurt me for my own sake because she wasn't any longer trusting me, but especially hurt – with a strong sharp pain I couldn't get rid of – for her sake because she'd hoped for so much, with her daughter reappearing, and instead I'd brought all this unhappiness on her. She was disappointed in me, and I felt so badly for her over that because I longed to comfort her and make her happy again and there was no way I could. Instead, the more she found out about me, the more she must be hating me. 'Don't fret,' I said stupid, 'I'll light out of here right this minute and you won't set eyes on me again. You suppose I might harm you? Then you truly don't understand me at all.' My voice wanted to shake but I managed to keep it sounding firm; that was the only thing I was proud of. That and the fact that I didn't hesitate or try to plead with her; obviously I'd got to leave, so I opened the door to the white outside world and the snow. That weather didn't faze me either; snow was a commonplace for us in the mountains out West.

'Don't you intend to take some luggage?' she said quiet.

I thought for a minute. 'Nuh-uh. You bought me the clothes and I'd feel like a freeloader.' This reminded me of something I wanted to be sure she grasped. 'I didn't come here with Les on the offchance of getting a bunch of rich possessions out of you,' I told her.

'Fair enough,' she said like an ironical underlining; I didn't know what to make of that tone. But I'd better not keep her front door open long, it was letting in a lot of cold air.

'Well,' I said, 'goodbye then.' I stepped through the door and started to close it. 'Hey,' I said, 'thanks. For what you've done for Les and me, I mean. I'm truly sorry things haven't worked out the way you'd hoped.'

'How do you plan on travelling?' she said.

She'd quite a point there. Sure, I was accustomed to driving in snow, but Les hadn't gotten around to putting the truck's snow tyres on; the weather was mild still when he got arrested. And these woods roads were hilly and cornery; I knew pretty damn well what the truck could and couldn't do, and I figured there'd be several places along the road where I'd have a problem. A skid-into-the-ditch problem, yeah. Couldn't fix the snow tyres myself, knew how perfectly well but without Les's help I doubted if I'd got the muscles. And, to be technically honest, the truck belonged to Les not to me; I'd be uneasy about bashing up something that wasn't mine. If I wrecked it I'd no money to get it fixed, and I surely couldn't expect my mother to cover the cost. Of that or anything else. Besides, I'd no money for a tow truck in emergency or for the next tankful of gas; I was leaving my purse behind. I'd feel wrong about walking out on her with clothes my mother had given me, and I'd feel extra wrong about walking out with her gifts of money. 'Why,' I said, 'I'll walk, what else?'

My two feet were good and reliable and I was all set to do that, just step out to the snow and keep going. I could hide out in some old cabin on the other side of town and go see Les, find out if he wanted me around when he got out. Eight years is a while, but if he behaved he'd get good-conduct time off. I could always hitch a ride in cars or trucks; if I picked a duff driver and he raped or killed me, what the hell? My mother wasn't any longer going to miss me. I might investigate dodging the fare-collector on a train too; folks said you could travel cross-country by rail without paying if you'd the right technique. And I'd all the confidence in the world; at fifteen, what can you lose?

My mother looked at me and I said, 'I've known a hell of a lot worse weather out West, damn it. And coped with it too.'

She walked across to the door where I stood and she said, 'Come back inside, blast you, and shut the door. And shut your mouth. I'm going to talk and you're going to listen.'

'No,' I said, 'I don't see any damn point in that. However much we talk, our minds'll never meet up.' Not with her knowing about Jeff they wouldn't. So I turned to go.

She caught my wrist and yanked me back indoors, caught me off balance and took me by surprise – otherwise she'd never have managed it, because truly I was much the stronger. 'Shut *up*,' she said, and she hit me across the face with the flat of her hand. Not hurting-hard but definite. Then she looked down at her hand and kind of shrank from it. She said, 'I've never in my life hit anyone before.' She locked the front door and slipped the key into her pocket, then she went across the room and crouched in a chair, hid her face in her hands.

I stood there like a fool, didn't know what to say or do except that I mustn't go near her. After a while she took her hands away from her face and she said, 'You're my daughter. I refuse to give up on you.'

But seemed cruelly imprisoning to her that she should feel that way. 'You don't need to feel so,' I said. 'Relationship's only a – what they call a technicality, isn't it? Like a bad debt, sometimes you've just got to cut your losses.'

Her face twitched then and I realised she was in a sort of

way smiling; to me that was the most heartbreaking sight. On account of this deep gulf between her and me, and none of it her fault. I dropped my old woollen gloves on the floor and I went across the room to her, but I was nervous because she knew I'd once used violence; I stood in front of her and I said, 'I won't touch you if you'd rather not.'

'Oh Cate,' she said, 'Cate Cate Cate.' From her tone I gathered she'd no special objection to me touching her. So I put my arms round her and she said muffled against my shoulder, 'You don't understand the half of it, child. You're not losses to me and never could be. You were my infant, bones and flesh growing inside my body, and after you were born I fed and washed and loved you those first three years. And also—' she held me at arm's length and gazed at me – 'for some unaccountable reason, and probably quite wrongly, I've begun to get fond of the new Cate, the person you are since your return. Damn it, as you'd say. Cate my fifteen-years-old daughter.'

Feelings shifted around in me like transcontinental trucks. I whispered, 'But I *killed* him,' and terror ran through her again, I watched it happen.

'Yes,' she said, 'that's changed everything. You're not the person I imagined you were. Not, probably, the person I've begun to love. But, dear God, you're going to stick around so I can find out.' She got tough again, she truly was one gutsy lady and something in me responded with a deep joy to this toughness of hers; I can't put it any less important than that. 'Take your coat and boots off,' she said, 'and let me think. You're definitely not walking out of here. Apart from anything else, it's snowing too hard.'

I started to tell her again about the snows out West, how this'd be nothing compared to them, but she said we might well be totally snowed in by morning, and she was right. She hadn't hardly spoken to me any more that day, only fixed lasagne and, later on, a sandwich, so we ate and watched television and went to bed. When I got up next morning the snow was three feet deep everywhere and the road silent. I said at breakfast, 'They'll plough it though, won't they, pretty soon?' I was damn nervous around her because I didn't know what she was thinking, what she'd got in mind to do. She'd spoken like her finding out about Jeff would change our whole life together, which was fair enough, only if she wasn't throwing me out I couldn't figure how.

She said terse, 'They'll plough it when they get around to doing so, which may take a couple of days.' She drank the rest of her coffee, pushed the cup away and said, 'At least the snow means there's no distractions. I want to hear the truth about this Jeff, Cate, and what happened to him.' Outside the world was silent like it listened too; no bird-song or wind, only an occasional shuffle of snow on the roof. She said, 'What are you waiting for? Start talking, blast you. And I'll know at once if you're lying.'

So I tried the line of talk on her that I'd used on Les – the illegal immigrant tale – but I ought to have foreseen that she was much too sharp a lady to swallow it. How long had Jeff been in the States? And where was he working – you did say he was working, didn't you? Where exactly did you say this happened? And what type of housing was he living in? Les hadn't asked me any of that stuff, so I needed to invent the replies to her as I went along; it was hard work and of course she noticed. I listened to my own voice and it sounded falser all the time. So I wasn't surprised – although terrified – when she cut across one of my explana-tions with, 'You're a very unskilful liar, Cate.'

The snow had started again and she sat at her worktable with the window behind her so her face was outlined against the falling snow; I thought how interested I'd gotten to be in her as a person and in what went on behind her face. A good-looking woman and a sharp lively brain, a mother you could be proud of. And the affection she'd been starting to feel toward me – but now I'd blown all the togetherness and warmth we'd been stacking up. I could cuss Les and blame him for telling her about Jeff, but the real cause that parted her from me was that I'd done the thing I had; it made her and me into two different sorts of person. You couldn't expect her even to like me after that, and love from her was out of the question. While I was thinking all this she'd gone on talking, asking questions and complaining about my silence, then she stopped and said, 'You're not listening to me.'

Beyond her the big wet flakes fell; there wasn't any escape. With three foot of snow already on the ground and more coming down, even walking the road would be difficult, and there'd be no traffic anywhere to hitch a ride from. Also, where would I go? There was nowhere to run and hide.

'Yeah,' I said, 'I was too so listening. I've blown my life and yours, haven't I? There's no altering that.'

She said, 'If only I knew the *facts*,' and she banged her fist down on the worktable so her pens and some little bits of wire and such jumped. She said abrupt, 'What do you plan to do with the rest of your life?'

I said, 'Keep running away and telling lies, I guess. What else is there?'

She took a long breath and turned her head away to watch the falling snow, then she said, 'No, I won't let you.'

'You mean to turn me in, then?' She swung around and gave me a blank stare and I said, 'To the cops, like?'

'No,' she said, 'I couldn't bring myself to do that. Perhaps I ought to but I can't. Not my own daughter.'

'Then whyn't you let me just run out?' She gave me that blank shocked stare again and I said gentle, like she was a kid, 'Wouldn't my running make everything easier for you?'

'Dear God,' she said, 'I don't want things made easier. I want to know where I stand with my own daughter, that's all. What sort of person she is and the full background and details to what she's done.'

But she wasn't going to get any background or details from me, and well she must have realised so. Only she was a fighter, wouldn't give up. I could be plenty of a fighter myself on occasion and about a good many things, but on this with her I felt damn sure I was licked before I got started.

'I truly did kill him,' I said gently. 'I can't see that the details need matter a hell's whisker to you. Who'd want a murderer for a daughter?'

There was the longest silence then and a swish of snow on the roof; the wind was getting up and the blizzard thickening along with it. 'I want my daughter,' she said at last, slowly, 'but I want the whole of her. The good and the bad about her must both be open to me, Cate, otherwise there'll never be any honesty between us. If you refuse to tell me why this – this thing you did – happened, I must take other steps to find out.'

'Les can't tell you,' I said quick, 'maybe he would if he could, but I never told him.'

'I realise that,' she said, 'haven't I just spent half an hour watching you make up one story after another and toss them away as soon as you realised I didn't believe you? No,' she said, 'there's only one way to find out the truth, and that's the way we'll take.'

'We?' I was standing and I'd backed so far a chair-arm was hard against my spine; I couldn't back further except out the locked front door. 'I can't help you,' I said, 'I won't. I don't recall the details anyway, I've long since forgotten them.'

'Then we'll learn them together.' Not brutal but unyielding as could be.

'How the hell,' I said, 'do you plan we do that?'

'It's simple,' she said. 'We'll travel out West, the two of us. Les told me the name of the town where this happened

– he was reluctant to but I pressed him. So we'll start poking around there and I guarantee I'll find out everything. If there's any detail you've genuinely forgotten, I'll make blasted sure you're reminded of it.' She stood up and shoved her hair back like she did when she was getting ready to chop logs or do some tricky jewellery design, only she wasn't looking at the logpile or the designs now, her gaze was fixed on me. 'As soon as the snow plough clears this road,' she said, 'I'll go into the city and make arrangements with a travel agency, get maps and pick up tickets. You and I are going to find out together who Jeff was and what happened to him.'

17

It took me a noticeable while to get a grip on my astonishment and fear. Then I said, 'You can't do that.'

'Not I, *we*. You're going with me.'

'But Les said—'

'I really,' she said, 'am not vitally interested in Lester's opinions any longer. He's in prison and likely to stay there for years, and anyway he's no blood relation of yours. He told me the bare fact that you killed Jeff, and I'm grateful to him for the information. As your mother, I certainly ought to know. However—' Her face was pale but fixed; I could tell there'd be no point in arguing with her. 'I need to know much more than the bare fact, Cate.' She crossed the room and stood in front of me. 'And since you'll lie your head off but not tell me the truth, how could I believe the truth from you if you ever did get around to disgorging it? So we're going back out there like detectives, we'll nose around and I'll discover the rock-bottom truth.'

'But they might notice us, they might get suspicious and arrest me.'

'Possibly,' she said level-voiced. 'I'd be ready to take a chance on that. You've never felt a hunger for truth, have you, Cate? A straightforward hunger and thirst as if you're lost in a desert and must find out certain facts to keep you alive?' She smiled at me then and I hated myself because I didn't in the least understand what she meant. 'No,' she said, 'I suppose you never have. Truth must seem relative when a person leads the sort of life you've had with Lester. But you and I are going to satisfy that straightforward hunger of mine, Cate; if I teach you nothing else I'll teach you the shallowness and uselessness of lying. We'll find the truth together and inevitably we'll take a few risks along the way.' She went away from me and started digging around in her bookshelf amid a pile of maps.

'But if they do arrest me——'

'For God's sake stop casting such longing looks at your coat and boots,' she said, 'neither of us is going anywhere till this snow lets up. Even if you don't feel at home here, can't you for both our sakes sometimes act as if you do? As a matter of common courtesy?'

'Sometimes,' I said slow, trying to avoid giving a truthful answer, 'I don't grasp a word you're saying. Why wouldn't I feel at home here?' But it was true, and she a smart enough lady to notice it, that I'd not settled into a permanent ease at her place although out West, with Les, I'd always felt at home. I missed Les something terrible since he'd been in jail; drunk or not, I surely to hell did long for the sight and sound and even the smell of him. My mother could touch me deep on occasion but it didn't last, after a while it'd go and later it'd come back but it didn't stay continually around. 'I can't do anything but hurt you, can I?' I said. But I kept my eyes away from where my outdoor clothes hung; at least I was willing. If I couldn't make her happy or always feel as much love for her as I ought, yet I felt a depth of sorrow toward her which I could hardly plumb. 'Only,' I said, 'if I do get arrested, that'll make your problems more complicated, won't it? It won't solve anything.'

She said, 'I'm prepared for that and I'll cope with it if it happens.' She threw a map of Arizona at me and opened the Rand McNally atlas on the table in front of herself. 'Sit down and shut up,' she said, 'except for answering my questions. You and I are going to find out the truth because I can't go on living unless I know it. What happens as a result of our finding out the truth – we'll deal with that when it arrives. Right?' But not like she cared whether I said yes or no.

So I sat there facing her across the table and this was a sort of lawyers' trial all to itself, with her as judge and jury and prosecution and me counsel for the defence – and me as accused person too. And, boy, do I mean accused. She wouldn't let the smallest lie or the littlest evasion get past her.

'This town,' she started out, 'where it happened – where's it located?'

I opened up the Arizona map next to her atlas; I pointed and she stared at the dot.

'How big a town?' she said.

'Holy hell, I couldn't say. Two hundred people maybe, three hundred? No, not that many. Two hundred at most.'

'What sort of people?'

I stared, not understanding her. 'Why, just *people*, I guess. Ordinary types like you'd meet any place out West.'

'You forget,' she said, 'I'm not from this country. I've never been out West, I know nothing about the people there.'

I'd gotten so accustomed to her bitty British accent that I never noticed it any more, never thought of her as coming from an altogether other country. So when she said this I only stared wider, which I guess didn't make her the happiest.

'What are the streets like there?' she said. 'The houses? Lester told me this happened in an apartment?'

And what the hell else had Les told her? Fresh bits were coming out all the time. 'Yeah,' I said, 'there's one apartment building in town, but nothing that you people on this side of the country would recognise as an apartment building. Two floors only, six apartments in all, could be an edge-of-town motel.'

'Go on,' she said, 'keep talking.' But I'd a vast amount more caginess than to do that.

'No,' I said, 'how can I guess at what you want to find

out? You ask questions about what puzzles or bothers you, and I'll answer.'

'You and Lester were living in town?' she said.

'Nuh-uh. Up in the hills.'

'Shacking out in somebody's derelict cabin?' And I nodded. 'But this Jeff, how did you happen to meet him?'

I started the tale about him being a wetback – it was the most believable way to explain what I did – but she shook her head. 'No,' she said, 'you tried that line of explanation on Lester but he soon saw through it.' She raised her head and her eyes nailed me. 'A college student, wasn't he?'

Les surely must have been shooting his mouth off to her – and have noticed a hell of a lot more than I gave him credit for in that apartment too. The books and study aids and notebooks scattered around there . . . Les hadn't remarked on them to me, yet he'd apparently seen them and wondered . . . How deep had he been mistrusting me ever since?

'Oh holy hell,' I said, 'I've really fucked things up, haven't I?' Then I tried to retrieve, not knowing what else to do. 'I've no notion *what* Jeff was. Didn't I tell you I was out driving the truck and it broke down and he came along, stopped his car, offered me a ride into town but instead of stopping off at a gas station he took me back to his place and raped me? Didn't I explain all of that?'

'Yes, Cate,' she said, 'you did. And your story's getting better with practice, it came out very nearly the same that time as the time before. Though a long way from the story you first told me.' She tapped a pencil on the desk, hooded her eyes and said, 'He was a college student but you weren't even attending school. How did you happen to meet him? And where was he at college? There wouldn't be a college in that little town.'

'I never found out that much about him,' I said quick, 'we never went into details.' Though of course I did know, chapter and verse, everything.

'You met him at a town dance perhaps?' she said – and for one awful moment I supposed she was laughing at me, because she'd certainly heard enough from both Les and me about my past life to realise that dresses and dances and such didn't figure anywhere in it. Not necessarily on account of lack of inclination, but of cash and facilities for keeping myself clean and tidy. I didn't answer because her question threw me so off balance, and then I watched her realise what she'd said, 'Oh Cate my dear,' and her gaze on me was pure as a child's, 'I'm sorry, I wasn't thinking.'

I longed to go around the table and embrace her, but who'd enjoy being embraced by a murderess? So I stayed where I was and mumbled that it was okay, and she went on asking questions.

'So you first met him along the road?' she said, and I managed to work up some spirit.

'What the hell does it matter where?' I said. 'The only thing that matters is, I killed him. For whatever reason and with whatever justification.'

'Or lack of one,' she said, and that did throw me; she was one tough strongminded lady when she wanted to be. 'Yes,' she said, 'you're right, the only important fact is that you did it, and why.'

'But I'd not dare go back there, it wouldn't be safe. Les said—' Her tough gaze stopped me.

'Because people around there knew you? You'd been in the town frequently?' I longed to say yes, but seemed like she could see right through me by now and any lie I told she'd spot at once. 'But you weren't living in that town?' she said.

'No. I already told you not.'

'You and Lester were living up in the mountains . . . You visited that town how often?' The tough stare again, that I didn't dare lie to.

'Not so often,' I said slow, fighting to keep her from finding out the truth. But she got to it anyway.

'*How* often, Cate?' A long silence, then, 'Had you ever been there before that night?'

'I can't exactly recall. I – Les and me, we might have driven through once or twice.'

'But you'd never shopped there?'

'No, we bought our stuff at one or another convenience store – little places in the valleys between the mountains. Vary your shopping place, Les always said, and don't shop at the regular highway stores unless you must.'

'Why would he say that, Cate?' But she could read my silences like they were glass-fronted. 'Because those stores have more surveillance cameras, perhaps even a store detective, and the two of you did some shoplifting?'

It sounded pretty crummy when she spoke it straight out like that. 'Only,' I said, 'if the money and food stamps ran out early, which they once in a while did.' My feet shifted themselves under her steady gaze and I said, 'A person's got to eat.'

'Yes,' she said, 'but there must be a better way of . . .' She filed that problem away for now, one more major gulf between her and me, and she said, 'So you'd never been on foot in that town, never seen anyone there close up who might remember you?' She watched my silence. 'No one saw you that night?'

'I don't want to think about it,' I said, 'please.' I had on a thick blue-and-white sweater and white ski pants, and all of a sudden I was hot like to die. I got up and walked around but that didn't make me any cooler.

'Where did he pick you up?' she said. 'Not in the town itself?' She saw she was distressing me and she didn't a bit care. I guess that was reasonable enough on account of what I'd done to Jeff, but the details of that night were packed away in my head and I meant to fight like crazy against taking them out for anyone.

'Not in town,' I said, 'no.' She waited, which forced me to go on. 'I walked down from our cabin and Jeff met me a mile down the track, at the bottom of the steepest part.'

'So no one saw you?'

I ran my finger around the neck of the sweater, trying to get air. 'Wasn't no one there to see. No cabins nearby and no traffic. Far enough from our cabin too that Les couldn't—' Everything I said made me sound cheesier, slyer, than ever. 'Jeff was already waiting and I got into his car. I'd expected we might – but he'd got this apartment in town and he said—'

'He said it would be more comfortable for what the two of you had in mind.'

It's a strange thing, I started sleeping around when I was fourteen, and I can't imagine ever flinching at the notion, but it hurt me like crazy hell to watch my mother take the idea on board and see her flinch.

'Roughly speaking,' I said, 'yeah. That's what he said.'

'So he drove you to his apartment and – no one saw you there?'

'Nuh-uh. Like I told you, it was a little shack of a building. He'd a downstairs apartment with its own entry from the parking lot, and there wasn't a soul else around. At least, I heard a television from one of the upstairs apartments when we went indoors, but we'd only been in a moment when it cut off and the guy slammed his door, came down-stairs and roared away in his car. Night worker at some factory out in the desert the other side of town, so Jeff said.'

'What all this boils down to is that no one in the town has ever seen you.'

'Not to my exact knowledge,' I said, sulky because she'd gotten me into a narrow place. Seemed to me Les was right and you oughtn't to go back to where it happened, oughtn't to take that thousand-to-one chance. But hadn't she said she was prepared to take the chance if necessary? Which meant she was involving me in the risk too. 'I can't be sure no one in that town's seen me,' I said.

'By the sound of it you're sure enough for safety.' She paused and then she said in a voice like a small breath, 'You had a knife, didn't you? And stabbed him. Lester told me that much.'

He'd told her too damn much altogether; I'd never supposed Les would. From fear of what I might do – sweet Jesus! Like I was a wild animal snarling. 'If you know everything,' I said, 'why d'you keep on asking?'

'Because I don't know the most important things yet, Cate. You and I both realise that. But a knife . . . and you killed him with one blow?'

'It was that sort of knife,' I said, chopping off each word because this truly didn't sound too good for me. And I knew what she'd say next, my own head kept on saying it.

'A knife you carried, that you took there with you?' And I nodded. 'So,' she went on in that breath that was hardly a voice, 'you went fully prepared. Did you have in mind to kill him before you went there, Cate?'

But to that I buttoned my lips and would give her no answer; there had to be a limit to the amount of shame and complicatedness and explainings I could get involved in for one day.

During those next days it stopped snowing and the sun shone brilliant but the plough didn't show up; when I complained my mother said it often happened that way around there. In those days she'd take an occasional rest from plaguing me but I swear her mind was always on the subject; I guess you couldn't expect anything else. Then she'd start up again; what happened when I left the apartment to fetch Les? And how about when he went back there with me and the two of us left again with – with what there was of Jeff? And the cleaning up we must have done in that apartment – she forced herself to imagine all this and I watched her forcing and felt terrible for her. But too late now; would I have done what I did to Jeff if I'd known

I'd got a mother that wasn't angry and rejecting but was warm and loving and hungry to have me back again? I can't say. Life would have been so altogether different, I can't imagine myself into that position.

Anyway. No, mother, I can't truthfully claim that anyone saw me. Or saw Les either, but if my mother dragged me back there the danger'd be all mine; Les was safely tucked away. Would be my mother's danger too, of course. I said to her, 'You don't want to get involved in all that mess,' but naturally she took no notice.

So she she asked me questions and I stalled but sometimes answered, and on the third morning after the snowfall she said, 'Oh, we'll be safe enough. No reason we shouldn't go and poke around there.'

'How exactly do you plan to work it?' I said.

She looked surprised. 'Go to that town and keep our ears open, get to know people, chat with them, what else? Look up the local newspapers and get further details of this Jeff, see what coverage there was.'

'But – you plan on staying *there*, in that same town?'

'Why not?' she said. 'There must be some sort of a motel either there or along the highway nearby. People still drive cross-country and want to stop off overnight, don't they? And I gather that Arizona is quite a tourist area.'

'Yeah, but—'

Then we heard a rattle and a roaring; something yellow clanked at the bottom of the driveway, by the roadside trees, and my mother picked up her purse and car keys. 'Get your coat on,' she said, 'we're going into town to make the arrangements.'

'But—'

She was already pulling her own coat on. 'The snowplough's come through,' she said, 'the road's clear. There's nothing to stop us now.'

18

We flew out there, no long overland drive for her. She said, 'You won't mind flying?' and then she shut her lips tight on the words, because how would I ever know? Everything in the way she'd lived was new to me, I'd needed to get accustomed to it bit by bit, and the notion of flying seemed no odder than anything else. People did stuff like that all the time, and if I was going to live around her – which I wasn't any longer sure of but she hadn't said definitely not – I'd better get accustomed to doing these things too.

I enjoyed the zoom up of the plane when we took off, that was a real happening and like we were free, going someplace unusual. The land under us looked to be a big exciting map when the clouds let us see it, but then I recalled where and why we were going and the happiness went away. We ate some chicken-scratch airline food and I recalled how Les and me'd driven pretty much this route going the opposite way, how we'd eaten cold cheapcut pizza and smelled the sage and cottongrass, and I got unhappy again. I started to think about what had happened before him and me took that journey, and, thinking about all that, I got scared as hell.

I couldn't hardly believe she meant to drag me back to those places, till the airport at Flagstaff showed up ahead and the plane tilted down to it. 'But we oughtn't,' I said to her under my breath while we fastened our seatbelts. 'Supposing you poke around too much and get yourself in trouble too?'

At this she gave me her tough glare and said, '*We*. The

poking around is going to be done by both of us, Cate.' So I could see there was no shifting her.

She'd garaged her own car in Virginia; she'd left Les's truck parked outside her cabin and arranged for the local mailman to keep an eye on cabin and truck both. At Flagstaff she picked up a rental car and we drove north, with me grumbling every mile of the way; I felt I'd a right to do that. But she took no notice; once she said, 'Do shut up, Cate,' but as if her mind was elsewhere. Those first miles out of Flagstaff are high woodland – aspen, ash and pine trees. Good-smelling, but I could hardly wait to get away from trees – any damn trees at all – and reach the bare open country that felt like home. Which didn't take too long; she was a good driver, steady but swift, and soon we were running between the red rocks and squared-off buttes of the Painted Desert. Being winter, and us heading north into lonely country, there was precious little other traffic and the air, when I let my window down, was colder than you'd ever want. I said, 'This is a hell of a season to come out here. You realise there'll be snow or the threat of it all the time?'

She gazed through me and said, 'I couldn't have waited till spring to find out.' She drove another five minutes, then she said, 'We've snow tyres on and chains in the trunk. We'll manage all right.' She didn't say any more till we got clear of the Painted Desert and were running along the bluff high above the river, then she said, 'We'll be there soon.'

Was an odd meaning of 'soon'. I said, 'In about ten miles we take a left-hand side road and then—'

She said, 'I know all that. I've got the map.' The sun glittered on the rock angles and the river far below, and she didn't speak again till we reached the turnoff. Then instead of going left she headed the car straight ahead, then right to a really minor road.

'What the hell?' I said. 'There's nothing along here except—'

'I *know*, Cate. A ramshackle group of cabins you've probably never seen before, and—' The high rock bluff fell away, the bare brownish-red slopes were all around us, and ahead the light glittered so strong it hurt your eyes even with sunglasses. 'And the lake,' my mother finished.

I said fast, 'But we don't want to stay there. We'll do much more comfortable, honest, along the other road.' Then I shut my mouth because I realised where protesting would lead me. Into telling my mother everything, that was where.

'No,' she said, 'I made some phone calls and I liked the sound of this place better. Convenient too, isn't it? The town where – where you were with Jeff – is only twenty miles or so along the road.'

'Thirty, more like.' Because didn't I know exactly? But I needed to be so damn careful; this visit was turning out already to be trickier than I'd ever expected, and we'd hardly gotten started yet. 'Be a better motel there,' I said weakly. I hadn't much relished the prospect of the two of us staying in the town Les and me had busted in and out of so quick that night, but here by the lake'd be worse in a way she couldn't imagine.

'Oh no,' she said, and pulled the car up at a sort of mock rustic lodge with little pine cabins lined along the roadway, 'I think this place'll do us very nicely. We might as well be comfortable.' Which I interpreted to mean that this place was pricier than the other. I'd not seen these cabins before – for what we'd needed to do that night we'd stayed away from buildings – but they looked to be new-polished if not new-built. The kind of motel that gets itself done up fancy and then sneaks into the guidebooks and travel agency recommendations.

She liked her comfort, okay, in a chic sort of way. But maybe she'd been having qualms too, about us staying in the exact same area where I'd killed him. She'd have a hell of a lot more qualms if she knew the true reason for my objecting.

She parked outside the office and strolled in – yeah, she'd already booked from Virginia; she wasn't a person to leave anything except the hugely important things to chance – and she came back almost right away with a cabin key in her hand. I had my own reasons for hoping it'd be a cabin looking out to the roadside, but nothing was working right for me then; she drove around on a pine-needled track to a row of cabins set behind. She got out, opened up the cabin door and looked at me where I still sat.

'Tomorrow we'll drive in and get started,' she said, 'but I decided this would be a comfortable headquarters for us.' She swung the cabin key and said, 'Come on, Cate, don't keep making everything so hard for me. Haven't you made things hard enough already?'

I got out of the car then, dragging my feet, and went across to her and indoors. The cabin was tarted-up rustic all right, with a couple of big deep beds and lots of Indian rugs and pine cupboards everywhere, which is okay if you're smitten with stuff like that and don't object to paying. The window at the front was okay, it looked out to the back of the roadside cabins. But there were two big windows at the back and one in the bathroom, and I knew damn well where they'd look out to. I went across – there's no point in not facing up to your troubles – and yeah, I'd guessed right. The lake in all its shining glittery length. It sneered at me in the sunlight like it intended to speak and I couldn't do a damn thing to stop it. Like it'd been *waiting* for me.

I opened my mouth then, I almost told my mother the truth so we'd get out of there. I wouldn't have cared where in the hell we went – except Jeff's apartment, of course – but I just didn't want to look at that damn sneery lake any longer. So I opened my mouth but my mother said something about the towels in the bathroom; I shut my mouth and after a while I answered her. Said nothing about the view, though I didn't see how I could live around it. Even if she'd not spoken then I doubt if I'd have managed to tell her; I was beginning to realise how little guts I'd truly got. You'd imagine that anyone who commits a murder must be a person who's full of courage and fire, but it's not necessarily so. Les was right about me; not a coward when I'd a long sharp knife in my hand, but if it was ordinary unarmed me against somebody that was armed or just extra courageous – why, I'd hold my tongue and crumble, every time.

I turned away from the window and my mother passed me; she said, 'Quite a view, isn't it?' and I was so paranoid by then I stared at her hard to see what she was thinking. But nothing special, by the calm of her face.

'It surely is,' I said, and recognised that – except for the one moment of the murder – nothing difficult or painful had happened around me before then; the tough part lay ahead. I could see it all piled up around us, waiting to happen.

19

We unpacked and then ate supper in the motel's little restaurant – tortillas and such – and that wasn't too bad because the restaurant faced roadward. I said to my mother afterwards, when we were back in our room, 'Was it a smart thing to do, to get chatting with the guy who runs this place like you did?' Because she'd talked and asked him questions as ready as could be I said, 'We don't want anyone around here to remember us especially, do we?'

She said, 'I don't care whether they remember us or not, I'm going to find out what happened. And if that includes picking up whatever gossip is still floating around the area – fair enough, I'll do that too.' But there was a sort of slight uncertainty in her voice, and I could guess why; here we were at last and finally, if she'd meant what she said back there in safe old Virginia, the risks had got to be taken. She couldn't just make big-sounding statements and put off the practical actions any more. Her asking this guy Elwood all those questions about possible crimes in the area most likely made her as nervous afterwards, thinking it over, as it did me at the time.

To test her I said, 'How do you plan to go about this?'

She looked at me and visibly toughened herself; of course she'd long realised she'd get more hindrance than help from me in digging up the past. 'Tomorrow morning,' she said, 'we'll drive over there and I'll find the local newspaper office. Those always keep their back copies, and I can read up on what was said at the time.'

'That sounds to me pretty damn suicidal,' I said, 'for you

and me both. Didn't it occur to you that someone'll wonder why in the hell you've suddenly shown up and gotten interested in all this?'

'There's no other way to do it,' she said. 'I'll dream up a likely enough story to satisfy them.' She turned suddenly irritable and said, 'How else did you expect I'd approach it – go to the local sheriff and ask him for details of Jeff's death and a list of suspects?'

'That'd not have surprised me,' I said, 'but dumb, dumb.' I laughed and after a while she managed a reluctant grin. But we'd both have wiped those grins off our faces pretty damn quick if we'd foreseen that the sheriff would be right there in the motel room with us next evening. Eyeing us up and down, asking questions. And us with no halfway watertight answers to anything he'd ask.

It happened this way. Next morning after breakfast she got the car out and we drove along to that town as she'd planned. It was a sunny morning and when we lost sight of the lake I felt pretty damn good for about five minutes – then I recalled that Les and me had driven this road in the middle of the night with Jeff's body wrapped in his rug and plastic in the back of the truck, and although my mother's car heater was blasting away I started shaking all over.

She said, 'What's the matter? Are you cold?' I think she was beginning to wonder what we'd done with Jeff's body, but she kept letting her mind run away from the question because she didn't like its possible answers any better than I did. A fine pair of chickenhearts we were, but she'd got the excuse that she hadn't wanted any of this, and I'd no damn excuse at all. If you pull out a knife and kill someone, you ought to be ready to follow through.

'Nuh-uh,' I said short, 'not cold.' We were driving out of the red butte country and suddenly we reached that big patch of salt desert that no one ever expects, that feels to me like my own personal territory. The high mountains off in the distance are sharp white in the sun, blue-black in shade; they stand up naked like the bones of some animal that died a very long time ago and will belong here for ever. And between you and the mountains are the salt flats, miles and miles where the crystals shine silvery all around you; they gleam like all the world's jewels and, where they've piled up against a scrubby branch of sagebrush or a bit of some-body's dead vehicle, they lift like prancing white spiders in the wind and blow bitter on your lips like a tricky some-thing that you urgently need to say. Not like anywhere else in the world, I'll guarantee; a place where you meet yourself and don't need make excuses. Despite the horrible errand we were going on, I felt myself very nearly relax.

We drove through this for a handful of miles, then my mother abruptly pulled the car off the road, saying no-thing. I said urgently, 'Don't kill the engine,' because in those remote areas if it didn't start up again, what would you do? This was a highway, yeah, but trafficwise not so's you'd notice. And cellphones aren't exactly reliable in those high-up ghost areas.

She left the engine running but didn't speak, sat with her hands in her lap staring straight ahead. At last she took a long breath and said, 'Look – there was a reason for what you did, wasn't there? Killing is always wrong, of course, but if he used violence to you first, if you felt your life was threatened—' But of course that didn't wear too well, because I'd carried the knife. 'Perhaps that's a common-place out here,' she said, glancing around us and sounding desperate, 'I can't judge. I hadn't realised how different—'

She rubbed a hand over the steering wheel like explor-ing. 'I'm familiar with the East Coast and its hinterland and parts of the West Coast, but that's it. When we crossed the continent we always flew.' She glanced round again, like the cops' hounds were tracking her.

I tried to imagine how this landscape must look to a

person such as her, that had never seen it before. 'Different,' she'd said, and not in a liking tone either.

I said, 'You mean you hate it here?' but she looked at me baffled, like the desert had wiped all emotions out of her.

'I don't know you,' she said, 'any longer, you're not the girl I thought I was beginning to get murmurs of, back in Virginia. You love this place, don't you? That shines out of your eyes as all this white stuff – what is it? Salt? – shines everywhere around us. You were scared to come back here because of what you'd done, but you're so happy now that it's almost made you forget your fear. A young wild animal, aren't you? Completely at home here.' And her fingers scrabbled over the steering wheel like she'd truly forgotten me. Or, rejecting what she now thought I was, had laid me aside. Which scared me to holy hell, because there was much more to me than that.

'Your daughter,' I said, 'aren't I? And a human person too, no animal.' She'd put such a gulf between us that I got insulted, though I was for sure not in any position to justify that. 'Trees and the lack of them,' I said, 'or the white shine of the salt – yeah, sure, but aren't those the things you knock out of the way when there's something really important going on?'

At least then she brought her attention back from the desert to me. 'Tell me you had justification,' she said, 'that's all I need to know.' She managed a sideways grin then, which near broke me down. 'I'm becoming more unscrupulous by the minute,' she said, 'if anyone had told me six months ago that I'd gladly help to cover up a crime, of course I'd have refused to believe them. But now, with you – and not only because you're my daughter—' But despite that grin I could see how this new land had thrown her, she wasn't sure of me or herself or anything any more. And she waited, like it urgently mattered, for the answer to her question.

'You'd want me to be honest,' I said slowly, 'so I better

not give you an easy happy solution, right?' Her grin and trickle of warmth faded, but seemed like honesty was all the two of us had got left. I couldn't throw that out too.

She said, 'You mean there was no justification for what you did?' Then she partway recovered. 'But Cate, Cate, you're selling yourself too low. You're not a stupid or naturally vicious person – I know you well enough to be sure of that – so you must have had *some* reason, a reason which seemed good to you at the time.'

'But it won't to you.' And, to be honest, it mightn't still to me; what I'd done to Jeff was plenty clear, but the why of it kept trying to become a muddle. I'd only my own judgement to rely on, my own sense of what he ought or oughtn't to have done and how I ought to have answered him, and in all my thinking afterwards I couldn't find solid ground. So now I closed my lips and said no more to her; she'd find out soon enough some of the things I'd tried to keep hidden, and she would make her own judgement on them.

She said nothing either; we drove on through that silvery desert and I stared at the far hills that, among the white-coloured rock, had a goodly amount of snow on. After a while the town sign appeared beside the highway, and ahead of us the single street of buildings. The town was exactly as I recalled it; okay, I'd only seen it that one night, but I'd not forgotten how huge and threatening the moon looked when it rose and outlined the main street. Like the moon had come to life just beyond, in the desert, and knew what Les and me were about, was aiming to follow and spy on and betray us. The buildings had stood out clear in its light and they looked much the same now under the morning sun. A few one-floor houses and old thrown-together cabins, none of any size. A small concrete building which was the post office, with a phone booth outside. A family-run hardware store – and feed too – and a Safeway with its doors too tired to shut tight and a double aisle fuller of ghosts than of people. Then the little apartment building; my mother tightened her lips again at sight of that.

I said, 'Hell, you might as well say what you're thinking,' which I guess was brutal of me to push her.

And she said, 'Cate, *please*. Let's try to keep something of our friendship intact through all this, until—' Which shut me up till she spoke again, because the one thing I was terrified of was that she would say she wholly regretted meeting up with me her daughter. I was pretty tough about most things, but I surely didn't want to hear her say that. Anyway – right at the far end of town, next to a battered stone church, the wooden shack of the newspaper office.

She pulled the car up out front and said, 'Let's get this over with.' Then I realised clear and deep what sort of danger she in her innocence was heading toward, and I had a moment of pure panic.

'No way,' I said. 'You can't possibly intend me to go in there with you. Double the risk and more than, wouldn't it?'

She hesitated with her hand on the open car door. 'But what'll you do while you're waiting? If you sit around here, it's rather—' Because there was a handful of people doing errands along the streets – in and out of the Safeway and the feed store – and once or twice a pickup truck passing by. And us in our rental car; being strangers we weren't exactly unnoticeable. She all of a sudden looked tired and unanchored past coping with, and I felt such a sorrow for her it near swamped me. But one of us at least needed to keep a sober head and make balanced decisions; if my troubles fretted her so they made her unable to do that, then I needed to.

So I said brisk, 'How much time do you figure you'll take? Because I can leave you here and drive the car around out in the desert while I'm waiting. On the highway, a car and driver won't interest a soul.'

'You can't do that,' she said like helpless, 'you may not be too young to drive in this state, but you haven't a licence.'

'Hell and damn it,' I said, 'you recall what we're here to investigate, don't you? And you're fretting over a *driver's licence*?'

'Oh Cate,' she said helpless, and at that moment someone stared out of the newspaper office window at us. That gave her the shove she needed. 'Just for God's sake drive carefully,' she said, 'so no one stops you. Stay within the speed limit and—' She handed me the car keys.

'How long for?' I said.

'Oh,' she said, 'say a couple of hours?'

'Holy heavens,' I said, 'it oughtn't to take you more than a half-hour at most. Got the dates, haven't you? Either they've still got copies and can turn them up or – no dice.'

She tried to sound confident. 'They'll certainly have them. But I'll need time to read and digest the details and get photocopies made. Give me an hour?'

As it turned out, that was a pretty fair estimate. I got back in just under the hour – had a damn good time driving around on those desert roads; I'd forgotten how good that cold bright air was, and huge space all around me, no trees or buildings visible to the horizon – anyway I'd sat out front in the car six or seven minutes when she came out. She'd a bundle of photocopies under her arm; she climbed into the car without looking at me and she was white around her mouth in a way I'd not seen in her before. Turned out it was an anger so strong it made her feel sick.

We drove off and I couldn't wait, I started to ask her little nibbling questions, but she said nothing except, 'You didn't tell me the half of it. What a fool I was to be taken in so.' I asked some more questions but she wasn't having any; she drove on beyond the town and we ate lunch at a hamburger joint on the grey-salt edge of nowhere. The sort of place Les and me could once have bought something to eat and not much cared for the flavour of it. Then we drove back to our motel, her taking a sideways route along desert roads so we wouldn't need pass through the town again. The sun glared on the snowy rock-faces and the patches of shade were hard like iron; she said, 'Dear God, what a landscape!' and there was nothing useful or honest I could say to comfort her in reply to that. Then she didn't speak again till we got back to the motel.

We went into our room and she spread out the photo-copies, they were the newspaper pages which covered Jeff's death and the autopsy result. She smoothed them out on the table and said, 'I won't claim that you didn't tell me the half of it, because the truth is you didn't tell me any of it at all. Did you, Cate my daughter? You've been lying to me all the way along.'

She pulled up two chairs to the table, in front of those damn newspapers, and shoved me into one of them.

20

There it all was staring up at me – the things I'd already known about Jeff plus some I'd not known but could have guessed. His high school record, stuff like that. And my mother didn't spare me, she physically shoved my nose down to the papers so I couldn't evade. 'Go on,' she said, 'read it aloud. First of all read what he was before you wrecked him.'

That wasn't hardly fair and I had to say so. 'I've a notion he'd already played around plenty, what makes you so sure I was the one who messed him up?'

'You were the one who killed him,' she said, and I couldn't deny. 'Read it,' she said, 'blast you. Read that.' She pointed to the column where the reporter visited Jeff's former high school and they told him what a brilliant student Jeff'd been, and what a clean-cut, honest-to-God pleasant all-American guy. I protested again before I started reading; this was really my life at stake too. At least it was my relationship with my mother, which was getting more important to me every moment.

'Haven't you noticed,' I said, 'how when someone gets killed young they were always just the smartest and pleasantest ever?'

'Oh, just read it,' she said, 'Cate.' Yet there was something about the way she said my name then, something deep-involved and caressing in spite of herself, and this really got to me. So I started to read without any more argument.

He'd been an honour student in high school; I didn't

plan to rub it in to my mother that I'd not a clue how important or otherwise stuff like that was, never having much attended school myself, so I just did the reading. Expressionless, not asking questions. He'd won prizes and such for various subjects. A wide-ranging intelligence, his head teacher said, a natural type to go on to college and do well there. Sports too, seemed like there was nothing he wasn't good at.

In the midst of my reading my mother said in a voice as toneless as mine, 'Wetback or drifter be damned. He was a person who *belonged.*'

'A wetback or drifter could be smart too if he got the chance,' I said, because I'd known a few of them while we'd travelled around, and they weren't lacking in brains. ''Course,' I said, 'they wouldn't get much chance, being outside the system.'

She glanced at me; I guess it sounded like I might be pitying myself, saying I'd not had much chance either, but that wasn't anywhere in my mind. So I tried to straighten this out between us and as usual messed it up.

'Look,' I said, 'if I'd been offered the chance of schooling, there's no way I'd have accepted. A bunch of damn sheep, that's what students are.'

'Just read it,' she said, 'don't try to talk smart.'

Okay, he'd won prizes, had gone off to college with all the glory a town this small could manage. They'd interviewed the college head too; Jeff was a terrific student, very bright and with a great future. I threw the paper down and said, 'Look, this isn't getting us anywhere.'

She said, 'We're getting close to what happened that night, aren't we? And you're reluctant to face it. But there's no point in getting sensitive about a man after you've killed him.' Her face twitched, she lifted her gaze from the newspapers and said, 'Cate, I'll do my best to cope with what happened – if only you'll tell me the truth. Why don't we forget these news details and you just tell me frankly what you did that night? And why, if you can come up with the reason.'

I was longing as hard by then to accept her offer as she was to believe me. I still felt a very considerable affection toward her, and she wasn't going to stop asking these questions till she'd gotten a credible answer. So I might best go along with what she wanted; at least that way we might salvage some of the comradeship we'd started to build up. I scowled, thinking, and she said soft, 'Take your time.' Almost gentle, like she still cared plenty about me.

'It's not that simple,' I said, not knowing where to begin.

She said in the deep tone which sounded caressing, 'I wouldn't believe you if you said it was.'

The silence sat around us; nothing to disturb it except an occasional car or truck going by and the breeze twiddling amid the pine trees which fringed the cabins. My mother saw I needed help and she started asking small useful questions. 'Where did you first meet Jeff?' she said.

On a desert road, that was where. I was out driving without Les, he was home resting up and smoking, and I was in the mood for an alone afternoon. I pulled off the road where there was nothing but desert, and I sat in the truck cab gazing around and feeling happy. Soon Jeff came driving along in his two-seater import; any girls he'd had before, he must have taken them to his apartment or where they lived. A cute little yellow car, but there was no room in it for anything like that. Not that he, maybe, was thinking of such when we first met. Nor, in the beginning, was I. He pulled up with a screech of brakes when he saw the truck, he strolled over like a real Western gentleman and asked had the truck broken down, did I need help?

My mother said, 'This was how long before – before that night?' Her delicacy, that she couldn't say 'murder' and be done, made me burn for her with a painful protective love.

'A week maybe. A handful of days. I never knew him

long.' She turned her face away and I said, 'Look, all this is hurting you too damn much, whyn't we just give up and you can say goodbye, dump me in the desert. I'll make out okay and if not – well, that'd only be what I deserve, right?'

She turned back to me and said tough, 'Go on explaining.'

The sun slanted through the rear windows; soon it'd be dark and time to go eat. A boat put-putted on the lake and that made me pull myself together; I couldn't possibly tell her everything, so might as well boost my courage and be honest with her about what happened up to the time Jeff got killed. To make up to her, I mean, for the evasions about what we'd done with his body.

'So I told him no breakdown, I just enjoyed the desert.' That was one thing about Jeff, he loved the desert the same way I did. If not, we mightn't have gotten so terribly tangled together. 'He saw it the same way as me,' I said, and heard the wonder still in my voice, 'the colours of the rocks, the glittery salt flats, the cactuses shoving their spiny arms and their flowers at you, and the wild creatures that creep and hide by day and rush out swarming at night.'

'Me and my forests,' she said, 'you and your desert. At least we're both capable of loving *something*.' Then she said kindly, 'Go on, Cate.'

So Jeff and me talked. 'And he said he was in college, yeah. The semester had just finished and, because his father was dead and his mother remarried, Jeff kept this little apartment in the town where he'd grown up. His true home, he said. Later in the vacation he'd be visiting his mother in California.'

When I said 'California' my mother stiffened again, because of the campsite where Les had stolen me. I gave her a minute to get over the worst of that hurt, then I went on.

Jeff and I talked, out there in the glittery salt desert, and something sparked between us. I'd slept with boys before – they'd wanted to and I was curious – but that's not what I mean. A deeper feeling by far. I labelled it, that first day, as how you'd feel if you loved someone and were pretty sure they loved you too. Finally we quit talking and he got into his car, drove off; I sat in the truck watching the cloud of dust roiling behind him and I said to myself, Cate you fool, there's nothing different about this. Yet I'd a gut feeling that our meeting had felt special to Jeff and me both. As it turned out I'd guessed wrong, but I'd not much experience to guide me.

'Excited and happy,' I said, 'that's how I felt.' And secretive; there was no point in trying to explain any of this to Les.

My mother said, 'How young were you when you first slept with a boy?' Sorrowful; I guess her own young years had been unimaginably different.

A year previous to Jeff, that was how long. No, more than a year. I said, because it sounded better, 'Fourteen.' Then that inconvenient need for honesty broke into me again. 'No, I guess basically thirteen – but not too far off my next birthday.'

She said nothing, only looked at me sad, and I knew she was brooding on how if she'd had the charge of me this wouldn't have happened.

'I was never promiscuous,' I said, 'there were only maybe three or four boys in total, before Jeff. I never went with a boy unless the sight of him did something for me. And of course—' urgent to get this clear, because she mustn't blame Les unfairly, 'Les never knew. I'd go driving without him, that was nothing unusual, and there wasn't any point in me telling him more than need be.'

She took a long breath and said, 'So you chatted with Jeff and he drove off. Then what?'

The setting sun turned her hair gold and made her skin

glow; made me remember the Vince up in Washington who'd fixed up our tests, how glad she'd talked with him on the phone and gone to eat dinner with him. Even if he wasn't a guy she wanted to spend her future with, yet there'd been *something*. Maybe she and myself weren't so different after all. But at least she'd not killed him.

'What then?' I said. 'Why, next afternoon I took our truck out again and cruised around the edges of town, didn't run the main street but nibbled along the dusty borders where the old broken-down shacks are that no one lives in any more.' Cactus in the back yards of them, and across the thin dry grasses and wire the desert wind blowing. I'd stopped the truck outside a couple of them and poked around, playing my favourite game of 'What if Les and me lived here?' But the game couldn't hold my attention that day, I was burning for Jeff. Not only body-hot but especially those warm unexpected feelings shoving at me. Didn't see him that day though.

'Oh,' she said, 'do get on. When did you meet him again and why did you kill him?' So I tried to explain to her how, without she knew the way I'd been feeling about him, none of what I'd done made any sense.

Anyway, 'A few days later. I wouldn't drive through town but I drove those edge-of-town unpeopled tracks every afternoon. Then one day I'd given up looking and was haring back through the desert to our dirt turnoff – and Jeff's yellow car came haring along from the other direction. He said he'd a vacation job and was driving home from it.' He didn't say he'd missed me and hoped to see me again, but I recall the feel of his fingertip running up and down my bare arm, and surely that's what the travelling fingertip was saying. 'Then we were in each other's arms, but it was full day still and – you've seen the wreck our truck is, and I told you about Jeff's tiny car. Out there in the desert, what the pair of us were thirsting toward wouldn't exactly be practical.'

'So you met that evening and he took you to his apartment.' Then she said very low, 'And you carried a knife.'

But I always had, whenever I was out alone. Because I surely didn't have character references from any of those boys. The desert can breed tough customers that look friendly enough on the surface, so this seemed a reasonable precaution. I told her so, and she was silent for a while.

Then she said, 'Cate my dear. Cate.' Like she was weeping and embracing me, only her eyes were dry and the two of us weren't touching. So I hurried along with my story.

'I'd never used the knife before, never expected a real use. And I'd always planned that if I did need use it I'd aim for an arm or leg, disable them without any chance of a major hurt.'

'But something went wrong.' She rocked her arms together, she held them tight around herself. 'What happened?' she said.

'We started out, in his apartment, to – to make love.'

I hesitated and she said sharp, 'Don't get coy, I've heard all the words before.'

'Yeah, well – so he'd no clothes on and me only my T-shirt.' Can't recall why I'd not taken that off too, would've been easier and a sticky night as it was despite the air-conditioning. Anyway I'd this T-shirt on down to my hipbones, and the sex was . . . yeah, I thought it pretty damn good. He was a fast in-and-out type without much consulting you, but all the boys I'd been with acted that way. If I'd hoped Jeff might be more subtle – well, losing that hope wasn't necessarily a major disappointment. 'We finished and he rolled off me. I thought we'd – I hoped—'

I stared down at my clenched hands and relived those silly hopes. I'd expected, to be truthful, that he'd make coffee or fetch a cold drink from his icebox and we'd chat a while, maybe about the desert since we'd that in common, and maybe afterwards about how we were starting to feel toward each other. He'd a fancy collection of books on his shelves, okay, and a computer and such, but what the hell? I was young and was ready to learn anything a guy wanted me to, if I cared about him enough. Anyhow he rolled off me and there was this silence. I lay with my eyes shut and I supposed he'd gone into the bathroom or to fetch that drink or whatever. Nothing happened and I opened my eyes; he stood staring down at me. He said, 'What are you waiting for?' and he reached over to a chair, picked my jeans off it and threw them at me. 'All done,' he said. He took a prissy smarming voice, like you'd use to mock a stupid animal. 'Thanks very much and goodbye,' he said in this hateful voice.

I said to my mother, 'So everyone claims he was Mister Nice Guy? He surely acted exactly the opposite to me.'

She muttered something about young men and 'You never can tell.' Then she said, 'Where was the knife all this time?'

'In my canvas bag, on the chair, under the jeans. You can see I didn't intend using it, wouldn't I have kept it handier if so?' She didn't speak and I went on, 'I was confused and – unhappy, I guess, because all this was turning out so different from what I'd dreamed of. Anyway, I picked up the jeans and my bag and I went into his bathroom with them.'

And sat on the edge of his bath and started to cry, that was what. I needed to get back through the desert up to the hills where I'd left the truck; without a vehicle it'd be an impossible long journey, and nothing except a collapsing old shack and the stink of Les when I got there. I was plenty accustomed to sun or cold and to staying up till all hours, but suddenly I was bone-tired from the whole lot of those. And never being able to get properly clean, let alone stay that way. In order to get ready for that night I'd taken the truck down to a desert gas station in the late afternoon and locked myself in their restroom to scrub my whole body over. I was there so long the proprietor came banging on the door and shouting insults, and when I got out he told me never to stop off there again. Then by the time I met Jeff there was sweat on my T-shirt, oil on my jeans; that was how Les and me lived. And no escaping from it ever, that I could see, because no decent man would want to stay around me.

I told my mother, 'Jeff pulled the bathroom door open and stood there sneering – not yelling so a passerby might have heard, but this quiet sneer so I couldn't even prove that against him – and it came to me this was how my whole life was going to be. Not entirely Jeff's fault, for sure, but he was the centre of it and he was standing right there in front of me. I was hurt and hating, wanted to scare him, and I heard the knife shift in my bag.'

There was the biggest silence in the world between her and me then; I said, 'I never intended to kill him,' and this was the bone-truth, although if I'd been her I'd not have believed me either. A thin voice with no conviction behind it.

She said, 'But you did.' And her face was open, waiting; I'd got to tell her the rest.

'He kept saying these things about me, how I'd sleep around with anyone and was the cheapest bit of goods he'd known. How I was dirt out of the desert and he couldn't imagine how I'd conned him into us sleeping together. How he supposed I was waiting for money from him and I could go howl for it. How I was a rotten lay anyway – which I knew wasn't true, from what other boys'd said. How I was coyote shit and he'd never slept with such a shitty lay.' I looked across at my mother and told her, 'When he said that, I'd truly got nothing left, he'd robbed me of everything. He was educated and he'd obviously been around, so I believed him and had to disbelieve those others who'd told me the opposite. He'd stripped me of everything and his damn voice kept on sneering at me.'

She said in a flat voice that came out of nowhere, 'So you killed him.'

'Not till he hit me.' When I'd said this I got an odd feeling that these words were what she'd been digging and digging to expect; now she'd unearthed them she could almost live with herself and me again. Her hands smoothed themselves out and her voice took a depth.

'He beat you up,' she said.

To be honest, not so, only the one tap of his sneery finger against my forehead. But that despising contact of his with my angry flesh was entirely too much for me; my rage and unhappiness ripped loose. Plus I was mortally afraid he'd forget to stay cautious and more blows would follow. I tried to convey some of this to my mother, but I got muddled and she was starting to hear what she wanted to, what would halfway justify me in this scenario she'd cooked together.

'He beat you up,' she said. 'Go on from there, Cate.'

'I wish I could say he ran onto the knife, but that wouldn't be true. What happened was, I sent the knife going forward to stop that damn sneery voice of his. And where the knife travelled toward, he was there.'

A pause, then she looked down at the newspaper reports and the hardness came back into her face, I watched it stiffening. '*He* beat you up?' she said, and there was a photo of Jeff the clean-cut all-American everything; I could see her point. I said, 'Not exactly beat me,' and she came back fast, 'But you do claim he verbally abused you and hit you?'

I said, 'Yeah.' Hopeless now, because I saw which direction she was heading. Sure enough she said, '*Him*? I'm aware people can be unexpected, but . . . and you've told me so many lies all along, Cate. You admit that, don't you?' She didn't wait for a reply there, knew she needn't. 'So many lies,' she went on, 'how can I ever pick out the truth in all this mess?' And her gaze went back to Jeff the basketball player, the sprinter, most-likely-to-succeed in the yearbook; I sat watching her and was beaten before I'd ever started. The room was full of dusk and evening silence; no point in me breaking that.

Then a banging started on the door.

2I

He stood just inside the door and glanced from one to the other of us; he'd quick sharp eyes – dangerous eyes. They didn't sit right with his build which was hefty, to be honest overweight, nor with the tough long jaw which all sheriffs seem to get, I guess from chewing gum or tobacco and acting mean toward suspects. But the voice matched his eyes; he'd a short definite way of talking, like he meant to solve each case in double-quick time and move on to the next. I sat staring at him and figuring that his success rate was most likely way up there – too damn unhealthy for us by half – and my mother gawped at him too.

He put sort of a quick grin on his face but it had a hard time staying there. He shut the door behind him and said, 'Elwood told me you were home. Excuse my busting in like this, but maybe you didn't hear me knock.' He didn't bother to try calling the grin back again. 'It's hard to believe of a sheriff, but I've been told I knock too gentle.'

Gentle, nothing. My mother stared like he was meaner than any movie sheriff in creation. Only she did need to brisk up, answer him back, say something; instead she sat there staring at his uniform like the gilt star and holster had drained all the life out of her.

'Mind if I sit a few minutes?' he said. 'Seems that you and me, ma'am, have an interest in common, and there's a couple of questions I'd like to ask you.'

My mother flapped her fingers toward an empty chair and he sat. He glanced across at me and his eyes had gone flat blue like the desert lake outside; I'd no notion what he was thinking.

Then he took his gaze off me and returned it to my mother. He asked her, 'Did you want to send this young lady to the restaurant or such while you and I chat?'

She found a brief husky voice from way inside herself and said, 'I've no secrets from my daughter. Whatever you need to say, you can say to us both.'

He said, 'Very well, ma'am.' He settled his hands comfortable crossways on his knees and leaned forward like he was studying us both; I felt like he'd already handcuffed us and we'd never get away. My mother's calm was, I guessed, mostly frozen fear, but I vastly admired her because she was putting up a damn solid front. Calmer and tighter controlled than I'd ever have been able to. 'About those records you were checking over today,' he said, 'in the newspaper office.'

'Yes?' said my mother. 'I hadn't realised there was any law against that.'

'No law, ma'am. Only—' He shifted his feet and cleared his throat, pretending a certain gentleness; at this pretence I got more afraid than ever. He didn't even care if we realised. He went on, 'That boy's death, might I learn what your interest in it is?'

'Certainly.' I'd been around my mother enough to sense that she was thinking desperate and fast; I only hoped this sheriff didn't sense that too. But she came up with her excuse so swift, I felt a real triumph for her. 'I'm a writer,' she said, 'fiction chiefly. Crime.' She managed a small smile. 'And plots aren't easy to come by – at least I never find them easy – so, as I'm on vacation in this area with my daughter, and somebody happened to tell me about that unsolved crime—' She stopped there, which was wise; she'd sounded just right. Like a woman who wrote that sort of thing for a living, did it off the top of her head and kind of enjoyed it but knew how silly and maybe hurtful her interest must seem to someone such as him who got truly involved with solving real-life crime. 'It never was solved, isn't that so?' she said in a casual little voice, like she hated bothering him to answer her.

'That's so, ma'am.' He crossed one thick leg over the other; he wore tall boots because of all the places he'd need go into and the scorpions and snakes and such. Half-ruined shacks like where Les and me had hung out, old mine workings, houses where drugs or the money from them might be stashed. His beat would never be the shiny casino area, the rich sunbelt further south. But he'd know his own patch much closer than he'd know the back of his hand, know every person in it and how they breathed, how they slept – or, if they didn't sleep some nights, most likely he'd have a pretty accurate notion of what they might be doing. And us, the odd folks from out of town, he'd work at till he fitted us into his picture.

He let the silence hang and I hoped my mother would defy him, would let the silence hang on her side too. But she, being nervous, rushed in. 'So I read the newspaper accounts but—' she shrugged – 'there's nothing in them for me. Nothing which suggests a full-length novel.'

'No, ma'am?' he said. 'And yet the boy died and no one's been caught.' He gave her a comradely grin you could see through a mile off. 'Seems to me there ought to be a story in that, ma'am.' I could see her getting ready to explain about fiction techniques and such (she'd have rushed into that too, whether or not she truly knew much about them) but he threw her off balance by saying first, 'May I know whereabouts you're from, ma'am? You've a local hire car, so I assume you flew in.' He didn't add, 'I can easy check with the airports, so don't bother lying,' but this must have been in all our minds. He said, 'Maybe you're visiting from England, ma'am?'

'No,' said my mother, 'I live in Virginia.' She gave him

the city name but not her full address; I expected he'd ask for it but he didn't.

'And you've lived over there how long, ma'am?'

'Seventeen years.' From eighteen months before I was born.

'You recollect the date of this crime of ours?' Then he acted like he'd just that minute spotted the newspaper copies lying all over the table. 'Ah,' he said, 'yes, they said you took photocopies. You planned to study them in detail, I guess, although there wasn't a good enough story in them. Might have second thoughts about how interesting the story was, huh?'

My mother's colour was coming back; she pulled her voice together and said, pretty much as tough as her usual self, 'If you disbelieve me, why don't you say so? I've told you the truth, and I can't see why you keep asking me questions.'

'Yes, ma'am,' he said, 'I've been told I do get led away into details. A good fault maybe – sometimes a little detail will make all the difference.' He leaned back and crossed his legs the other way, like relaxed, but I didn't for one moment believe that either. He said, 'I was a geologist by profession before I got into law enforcement, and the shine of a few crystals on a rockface or the twist of layers on a creekside bluff – those could lead to something deep-hidden but vastly important, time and again.' He brisked himself up as if he might have gotten wistful sometimes for those geologist years, and he said, 'But my poking around can be tedious for the folks I inflict it on. Such as you, ma'am.'

'Poke all you want,' she said with a spirit I admired and loved her for, 'but if you're going to ask where I was at the time and date when he was killed, yes, I was in Virginia and I could certainly produce witnesses to that.' She put her arm round me so smooth and casual I admired her more than ever. She said, 'My daughter was there too. And neither she nor I had ever heard of this place or the youth who was killed. We were busy leading our own lives.'

I longed to tell her she'd played this exactly right, but of course I was forced to keep my mouth shut; for me that was the only safe thing. I'd sense enough to realise that if I talked much the sheriff'd pick up that my accent and grammar weren't the same as my mother's; I was just thankful that when she'd chatted in the motel restaurant with that Elwood who ran the place, I'd kept my mouth shut all the time. Anyway she mentioned me so casual now, the sheriff didn't shift his eyes to me for an instant. 'Well,' he said, 'to be truthful, I didn't suppose you'd travelled out here and killed him, ma'am.' He gathered those hefty legs together and got up. 'Okay,' he said, 'I was obligated to ask questions, and you've given me good straightforward answers. I'm sorry to have taken up some of your vacation time, ma'am.' He got himself as far as the door, stood there with one hand on it and said, 'Good luck with your story-writing, ma'am. If you'd like details of any long-ago crimes in this area – old-style miners and such – just let me know. Long before my time, but we've a rich collection of those.' In the open doorway he turned around to say, 'Have a good vacation, the pair of you.' Then he left.

22

'Let's get out of here,' said my mother as soon as the sheriff had driven off, and for one crazy moment I thought she meant we'd run, rush back East and hide. That would have been a huge mistake to do right then; I should've realised she'd got more sense. Turned out, what she did mean was we'd go sit in the motel's little restaurant with cups of coffee and she, for sheer relief, would move her mouth to anyone that happened along, about – I hoped and was sure – anything on earth except what we were doing here and the fact that the sheriff had come visiting.

But, as our weird kind of ill-luck would have it, the only person there was this Elwood that sort of ran the place, and he already knew about the sheriff's visit. Also my mother was so relieved and still terrified – this was all new territory to her city-bred closed-in mind in a way that it'd never be to me – that the one thing she longed to talk about was this interrogation that'd just happened. She tried to act cautious and keep a guard on her tongue, and a couple of times I kicked her under the table, but this Elwood didn't make my job any easier.

Because he was so quiet, so fade-into-the-panelling himself, and yet such an open ear, that he more encouraged her talking than reined it in. I'd not taken much notice of him earlier except to think that she oughtn't to ask all those questions and it was damn fortunate that this quiet-spoken guy seemed almost bored and not much interested in why she wanted to know. But now I took a closer look at him, and listened to the pair of them, and I started to get worried.

He was a clear twenty years older than my mother; he wore glasses and had thin grey hair and he looked like any kid's grandad. A pleasant shy-seeming smile when you got to see it, which wasn't often because he most often looked pretty serious.

Anyway my mother, after asking him what hours he worked and all – he said this time of year he was mostly on duty because short-staffed; he'd take on more help when the busy season got near, several months further on – she had to spill out her nervous relief somehow to some person, like himself, that'd be educated enough to understand it; talking with me wasn't the same at all. Anyway, wasn't I the one that had done the killing? That, now we were in Jeff's own territory, kept reinforcing the barrier between her and me. So she started yakking to this Elwood and I listened.

'The sheriff needed some convincing,' she said with her pretty, meant-to-be-meaningless laugh, 'but I think in the finish he realised that, as well as having an unbreakable alibi, I'm not the type to commit a murder.'

'Oh,' this Elwood said, 'you never can tell.' He shoved those silly glasses up higher on his nose. 'The sheriff – I've known him most of my life and we often chat, 'course we're all friends around these parts and everyone knows everyone else – anyway he says there's some killers he can spot a mile off. But the ones that surprise you are what he calls the mischance killers. And I agree with him they must be the toughest to spot. The ones that weren't truly oriented toward murdering, but something nasty came along and shifted their allegiance. Like when a woman's sleeping around and her husband thought she was shiny clean but he catches her at it and finds out different.'

'But,' said my mother, 'I know crimes of passion happen, but still—'

His mild gentle voice went on, near smiling now. 'Did I say it was enough excuse, ma'am? Myself, I looked in the mirror and decided she had reason for preferring the other guy, so I moved out and filed for divorce.' He gazed at my mother calm as a nighttime squirrel in a treetop and he said, 'But there's all sorts of mess-ups, and as many reactions to them as there's people.'

My mother's face softened while she listened; when he finished, her eyes got large and glowed on him. And – this was what worried me far beyond ordinary worry – I suddenly realised she was starting to get interested in him.

Like she'd been with meeting that Vince in Washington, yeah, all warm and excited, like. This new man – could he possibly be *the* one? I don't mean she would fall for any unattached man that happened along. I guess she'd stayed hungry for sex; what good-looking woman isn't? But over the years she'd learned to cope. But once in a while, like now, she would interest herself in a guy as a person, she'd recognise that him and her owned something of the same mindset. Anyhow I watched her falling into this affection for him gladly, like a ripened fruit, as if she might forget our personal danger.

She said soft, 'You can't tell me anything I don't already know about betrayal and separation.' Then the two of them went back to the sheriff's visit and talking about Jeff, but this glow sat around the two of them and I longed to get her on one side, say to her You can't intend this, don't you recall the reason why we're here? And all these folks so damn friendly to Jeff? As this Elwood in his soft voice was explaining to her.

'An old crime,' he said, 'you may wonder why the sheriff and the rest of us still care. But Jeff was different.' Her silence hung wondering and Elwood went on, 'Okay, there was never anyone got killed that deserved to, according to their family and friends. But Jeff was a good kid and he aimed to do sheriff work someday. He was studying law in college but he aimed to use his knowledge in one of these rural areas where he'd work alongside folks like us.'

'I didn't know that,' said my mother thinly.

'It just shows the sort of company he wouldn't be keeping.'

'But,' said my mother, 'he was barely out of his teens. You can't be sure what young people of that age are doing, twenty-four hours a day.'

For sure she'd forgotten me then, but he gave me a small apologetic grin. I'd have liked him quite a lot if it weren't for the dangerous spot my mother and me were in. I arranged a quick grin in return and he said to my mother, 'I'm with you there, and I've no notion what he was up to during termtime, his semesters down in college. But vacations he always spent up here. His dad was dead – was always a fast traveller and moved out one day, then wrapped his auto around a tree down in Mexico – and Jeff's ma married a San Diego man, moved to the coast. Jeff took that little apartment and said he regarded it as his true home. And us as his true friends also. So you could say this area adopted Jeff and he adopted us. A real messy loss, to find someone had up and killed him.'

23

The two of us ate in the motel restaurant – chipolatas, corn and French fries – then we went back to our room and watched television. When it was late enough we went to bed. My mother didn't say anything to me all evening except, 'Do you want a double portion of French fries?' and about which programme we'd watch. Not till we were in bed with the lights out, then into the darkness she said, 'None of it adds up.'

'Careful,' I said, 'they might have this room bugged.'

She said, 'I profoundly doubt that.' But she didn't speak to me again till after breakfast next morning; it was one of those brilliantly sunny cold mornings you often get in the desert winter and while we walked back from breakfast she said, 'We're going for a drive.' She gave me an expressionless sideways look and said, 'At least you can't claim they've bugged my car.'

She didn't ask me where we'd drive to, she propped the map on her knee and drove glancing at it. West and then north, till we got into the salt flats again. The sun shone blinding there (to hurt your eyes if you left your sunglasses off for half a moment), the dry miles of salty ground glittered and in the middle of the flats was a shallow lake where each puddle caught its own sun. I'd tasted salt flats water once; bitter, bitter as hell, and I'd gotten sick after it. My mother pulled the car off the road near these salty shallows; I sat staring at the glary water and the brown dead bushes round its edge.

She said, 'So he was a brute no-nonsense grabbing

person who mightn't care if he got on the wrong side of the law?' I'd hoped she would go on talking so I wouldn't need think up an answer, but she stopped right there.

I said, 'If this Elwood was a woman and nearer Jeff's age, he might tell a different tale.' She didn't speak and of course I'm not one for lasting through her silences. 'Look,' I said, 'I can only tell you the truth, how it happened between him and me. If you or the world won't believe me, there's damn-all I can do more to convince you.'

'He was a good honest boy,' she said, 'a college student who loved the desert not as a racing track or for drug storage but, God help us, because he found it interesting and beautiful. A boy who liked people in general and the local community, who wanted to live around here or a place like it, and to serve his neighbours as a sheriff. A boy who didn't have any reputation for beating up girls, or these people would have heard about it.'

'Holy hell,' I said, 'Jeff owned a penis, didn't he? And urges, just like all the other guys.' I stared out at the brittle bitter-tasting world around us and I said, 'You can keep me in this salty dump all day arguing, but I won't say any-thing different. Can't. If you refuse to believe the truth when you hear it—'

'You claimed to love the desert,' she said, and her eyes on me were blank like I wasn't her daughter at all.

'Not when there's a murder charge hanging over me. Some things have got to get resolved before I can relax and feel comfortable.'

'Well,' she said, 'that's why we're making this explora-tion, isn't it? So that the pair of us can find out the truth and relax. Or otherwise.'

'Would you rather I'd never shown up?' I said, and I opened the car door. 'Because I can walk away right now if you'd rather, I can walk and hitch a ride to some town and you can go home, fix your own life the way you want it.'

'No,' she said, 'you've demolished that. I was unhappy and barren and settled; now I'm not happy or settled but I'm not barren any longer and there's no going back on that. If you walk out on me and keep walking, I'll still be obsessed with the fact that you exist.'

I got out and stood by the open door; I couldn't grasp her meaning. If knowing me was so uncomfortable for her, surely she'd rather not have me around? The cold air seeped past us both like we were a couple of statues, and nothing moved in the whole desert except a large bird way off, high up near the hills. Condor maybe, rare but there's still some of them about.

Then she reached across and held out her hand to me. 'Cate,' she said, 'Cate, Cate.' She kept on holding me tight and saying my name. 'Get back in,' she said, 'it's cold.'

We sat a while longer and I warmed up some, then I said, 'You like this Elwood, don't you?'

She turned to me like a kid on her first date, innocent and scared rigid. 'Was it so obvious?' she said. 'What a fool I make of myself.'

'No. Only obvious to me because—' I was her daughter and a certain amount of emotion attached between her and me, that was why. 'He likes you too,' I said, 'if that's any comfort.'

She gave a tiny snort of laughter. 'The prospects for him and myself aren't too good,' she said, 'are they? I'm conniving with my daughter to cover up her—' she couldn't say 'murder' or 'crime' because it truly wasn't in her to deal with those things. But because I was her blood and bones, she meant to do her damndest. She shook her head and left the words hanging.

'If he asks you out,' I said, 'will you go?'

'There's no chance he will.' She said this much too quick, so she and myself both knew she'd brooded on the possibility. But then she brushed the thought of him aside and she said, 'To be honest, I'm at a loss to know what to do next. I expected we'd come out West and discover the truth and—'

'And somehow it'd clear me?'

'Perhaps. At least that I could learn to live with it. I thought there'd be a solid reason for what you did.'

'Seemed to me there was.' And it still, by my reckoning, did seem that way.

'Yes,' she said, 'poor Cate. Your life, all these years, has been so different from mine. I hadn't bargained for that, and I keep wrenching my mind to try to square the reason you've given me with this other picture of a boy who just didn't have that kind of cruel hateful behaviour in him.'

'If you ask me,' I said, 'every man's got it somewhere. Every male I ever met, anyway.' Except Les, who was older and had always seemed pretty much non-sexed.

'You've met a limited range of men,' she said. 'Your father's not like that.' 'Your father' – how odd those words always sounded. 'And,' she said, 'I doubt that Elwood is either.'

'But he'd like to get you into bed.'

She flushed then, she looked real pretty and I was scared for her all over again because men mattered to her so much, she was thirsty not only for bed but to get loved and admired by some man; could she walk into terrible danger and not notice? She released the handbrake, pulled the car onto the road and said, 'I've got other things on my mind, Cate. Have you forgotten what we came here for?' She speeded up the car on the empty road and said fast, like she was getting rid of something, 'I know what we'll do to find out more about Jeff. We'll go and find his university friends.'

At least that gave us something new to argue over. She said I didn't need go with her, that she'd likely be only a couple of days gone and she'd be keeping this motel room on anyway, so I could stay there and wait for her return. I was startled, I said, 'You'd trust me enough to leave me staying alone in these parts?' and she took an apologetic little grin.

'Yes,' she said, 'of course I would, why not?' Which meant at least she didn't suppose I was a murderer by habit; this was a huge comfort to me. I thought about saying, Anyone can make a mistake once and kill a person, right? But I didn't say it; the area of behaviour she was coming from, there were no excuses for even one killing. She wasn't into frontier territory and she was bending the rules she'd lived by as far as she decently could to make excuses for me because I was her daughter. She said, 'I'll go and find his friends there, I'll put up some story to account for my interest, and young people talk readily. I'll soon learn the truth from them.' She showed me that apologetic face again and she said, 'They perhaps saw facets of him which he never showed here.'

Facets the hell; maybe they caught sight of him in different ways from me, but I knew how he'd acted with me and no one was going to budge me from that. Also I'd be bored and restless without her; she'd take the car and what'd I do for those two days except eat and sleep? And I'd pretty damn soon get fed up with doing those. For sure I wouldn't be taking walks along the lake shore to pass the time. And – a little niggly reason maybe, but important to me – I wanted to stay tuned to whatever things these folks from Jeff's college might be telling her. After all, this was my crime, right? And she'd only gotten involved in it from, you could say, courtesy. 'I'm going down there with you,' I said.

She drove careful for at least five minutes, then she said, 'You still don't trust me.'

'Trust, the hell. That doesn't enter in. This is my doing really, right? My problem, my – if he'd any reason for his attitude, I'd like to know about it too.' A reason wouldn't excuse how he acted with me, but it'd help me understand. 'I want to hear those college kids firsthand.' She opened her mouth but I said, 'Look, I trust you totally, never have trusted anyone so—' now that Les had ratted out on me, that was pretty much true – 'and I fully believe you'd tell me everything they say, but why should you do my dirty work?'

'All right,' she said after a while, 'you can go with me and we'll arrange the conversations so that you can listen. But not appear openly, and not a one-to-one discussion between you and them. That wouldn't be safe. We've taken precautions this far and I won't let you convict yourself out of your own mouth.'

'You suppose I'd do that?'

'Young people get talking together,' she said, 'especially girls who've slept with the same boy, and it could easily happen. You might say too much, Cate, and I refuse to risk that.'

I thought the arrangements would be tricky to make but I'd forgotten what a swift efficient lady she could be when she put her mind to it. She and myself drove down there; the ride – before we got to the hot southern desert – was all pine woods and hills, snow on them, not dense forest like hers in Virginia but kind of pretty if you like scenery that shows you its heart and smarms to you. We found a motel and she made me stay there while she went off to the university to make contacts: Jeff's former adviser and his year's counsellors and such. I didn't ask her afterwards what tale she'd spun them; maybe she should have been a fiction writer after all. She certainly could persuade folks to tell her things there was no reason they should.

Anyhow she got the names of a half dozen of Jeff's college friends. She came back to the motel and got on the phone, one by one arranging how she'd meet up with them all together. She played a smart act on that, she fixed to meet them in a big coffeehouse near the college – with me already installed out of sight in a nearby booth. The arrangements went so smooth she said to me, 'You see?

This was *meant*.' I didn't contradict her but I did feel she might be getting herself involved in hunting up deeper information about Jeff than she'd truly want. That was her problem though, the hunt was hers and I couldn't shake her.

The meeting was for early that evening and I holed up in the coffeehouse twenty minutes ahead of time; that worked out easy. They'd these little booths sectioned off by partitions, and every once in a while a big table taking the place of several booths, so though I couldn't see them for the booth divider I'd clearly hear them. But I groaned inside myself when I heard them come in and what sort they were. Four boys and only two girls, that was what; she'd not get the truths she needed, with such an imbalance. So I felt disappointed from the start, although it was kind of interesting hearing what they'd all say about him.

Nothing but the best, that was what. You never could believe there'd exist such a great guy as Jeff had been. A true loyal friend, great at games (I can't figure why that means so much to men, but it sure does. The guy hunts, shoots pretty straight in the forest or on a rifle range and he plays basketball too, baseball? Skis a regular furrow? What a great guy he is. No option allowed, he's just tremendous).

I got through a lot of coffee, listening to this, and maybe my mother sensed my disapproval, for she started pressing them harder. But no, the boys had nothing bad to say of him. He'd been a damn good friend. And if they could help . . .

I ought to explain that my mother had presented herself to this bunch not as a would-be novelist – she'd told me they probably knew a lot more about fiction techniques than she did, and anyway she'd seem to be cashing in on his family's grief – so instead she made out, with all sorts of little hints, that she'd been called in as a private investigator by someone closely concerned. (Which was true enough, except she'd called herself in.) That way she could ask blunt questions and make it seem like she was at least semi-officially hunting his killer. I admired her technique, she didn't exactly tell lies but the little soft words she spoke made a different impression from the way things truly were. Yet she was quite tough about the questions she asked these boys – and she got nowhere. So then she started on the girls.

She asked about his split family but these kids shrugged; lots of kids their age come from busted-up homes and maybe don't have a lot of contact with their families.

'Yeah,' one of the girls said quietly, 'a normal enough situation.' But she went on, hesitant, 'I don't know how the others felt about Jeff but to me there was something a bit . . . oh, I can't express it. *Ignored*, maybe. As if he'd not gotten enough attention in the past and was determined to make something special of himself.'

My mother said, 'He apparently had some notion of becoming a sheriff?'

'Uh-huh,' said the girl, 'yeah, that would be pretty much what I'd expect of him. He kept quiet about that sort of thing around here, but I personally could never imagine him fitting into the businessman or college professor mould. A guy who'd chart his own route through life no matter what. A guy you might never get to know well, who might have unexpected things inside him. I wouldn't exactly say he'd *dark* things inside him, but—'

The others jumped on this concept of hers and started to slaughter it; the other girl said she'd never noticed anything of that in him, to her he was just an ordinary regular guy. Good-looking, of course, and a good lay (only she, being college, put it more delicate) when he chose to invite you, but selective. A gentleman though. (I was sorely tempted to jump up and hit the whole bunch of them over the head when she said this, because what they were yakking on about had no relevance to his experience with me. Sure, he'd act polite to these clean well-dressed good-speaking girls from his own college – girls that weren't scruffy desert fly-by-nights, that he knew he'd be seeing around again on campus. But me, I was different. Listening to them, I realised for the first time *how* different. Which made me long to bang them all harder or dump my face into my coffee-cup and howl.)

The other students cracked on at the first girl about amateur psychology, made all these in-jokes about their and her college courses, and in the finish she weakly backed down. But she had said those things about Jeff being different and wanting to fight through; they were a fragile help to us but they were the first indication we'd gotten that Jeff had a less-than-orthodox side.

In our motel room that night I said as much to my mother; we planned on driving back up to the sheriff's territory next morning because there seemed no point in us hanging around the college, but I could see she was disappointed. This leg of the journey had hardly seemed worthwhile. We sat discussing it and wrangling, then the phone rang. I said, 'Who the hell knows we're here?' and she said, 'Must be Elwood.' She'd given him the number (for her own, romantic reasons, I guess) and she'd given the sheriff's number to the girls in case they came up with more useful memories – but she and myself both knew they weren't about to do that. So she said, 'It's Elwood,' and she went across to the phone quickly; she was already colouring up. But it wasn't Elwood, it was some girl we'd not heard of.

24

The girl showed up a half-hour later (my mother said, 'You can't tell from a phone call whether people are lying,' and I agreed). She'd got sandy stick-out hair and pale skin, thin figure, tired-looking; not the sort I'd imagine Jeff going for – but what had I known about him anyway?

She sat down, wound her skinny hands into each other and said, 'My sister told me you was asking about that student that got himself killed. Murdered, wasn't it?' She'd a cagey flattish voice too; no, I couldn't see the attraction. She went on, 'My sister works waitressing up at that big cafe where you all met today. That's how she knew, she heard you talking.' She leaned forward and tightened her bony fingers on each other. 'My sister knows the kids that hang around there, she asked one of them afterwards where she could locate you. On account of she wanted you to hear what happened with me and that – Jeff, was his name?' She gave a bitty skinny frown and said, 'Yeah, Jeff. That was it. From—' and she mentioned the name of the sheriff's town.

My mother whipped the newspaper picture out of her purse – it was a good clear picture, full-face and him smiling that wide honest smile, real clean-cut American boy – and she said, 'Was this him?'

'Yeah,' said the girl, 'oh yeah, no doubt about it, that's the guy.' She held the picture and her face took a silly smirk. 'Handsome, ain't he?'

'I'm only interested,' said my mother, 'in what happened. I don't intend to pass judgement one way or the other, and if you're nervous at talking about these matters – well, I've probably heard it all before. The facts are what I want.'

'Oh, not *kinky* or anything of that,' said the girl, handing the picture back, brushing imaginary specks of dust off her black jeans, black T-shirt, then tightening her fingers cagier than ever. 'I never knew him long enough – but I wouldn't go for anything like that. Him and me only slept together, I mean like ordinary sex. Is that what you wanted to find out?'

I cast a sarcastic look at my mother, like Does she suppose the sleeping with Jeff was a crime? But my mother had all the patience in the world; listening to her talk and question made me realise there might be some point to holding your temper tight in and stalking folks cautious. Get more results out of them that way and be pleasanter for all concerned. Like when Les kept on questioning me about Jeff and hauled out some at least of the truth – though you couldn't call those talks of ours pleasant. So my mother stalked this Ulla cautious and sweet, and I admired my mother more than ever. 'You slept with him,' she said, 'was that all? Nothing else happened?'

'Oh *yeah*,' said the girl with a strange pale energy. Like she was fascinated by herself saying these things, watching herself like she was an insect performing. And thinking all the time how daring she was to talk about these things, how strong my mother'd sympathise with her when the story was told. 'Oh,' the girl said in her toneless flat voice, 'I mean sleeping – that's nothing. No, it was what happened after.' She rubbed a skinny hand along the line of her jaw and my heart began to pound.

'So what did happen?' said my mother cautious.

'I'd need to explain from the start. Him and me happened to meet,' the girl said, 'in that coffee place, see? Where my sister works. She's no looker though,' she said reflective and passed a hand over her hair which stuck out matted like, to be honest, it needed a damn good wash. (Living around my mother and following her habits had gotten me used to noticing stuff like that.) 'Late at night it was,' said the girl, 'and no students much in there. I'd gone in to chat with my sister, her and me was sitting at a table and Jeff came in. Customer, see? So she got up and served him. Then a couple of men came in and my sister got busy. Anyway the boss don't like her chatting unless the place is cold empty. So Jeff and me talked, and one thing led to another. You know how it goes.' Her bony hand went up again to mess with that ugly hair.

'And then?' said my mother.

'It was all physical, if you know what I mean,' said the girl with that stupid earnestness, 'I mean him and me talking and that. What we said didn't mean a damn thing, only he started stroking my arm and such and it felt good. He wasn't my usual sort of guy and I'm not one for sleeping around promiscuous, if you get my meaning, but we talked easy and he smiled and I thought Why not? So we went back to his place like he suggested, and he was a slick act in bed. Kind of quick-and-over-with, but what man isn't?' A selection of tears came into her eyes and she kept them hanging on the lashes real decorative, if you admire that old-fashioned stuff. Personally it was too damn pat and smoochy for me; the floods of tears from my father's Louise had looked a hell of a lot more natural.

'Well,' my mother said briskly, 'what then?'

The girl dried up her tears and primmed her mouth; her eyes went hard and I could see she'd be one tough broad when she really grew up and pulled her act together. She said in a sudden strong voice, 'My sister told me I ought to notify the cops but I didn't. Was scared to, I guess. You know how cops can be.' She turned her eyes full on us and they were blank, blank as the desert after a duststorm. 'He got up off the bed,' she went on, 'and I made some kind of joke. Meant nothing by it, only he took it the wrong way. I said something about how it was good to go to bed with a college boy for a change. Praising the way he'd been in bed. I'd never do other than praise a man, even if I knew him real well. Just a silly friendly little joke, I don't recall the exact words. Only I remember college came into it, and me not being college myself. So he stood across me on the bed and he started to hit me, told me to get out. Said I was garbage and he'd no use for me.'

My mother began a sigh that came from deep inside her, then she caught herself back. 'Go on,' she said.

'Nothing more to tell.' The girl twisted those bony hands and, so help me, I couldn't figure what Jeff had seen in her. Maybe it was the sandy hair. And, to be honest, what had he seen in me? 'I was taken aback,' she said, 'him having acted so ready and pleasant before. And I'm not in the habit of men hitting me. So I lay there, didn't get up at once, and he swiped me some more – not across the face then, where it'd show, but on the ribs. I could find the bruises,' she said with a sort of tough pride, 'for a week after.'

'Yes,' said my mother. 'Yes. And then?'

'He chucked my clothes out to the hall of his apartment and told me to follow them. So—' she raised her bony shoulders and let them drop – 'I did, and pretty quick too. I was scared he'd really beat me up.' She turned those blank eyes on my mother and I watched them harden. 'Do you suppose I ought to have told the cops?' she said.

'No,' my mother said at last, and her voice came from a far distance. 'I suppose not. They're snowed under with domestic happenings. And perhaps not enough happened for them to base a charge on.' She went back into her distances but I suspected I could follow her at least part-way.

'Well,' said the girl, and raised those skinny shoulders, 'that's all. Not anything you could base much on, is it? Did you say you're some sort of detective?' She stood up and pulled her shiny raincoat on. 'I've not been much help to you, huh? Only when my sister told me the polite things those students were saying about him, I got angry and I thought, Polite be damned, one person in that dumb city'll speak the truth about him.'

'The students probably were,' said my mother from her immense distance, 'being truthful. According to their lights.'

'Yeah, well—' So the girl said goodbye and my mother went with her to the door. My mother offered her the carfare but the girl, to her credit, did refuse that. She said it'd been good to tell someone what she thought of Jeff, she'd not told anyone but her sister, and she didn't want to be accused of hiding things from the cops or investigators, she was a good girl. All that stuff. My mother saw her out and shut the door, sat down opposite me.

'It's not a justification,' she said, 'nothing's a justification for killing. At least she didn't carry a knife and use it. But her story does—'

For once I could find the exact word quicker, because I'd lived with the memory and the guilt of his death so long. 'It's sort of a reinforcement, right? It means that maybe I didn't wholly lie. That's all.'

'Yes,' she said, 'it does mean that.' She came across to me and knelt, put her face against mine; she didn't weep but you could tell the feeling was there. 'My daughter,' she said, 'I do believe you. I'm appalled and saddened that you did it, but I do believe I partly understand why, and that's a help. Dear Cate,' she said, and the two of us held each other close.

25

We drove back up, through the desert and pine forests, to the lakeside motel. After I was in bed with the lights out I heard our door open, then close. This startled me because my mother had undressed for bed too, so I got up and looked out front. She'd slipped her pants and sweater back on and she was ringing the doorbell at Elwood's private entrance. He answered, she went in with him and was gone twenty minutes. I went back to bed and lay thinking Can I trust her? With my history, how could I not wonder that? When she came back in I feigned sleep; in the dark she undressed and climbed into the other bed, and it seemed to me the two of us were further apart than we'd ever been. I lay awake most of the night, wondering and fretting, but sounded like she went into peaceful sleep after not very long.

Next morning at breakfast she said bright, 'We're going on an excursion today. A breathing-space for us. I thought it would be a pleasant change.'

'Oh, we are?' Yeah, I sounded wary; how would anyone in my position not? But attack was the only sensible option, so I said, 'What'd Elwood say when you talked with him last night?'

She gave me a startled glance. 'Oh,' she said, 'we just chatted.' She put some more butter on her hotcakes and said, 'Actually it's him we're going on an excursion with.'

I felt like she was baiting me. What had she told Elwood, and he answered her, if it wasn't about me and Jeff and what I'd done? I imagined the two of them filling each other in on details and her saying of course he'd need to tell the sheriff but she hoped the law'd treat me gentle. Although the law must . . . and so on. I shoved my chair back and said, 'The hell we're going anyplace with him. What have you and him been cooking up?'

She gave me another of her quick glances, like I was getting totally beyond any place where she could understand me, and she said quiet, 'Sit down, Cate. The men at the counter are staring.'

I said, 'Let 'em stare,' but I did sit down. I'm not sure why; something in my mother's face, I guess. 'What excursion?' I said lower-voiced. 'And to where, and the hell why? How come he can take time off all of a sudden?'

She said, 'Even the man who runs a motel gets time off once in a while. He'd talked about this with me before you and I drove south, and since today's the day another man fills in for him, there's no problem.'

'Where're we going then?' I said and she actually relaxed, she truly supposed I'd enjoy this so-called excursion she and him had cooked up.

'On the lake,' she said, 'he's getting a boat from the little marina for the day and taking us out on the lake.'

'Holy God,' I said, 'but the lake—'

I got up and went outside, was so blind with fear I couldn't do any other. One of the men at the counter laughed when I yanked the door open, he said something about 'damn teenagers' but he didn't know the half of it. The air outside was chilly despite the sun, and I stood there shivering.

After a couple of minutes my mother came out; I'd heard of people going white to the lips – like in adventure stories – but I'd never seen it before. She said, 'I didn't know. God forgive me, Cate, I didn't realise. I noticed you didn't like the lakeside, but I assumed that's because there's occasional visitors around at the boat store and marina. I thought you were nervous of people in general and that was why—'

'Not of live people,' I said, and shivered harder.

She led me away from the motel toward the roadside where there was no chance of anyone overhearing us. 'What am I going to do?' she said. 'What excuse can I give him? I can't pretend that either my daughter or myself has suddenly become afraid of water, and if I give any other excuse – he's no fool. I'm sure he doesn't guess yet, but if I start hedging he'll begin to wonder. After all,' she said, 'my story about why we're here is rather thin. If Elwood starts to suspect—'

At that moment Elwood opened the side door and called, 'See you down at the marina in ten minutes?' My mother nodded – I guess she couldn't figure what else to do – and he disappeared back indoors.

My mother said, 'What the *devil* are we going to do?'

Some of the colour had come back to her face, she looked pale still but not as stricken; only the shock had obviously slowed her brain down. I was thinking fast and I began to see how we might bluff this thing through, if she could hold her nerve. Only I wasn't sure how deep she felt about the guy. To test her I said, 'You're interested in him, aren't you?' and she didn't contradict, she only said short, 'Whatever that has to do with anything.' So I feared she was in deep enough; I bled inside for her but I couldn't go in a boat on that damn lake to save her or me or anyone else. 'I'd get green and throw up, spill the whole story,' I told her, 'and riding in a boat I'd feel especially trapped.'

Even that night when Les and me were there it had been bad enough; I still couldn't get out of my head the sound of the water lapping, along with the other small necessary noises Les and me were making. We hadn't dared go near the marina, it being summer and full of padlocked boats and a security man on duty at the jetty, so we prospected along a track the other side of the lake and by the grace of – like Les said after – the devil, we found a leaky old rowboat that no one had figured to be worth the locking away. I had to help Les with the . . . body, I guess, him not being too strong in the muscles, and it sagged something unpleasant between us. And when we got away from shore we'd to ease the . . . thing . . . into the water quiet so no one'd hear. We'd weighted it, of course, but the weights caught; seemed like he clung to us and would never leave us be. And I guess that was pretty much prophetic too. I didn't feel well or happy after but I was so sorry for Les, that I'd gotten him involved. Poor Les, that hated even the least bit of violence.

I said frantic to my mother, 'I can't go on the lake, don't ask me,' and her colour faded again, she went so white that seemed she must be reliving the wrapping and hauling and chucking that Les and me had done that night. Enough to make her reject me for ever. 'But,' I said, 'can you endure to go? Out of sight of this end, you'll be good and clear then.'

'Yes,' she said past her whiteness, 'I'll go. And I'll tell him you've an upset stomach, you want to stay quiet.'

'Tell him,' I said with a flicker of friendliness, 'I refuse to play gooseberry.'

'I can't tell him *that*, Cate.' But she was one tough lady; for all the horrible turns I'd done her, she pulled herself together real strongly. 'I'd better go or he'll suspect . . .' She put her hands up to her face and said, 'Cate, now that I know, how *can* I?'

'Get him away from this end of the lake,' I said, 'soon's you can. Out of sight round the curve and the big rocks. You'll have no problem then.'

She nodded with her white face; I put my fingers to her cheeks and rubbed some colour into her and then she went away, walking firm and steady toward the man who, with what she might unmeaning let out to him, could easy gossip me to jail.

That was the longest day I ever spent. I hated any glimpse

of the damn lake but I had to watch them go, see if she'd collapse pretty much as soon as she got on the boat. I ought to have trusted her better; she bent with him over a map and then the boat swung out from the marina, she pointed to things on shore past where he sat at the tiller and she spoke to him, like making conversation. With all she'd buzzing around in her head, it did take some doing.

Being winter there weren't many boats on the lake, but at least that time of year you get plenty sun and not much in the way of storms. I watched their boat till it rounded the curve of the lake and was out of sight. That shore both sides is all bare rocky piles of red sandstone lying around like someone's forgotten to prop them up level, but in the little side canyons beyond the curve there'd be beaches. Red sand beaches with a scrubby bush or two you could pull twigs off to make a campfire, grill the fish you'd caught or frankfurters you'd taken along. A pretty damn pleasant way to spend a sunny day – only pleasure in that sort of place was barred to me once for all. My own doing, yeah.

When they were out of sight I went back to our room, switched on the television and tried to think about nothing.

Late that evening, when the sun was setting, they got back. I'd expected them sooner – him ready to tell his pal the sheriff and get my future sorted. The sun started dropping and I went out to that damn lakeside again. I watched for the longest time and then with the last red glitter of sun on the water their boat came into sight; I slid into a gully between two rocks with only my eyes peeking over, and that's how come I saw him kiss her in the marina. I guess they figured nobody was watching, or maybe by then they didn't care. Anyway – a long kiss, and she wasn't exactly non-responsive. Then they climbed out of the boat and I ran back to our room, ready to wish her well and head away from there. Seemed like if I wanted her to be happy there wasn't any choice.

26

She must have stayed a while at the marina helping him stow the boat and chatting; by the time she came in I was ready to go. I couldn't decide, though, which would be least unkind to her – me telling her and walking out right away or me sneaking out in the middle of the night and leaving a note for her. I didn't much care for the sound of either one, and I was still chewing them over when she came in. She took one look at my face and said, 'So what's the problem?'

'No problem.' I shoved my purse back onto my bed and sat on it. 'You had a good day?'

'Believe it or not, we did. We landed in a little side canyon and explored rock formations and . . . various other topics.' The sun had caught her face and given her plenty of colour; she wore white jeans and a bright aqua shirt and sweater and she looked damn good. *Alive*. I told myself it was bad luck the folks in these parts all being so talkative with each other and so damn fond of Jeff. Fine for them, but near lethal for me. She said, 'Why are you sitting so stiffly and staring like that?' She switched my purse out from under me; it was a big black affair and while I waited for her I'd shoved spare underwear and such inside it. She said, 'You certainly do travel around prepared,' and she chucked the purse back on the bed upside down so most of the contents fell out. She turned away, pulled her sweater off and started to brush her hair; with her back to me she said, 'You intend to walk out on me?'

'So you can have a – uh – halfway decent life. So I won't

get in your way with this man or whatever else you want to do.'

'Just a neat little bundle of philanthropy, aren't you?' she said, still brushing.

'What the hell does that mean?'

'It means I profoundly suspect your motives.' She plonked the hairbrush down and faced me. 'Unselfish, are you? I'd never have suspected it.'

I said, 'Guess I deserved that, one way and another.' I picked up my purse and started shoving stuff back into it; she could call me all the names she wanted to but nothing had really changed. I said, 'Let's the two of us be honest with each other now, if we never have been before. You'd prefer me to get out of your life, wouldn't you? How could you not? Boyfriend or no, you must admit I've been one hell of a disappointment to you ever since I showed up again. You must want to chuck me and pick up the pieces of what you had before. That makes good sense.'

She heard me through. Then she said, 'Common sense went out of this situation when Les stole you, Cate.' She pulled up a chair to face me, she sat down and leaned forward. 'My daughter,' she said, 'it hasn't for one moment occurred, has it, to your busily scheming mind, that I'm every bit as much a human being as yourself and that I really do have desires and wishes of my own?'

I said, 'I don't get your meaning. Isn't that what the hell I just got through talking about?'

'No,' she said, 'it's not.' She took a long breath. 'I've tried to be honest with you,' she said, 'Cate, from the moment of your reappearance. Of course it shook me to learn that you were alive, and of course it delighted me too; there aren't any words strong enough. And as soon as it was proved that you really were my daughter, I tried time and time again to show you how glad I was, how we'd make a future together despite any remaining problems.

But you . . .' The long breath petered out; she looked tired and shot. Grieved, you'd say.

'Me ditto,' I said. 'But the way I talk and act that's different than you, the things you enjoy and I don't – all these would have gotten in between you and me even if there'd been no problem over Jeff.'

'You're a great one for euphemisms,' she said. 'Problem, my God!'

She'd never before used long words that shut me out. I opened my mouth but she went trampling on.

'I feel I don't *know* you,' she said. 'Not because of Jeff, I can understand what happened with him easier than I can anything else about you. But you won't allow me to know you. You haven't let me, ever since you reappeared.'

'I don't follow your meaning,' I said uselessly.

She flung a hand out at my half-packed purse. 'That's an example of what I'm talking about. You'd walk out on me, wouldn't you, rather than stay around so you and I can build our future together?'

'Holy hell, no,' I said, 'but I was so damn sure you'd want me gone. And this guy, this Elwood—'

'We kissed goodnight very sweetly,' she said, 'and I told him there was no future for him and myself. He's an adult too, Cate, he's knocked around the world as I have, and he wasn't overwhelmingly surprised by what I said.'

'But if you truly like the guy—'

'There'll be others,' she said, flushing prettily, 'you must have noticed I'm quite susceptible. There'll be a man elsewhere, sometime, in a place that's less dangerous for us and without any urge to ask difficult questions. If it turns out there's never another man – well, at least I've got my daughter. Unless, that is, she decides to run away again.'

'But this business over Jeff—'

'I've told you how I feel about that. It was a big knock, but I've recovered my balance now and can see it clearly. And I do realise that it knocked you sideways after you'd done it, just as much as the finding out about it did me. Isn't that so?'

'Yeah, I guess.' She felt I'd been uncommunicative with her, so I really tried to open up over this. 'To be honest I can hardly remember how I felt inside myself, how it felt to feel normal, all those years before I killed him. Since then, every time I start to like myself even a tiny bit, a voice inside me says But you've killed a man. And then I know that however cheap and mean and dumb anyone else is, they're glory in heaven compared to me.'

'Yes,' she said, 'for once I've guessed right. That's how I imagined you felt.'

'But what can I do? I can't own up, I'd go crazy if they shut me in a jail. And Les is in enough trouble, I can't involve him.'

'Do you trust me?' she said, and I stared because what did that have to do with anything? 'Do you want to stay with me?' she said. 'Let's start from there.'

'Oh yeah, if you'll let me stay, no question I do.'

'*Why* do you?' She sat very still and the room was dusky, I could hardly see her face.

'Why do I?' How could she need reasons?

'Yes, why? Is it because you think I can in some way protect you from the law, or because you suppose our blood relationship ought to mean something, or because you were tired of you and Lester scraping a bare existence and you wanted to live more comfortably?'

I said, 'That's a pretty insulting set of reasons,' and she gave me a tiny sneaky grin. Then she got serious again.

'Or is it because you realise Lester won't be taking care of you any longer and you feel you're not quite ready to manage on your own? Am I a convenient stopgap?'

'Hell,' I said, 'it's none of those, how could it be? You recall how Les dragged me to Virginia and you, I'd no choice in that. And I'll admit I was ready to turn around and leave again, soon's him and me could. But—' Then I burst out, 'Why d'you make me say it? Can't you believe the reason unless I spell it out to you?'

'Cate,' she said, 'you've no idea how impenetrable you are, how that offhand manner of yours conceals everything you're thinking and feeling. I simply couldn't guess at what your motive for wanting to stay is, unless you tell me.'

'Okay then.' Now I was the one to flush, and I practically never do that. A deep uncomfortable flush which made me shake. 'God,' I said, 'some people sure do take a hell of a lot of convincing. I got sort of accustomed to you, decided you were a neat-acting lady and pretty tough inside too, and I admired that. Also—' I stared down at my fingernails – 'how does a person feel toward a mother, how does a person want to act toward a mother? Mother and daughter is kind of a special feeling, right? At least I've heard it's so. What the hell do you want out of me – blood? You're my mother and, dammit, I'm extremely fond of you, attached to you not because of money or the possessions you own but because of you yourself.' I stopped, then I said, 'Is that enough blood? Are you satisfied now?'

'Oh Cate,' she said, 'yes. And I'm sorry I pushed you, but you're very nearly totally unknowable and I'm as vain and nervous as the next person. I had to be sure.'

'So you're sure now, right? I want to stay because I like being around you, and I hope some of the reasons for that aren't selfish ones.'

'Okay,' she said. 'And I believe Ulla's story – I *choose* to believe it, that's my decision. We won't explore the fors and againsts of it any longer.'

'Right,' I said. If she still loved me, after what she'd heard and must have guessed, who was I to complain? I certainly didn't want to discuss it any more. I said, 'And you're being honest with me about this guy? You genuinely wouldn't prefer to dump me and run off with him?'

'Honest as the day is long.' She gave me a wider grin

than before – not wholly confident, she wasn't the sort who'd ever be that, but a grin you could live around and be happy – then she took a shower and the two of us went to eat. Steak and fries and apple pie with cheese, an all-American meal. When we got back to our room she said brisk, 'Right, now we've some planning to do.'

I guessed we'd be going back to her Virginia place; we'd visit Les once in a while and I'd get accustomed to all those damn Virginia trees. I only hoped she wouldn't start on again that I must go to school; some notions are so far past their sell-by date there's no saving them.

But she certainly was a lady full of surprises; she said, 'I had it in mind the two of us might do some travelling. Abroad.'

I looked at her sharp but then I realised the reason; she was nervous about these folks' passion for finding out the truth. She hadn't betrayed me but maybe her enquiries had stirred up some mud and while she was in the same country she wouldn't feel comfortable. She'd taken on some of that hunted feel which I'd tried to keep to myself; I was the only guilty one and didn't seem fair to burden her. But she'd caught a breath of it, like an illness, and for that I was permanently sorry. A grief, to be part of my punishment.

'Whereabouts did you have in mind?' I said, and she looked vastly relieved because I'd not rejected the whole notion out of hand.

'Europe maybe,' she said, 'perhaps Italy.' Her face took that mischievous gleam I was getting truly fond of, and she said, 'Olive trees don't have very much foliage on them, you might get used to those.'

So then I knew things were going to be okay between us, a hell of a lot better than I deserved. But I hadn't stopped myself from doing the bad, and I couldn't rightly stop myself from accepting this good either.

That night she pulled out the little atlas she always travelled with; she said there'd be lots to arrange. For the first time she talked to me about her finances, and I felt ashamed all over again because I'd never wondered about any of this, I'd just assumed she had for always all the money a person could ever need. But she said no, she'd refused maintenance payments from the man my father because she'd some private income of her own, but she needed to work at the jewellery or something to have enough income for us to manage on. 'I'll start up again in Italy,' she said, 'there's plenty of fashion houses there.' And the Virginia place was half hers, half my father's. 'I'm going to get a divorce,' she said, 'there's no point in hanging on hopelessly. I was deceiving myself in thinking that he and I could ever have a long-term future together. Our problems had already started before you disappeared.'

I recalled then what she'd said after we met that Louise, how she was fitting for him because of being soft and accepting, and how my mother had instead tried to toughen him.

She said, 'That is, I'll get a divorce unless you have an objection. After all, Brad is still your father, you should have some say in this.' But I said no sweat, I'd barely had a chance to start thinking of him as my father before he up and ran, so whatever she did about him was okay by me. She said right, she understood that.

Then the Virginia place could be sold or whatever, anyway she'd get her half of the money and that would be plenty to take us travelling, set us up somewhere else.

She sounded sort of sorrowful about my father but as if her mind was made up, like she'd decided he was a part of the past that wasn't ever coming back, and because of me and for her own happiness she'd need to untangle herself and look to the future.

I couldn't easily or happily cut my thoughts off from remembering Les either. Right or wrong, he'd reared me all those years and taken as good care of me as he, poor man, knew how; he'd fed me and taught me to read and all; we'd had jokes and things we both cared about doing and we'd been, in our own sort of way, a family. I couldn't expect my mother to understand that, and of course Les was shut away from me now because of something he'd done wrong, but there was a hole inside me when I thought about never seeing him any more. No help for it though, he'd handed me back and basically he wanted for me to be with my mother rather than with him. But he might be unhappy for a minute when we told him we were going; I didn't want to think about how he'd look then. Him gone from me, and Brad my father gone; truly there was no one left but my mother.

Of course we'd visit Les before we left, we'd explain to him. I said, 'He wants no part of me any more,' and she didn't try contradicting that because it was the rock-hard truth. When all these arrangements were through with we'd buy tickets and go, tell the man her former husband that we were going overseas but not the details, not tell anyone those. She'd no close family in England any more, so it wouldn't matter much to anyone there. I said, 'We'll be running away,' and she said, 'Sometimes you don't need to apologise for doing that.' If she felt that way about it, that was okay by me.

I've kept on saying 'okay', like 'things were going to be okay between us,' but now that we've started running it strikes me 'okay' is much too slick a word, it supposes much too simple a solution. Her and me'll get along fine for a while, sure; we've enough in common, and enough affection, to make that happen. And I'll do my damndest to make it keep on happening, but there'll be problems crop up that neither one of us can control. Like, we'll both get homesick – for two different places. She'll meet a man she truly cares about, and she'll get nervous on account of me all over again. Or she won't meet anyone she cares that much for, and she'll start recalling this kindly guy out West and how, when the two of them were on the lake that day, he asked her – what? – and she'll recall how she felt obligated to answer shifty and untrusting. She could easy, honest person as she is, truly deeply hate me for that, someday. Then maybe there'll be money problems too, also maybe I won't turn out to be the sort of person she'd want me as. For all that I'll struggle to, there's an awful lot of gaps in this future.

Anyway we've started running and I guess that was unavoidable. And none of these possible problems arrived inside my thinking at first; they've started building up since. Could be I'm wrong and none of them will happen at all. For sure the future looked clear and bright and pretty good and shiny to me that evening when we lay on her bed and studied the maps and in our heads, both of us pointing to various places and routes, we started travelling.